# Across the Table

**Center Point
Large Print**

**This Large Print Book carries the
Seal of Approval of N.A.V.H.**

# Across the Table

 ❧

# LINDA CARDILLO

## CENTER POINT PUBLISHING
### THORNDIKE, MAINE

This C                     ꓺdition
is published ... ᴛᴠ ʏᴄᴀʀ ᴢᴜᴛᴜ ᴠʏ ᴀᴛᴛᴀᴛɢement with
Harlequin Books S.A.

The text of this Large Print edition is unabridged.
In other aspects, this book may vary
from the original edition.
Printed in the United States of America
on permanent paper.
Set in 16-point Times New Roman type.

ISBN: 978-1-60285-847-3

Library of Congress Cataloging-in-Publication Data

Cardillo, Linda.
  Across the table / Linda Cardillo. — Center Point large print ed.
    p. cm.
  ISBN 978-1-60285-847-3 (library binding : alk. paper)
  1. Restaurateurs—Fiction. 2. Veterans—Fiction. 3. Boston (Mass.)—Fiction.
  4. World War, 1939–1945—Fiction. 5. Domestic fiction. 6. Large type books.
  I. Title.
PS3551.U839A64 2010
813'.54—dc22

                                                    2010016145

To my aunts—Angie, Beulah, Carmella, Cathy, Clara, Corinda, JoAnn, Kay, Lydia, Mary, Rita, Rose, Ruth and Susie

# Across the Table

# ROSE
## 1939–46

# A Lifetime Ahead of Us

I HEARD THE SCREEN DOOR slam shut against the wooden doorjamb and the crunch of Al's work boots on the conch-shell fragments that surrounded our cottage a quarter mile from the Chaguaramas airfield on Trinidad. It was 5:00 a.m. The tanagers that nested in trees beyond the field where we enlisted men's wives hung our laundry had just begun their morning song.

I rolled away from the empty hollow on the bed where Al had been sleeping only fifteen minutes before. The sheets were damp with his sweat. Nothing stayed dry in that climate.

I figured I might as well get up, too, put on a pot of coffee, start cooking before the temperature climbed. Thanksgiving Day and it was already seventy-five degrees outside. It would rise to one hundred and twenty degrees in the shade before the day was over. Al had hung a thermometer for me outside the bedroom window so I'd know as soon as I opened my eyes how hot it was. I'm not sure why it mattered so much, but it helped. Gave me a little piece of knowledge that let me feel some control over my life. Hah!

I wrapped myself in the navy blue embroidered kimono Al brought me last year when he was on furlough at Christmas and managed to get back to Boston for ten days. It seemed like a ridiculously impractical gift at the time, the middle of winter in the Northeast. I was wearing flannel nightgowns and wool socks to bed, for God's sake.

But then he'd asked me to marry him. Al Dante and I had been keeping company since we were in high school. He was a year ahead of me, one of my brother Carmine's friends.

The ring was in the pocket of the gown.

"What's this?" I asked when I felt something hard and lumpy against my heart. I'd just put the kimono on over my powder-blue sweater set in my parents' living room.

I slipped my hand into the pocket and retrieved a velvet box.

"Open it, Rose." He was sitting on the edge of his chair. He had his uniform on, the petty-officer stripe he'd earned a couple of months before neatly displayed on his arm below the Seabees construction insignia. He looked sharp, my Al did.

I held my breath as I lifted the hinged top of the small box. Inside was a diamond sitting high on four silver prongs. I let out a quiet gasp and my eyes filled up—for all the nights I'd lain awake, wondering how he was doing so far away, building an air base as the world descended into war. Trinidad. Al told me the U.S. Navy had leased territory there from the British because of its strategic location in the Caribbean, a base for planes that escorted convoys and patrolled the sea lanes. I had to go to the library to look up where it was.

My nose started to run. I was a mess. Tears streaming down my cheeks, me sniffling. Who knew this was what love does to you.

"Will you marry me, Rose?"

We didn't have much time. But I wasn't going to let him go back to Trinidad for God knew how long before we could walk down the aisle at St. Leonard's. Neither of us wanted to wait. We talked to my folks that very night. They were wary about the rush.

Mama got me alone in the kitchen for a few minutes.

"Rosa, be honest with me. Are you gonna have a baby? Is that why you gotta go to the priest so fast?"

"No, Mama, no! I swear on Nonna's grave that I'm as pure as the snow that's falling outside. It's just—I can't bear for him to go away again. The navy will let me go with him if we're married."

"He's gonna take you away to that island! Your papa will not agree to that, Rosa. You belong here, with the family. It's too far. Too strange. Another country."

"Mama, you left your parents to go with Papa to another country when *you* got married. America was a lot farther from Italia than Trinidad is from Boston. Please, Mama. Understand. I love him. I've waited already, worrying about whether he'd come back alive. I don't want to wait any longer. Talk to Papa. Give us your blessing!"

Mama put her hands on her hips and looked at me, measured me. She was from the old country, but she'd been in Boston a long time—thirty years.

"I didn't want to leave back then. It broke my heart to say goodbye to my family. I was pregnant, don't forget, with your brother Sal. But the last thing I wanted was to be separated from your papa. I'd seen too many men leave the village on their own and get lost in America, find another woman, forget the family they left behind. I was scared, but I knew I had Papa to depend on, protect me and the baby. With his skill as a stonemason, he knew he could find work in America. But when we left, my mother cried and cried as if it was my funeral. I won't do that to you, *figlia mia*. I'll talk to Papa."

She made the sign of the cross on my forehead and went to talk to my father.

We got married on New Year's Day. I wore my mother's veil and my sister-in-law Cookie's dress. My best friend, Patsy, stood up for me. It

14

snowed the morning of the wedding. Huge flakes came in off the harbor and by the time we went to church there were three or four inches on the ground. I had to put on galoshes and hold my skirts up as we walked the two blocks to St. Leonard's. Fortunately, Father Giovanni had gotten somebody to shovel the front steps. My cousin Bennie, with the voice of an angel, sang the *Ave Maria*. Instead of his overalls covered in granite dust, Papa had on his good black suit and waited in the back of the church while I changed my shoes and Patsy fixed my veil. She licked her thumb and wiped away a fleck of soot that had settled on my cheek. I peeked into the sanctuary through the little glass panes in the doors and could see Al up at the altar in his uniform.

I bit my lip, squeezed Patsy's hand, then took Papa's arm. I stepped across the threshold and headed into my new life.

After the Mass, we went to a restaurant on Salem Street that had closed for our private party. The meal wasn't elaborate; after all, this was still the Depression, and the rest of the world was at war. But they did a nice job for us—escarole soup, manicotti, a cacciatore made with rabbit, fagiolini and broccoli rabe on the side. The wedding cake came from Caffe Vittoria, but the cookies Mama baked herself. It took her three days. Mostaciolli, anise cookies, pignoli cookies, honey fingers. She even managed to find sugar-coated almonds, and I sat up with Patsy two nights before the wedding and wrapped the pastel-colored nuts—blue, green, pink, lilac—in circles of white netting that we tied with thin strips of white satin ribbon as wedding favors.

Al and I spent our wedding night at the Parker House. They brought us a bottle of champagne and a fruit basket on the house because Al was a serviceman. I'd never had champagne before. It was New York State, not French, of course, because of the war. It wasn't what I expected. But then, most of what's happened in my life wasn't what I expected.

The hotel wasn't far from the North End, but it might as well have been a foreign country. Very old Boston, with a snooty bell captain and a dowdy lounge. Not that we wanted to spend any time there. It was all we could do to get up to our room and get the key in the door, we were so excited. I was nervous, with a lot of butterflies in my stomach. I'd hardly eaten anything at the reception. I'd been busy moving from table to table, kissing and being kissed, thanking everyone as they slipped their envelopes into my hand and I put them carefully into the satin-and-lace *borsa* Mama had carried on her own wedding day. We didn't count the money until the next morning. We had other things on our minds that night.

Although she'd given birth to seven children and therefore must have known *something* about the sexual side of marriage, Mama had offered me nothing in the way of preparation. Her only advice to me was, "Don't ever go to bed angry. When you fight, make up before you fall asleep."

But right then, I couldn't imagine fighting with Al. I'd known him since we were kids and never in all those years had we ever said a sharp word to each other.

My sister-in-law Cookie, in addition to handing down her dress, had given me a smattering of advice, although I tried to avoid the image of my brother Carmine doing to her what she was trying to describe.

"That was the first time I'd ever even seen one," she said of her wedding night. "You'd think, growing up with five brothers, that sooner or later I'd have caught a glimpse. So it was kind of a shock. Try not to react too strongly when you see it, 'cause men are very sensitive about that. And try not to worry or build the whole experience up into something that's got to be perfect the first time. More than likely it won't be. But it does get better." And she smiled this knowing, secret smile and patted her belly. She was just starting to show.

So we made it into the hotel room with these goofy smiles on our faces. We looked at each other and then Al swooped in, picked me up and carried me to the wing chair by the window and sat down with me on his lap. We looked out at the city, coated now in a thick blanket of snow that softened the edges of everything and hid the shabbiness.

It was magical, that whiteness. The world seemed fresh, unmarred by weary footprints. A good omen for us, I thought.

Al nuzzled my neck in the spot he'd discovered when we were sixteen and he first kissed me. He'd begun with my lips, but then moved to cover my face with his kisses—my eyelids, my cheeks, my earlobes and, finally, right below my ear. It had sent shivers through me then, and he'd known ever since that was how to make me melt.

He lingered there for a few minutes and I leaned back against his chest. All the nervous energy that had gotten me through this frantic week dissolved into his tenderness and strength.

"Oh, Rose," he whispered.

And then he began to unbutton the twenty satin-covered buttons that ran up the back of the dress from below my waist to my shoulder blades. I knew he wanted that dress just to slide off me like the waterfall in the middle of the island he'd described for me—heart-stopping ice-cold water plunging from cliffs so green you thought they'd been colored by a child-giant with a box of crayons.

But there were so many buttons! Not only up

my back, but on the sleeves, as well, marching up to my elbows. Painstakingly, one by one, he slipped the loop fastener over each button to release it. While he unbuttoned, he continued to nuzzle my neck, his breath hot and urgent against my skin. Finally the buttons were all undone and he drew the bodice off my shoulders. I stood and let the whole thing drop to the floor and turned to face him in my bra and slip and panties.

I had a negligee in my suitcase that I'd bought at Filene's the day after Al proposed, all filmy white nylon with pale blue flowers embroidered around the neckline. But I could see from Al's eyes that I wasn't going to put it on that night.

Those eyes swept over me from head to toe and back again, coming to rest on my breasts. He broke into a broad grin.

"You're beautiful, Rose!"

It brought tears to my eyes, how adored I felt at that moment.

He picked me up again and carried me to the bed. Nothing Cookie had told me prepared me for the rest of that night—for how I felt lying against the pillows, watching him undress; for all the revelations about my body and his that followed; for the absolute peace of sleeping in his arms.

As he stood by the bed, undressing, the stiffness and formality of his uniform gave way to the soft curl of black hair against the smooth browned muscle of his arms and chest. The work he'd been doing on that tropical island had given him a sleekness and a strength I'd never seen in him before, not even when we'd gone to Revere Beach during the summers we were in high school. He wasn't a boy anymore, not in his body, not in the way he wasn't embarrassed to have me watch him, not in the way he touched me when he got into bed next to me. I wondered—fleetingly—if he'd gained that confidence from being with another woman. But he dispelled any doubts I had about being the only one in his life from that moment on by his tenderness and his passion. His patience with the buttons had only been the beginning of his willingness to take it slow for me.

We didn't sleep much that night. It was as if we had to fill ourselves up with each other, fill that emptiness that had gnawed at us all the time he'd been away. We didn't fall asleep until early morning, the sheets twisted around us. I woke up first, disoriented by the strange bedroom. I eased myself out of the bed to wash. There was a bit of blood, but not as much as I'd thought there would be. I looked at myself in the mirror over the sink. The bride who'd anxiously bitten her lip and walked with nervous hope down the aisle was still there. We still had a lifetime of unknowns ahead of us. But one question had been answered for me during the night. I had the certainty—don't ask me where it came from—that if things were okay in bed, a couple could weather whatever else life threw at them. We were going to do all right, Al and I.

We couldn't afford more than one night at the Parker House, so we spent our last night in Boston and the second night of our married life at Al's parents' apartment. My mother-in-law, Antonella, invited my parents over for dinner. We'd spent the day walking around the city, arm in arm, Al helping me over the snowbanks, as we talked about the life we hoped to have. God willing, the war would end before the United States got pulled into it, and we *could* have a life.

When we got to my in-laws', my cheeks were red from the cold and I heard a lot of ribbing from both the Vitales and the Dantes about being the blushing bride. Al just took me in his arms with a grin and planted a big one on my lips in front of everybody. Then everyone had to kiss me.

Eventually we sat down to eat. Al's mother is Calabrese, so her cooking is slightly different from Mama's. She made tripe in a pizzaiola sauce and her own fettucine. Papa had brought a jug of Chianti filled from the cask in our basement, the wine made from my uncle Annio's grapes that he grew in his garden in Everett. The toasts were endless, each family raising their glasses to our safe journey, long life and many babies. The meal was raucous, a celebration but with an undercurrent of melancholy as the evening wore on and our mothers, especially, worried about our departure the next day. Nobody wanted to say good-night. But at last, Antonella, Mama and I cleared the table and began washing up and putting the kitchen back in order. Around eleven, with another round of kisses—and, by now, tearful embraces—my family headed down the stairs. I went to the front windows, Al's arm around my waist, and watched them walk down the block. Before they rounded the corner, Mama turned and looked back. I blew her a kiss, but I don't think she saw me.

We sailed early the next day, first to Miami and then on to Trinidad. Off in the distance we could see the escort ships protecting us. We weren't allowed to photograph them, a reminder that even on this side of the Atlantic, the world was a dangerous place. I was seasick the whole twelve days of the trip, throwing up in the cramped stainless-steel toilet in our cabin. When we had a practice emergency evacuation drill, I crawled up to the deck with my life jacket on, but at that moment, I didn't care whether I lived or died, I was so sick. The tugboat horns indicating that we were in the harbor were the most beautiful music I'd ever heard.

Little by little, I made a home for us on Trinidad. The first thing to adjust to was the heat, since we were practically sitting on the equator. I pinned my long hair up on top of my head and made a few sundresses out of some cotton I found in a shop in Port of Spain. But before I sewed the dresses, I cleaned.

The cottages assigned to the married couples were newly built, like the airfield Al and his platoon were carving out of the peninsula. But left empty for even a few months they became overrun with wildlife, large and small. Our cottage had two rooms, plus a small kitchen and a lavatory. The shower was outside. When I first saw our home, I hadn't held down any food to speak of in more than a week and I was covered in a layer of dust from the open jeep ride to the base. The sweat was pouring down my neck, leaving a trail of narrow brown rivulets.

Inside the cottage, cobwebs hung from every corner, the husks of giant beetles and unidentifiable insects trapped in the sticky silk. Something had made a nest under the kitchen sink. Geckos slithered along the edges of the floor. If there'd been a clean place to lie down, curl up and cry, I would've done so. But there wasn't. So I put my bags down on the porch and immediately dug out a housedress and a bandanna to tie up my hair.

"You got a broom, some rags and a bucket?" I said to Al.

God bless him, he scrounged around while I changed and came back with the basic necessities. He told me he had to report to his commander and then left me for the afternoon.

I put all my years of Mama's training as a housekeeper to use that afternoon and for days afterward, sweeping and scrubbing that place until it was something I could be proud of. It was my first home, after all—but let me tell you, it wasn't like anything I'd ever imagined.

The blue of the sea, the purple of the bougainvillea, the red of the Chaconia trees—I'd never seen anything like them. The colors of the land, the smells of the sea and the flowers—everything was heightened by the heat and the moisture. The same was true of the food. The tastes were both strange to me and exaggerated.

The base had a commissary where we could get tins of evaporated milk, peas, potted beef and Spam. But I longed for fresh, so soon after I arrived I walked down to the little village that was halfway up the hill between the base and the harbor. I'd seen chickens pecking around a yard the first day, and vegetables I didn't recognize growing in a field. I knocked on some doors, talked to the old mama who had the chickens and walked away with a basket of greens, some eggs and a packet of spices—cardamom, cilantro, some dried chili peppers.

They eat spicy in Trinidad. Al was used to

Calabrian cooking and that was spicy, so I gave the local things a try. If I had to open another can of Spam and make it into something recognizable, I thought I'd shoot myself. Or we'd both starve.

But fresh eggs I knew what to do with. I had some potatoes and onions and made a pan of frittata, with the greens on the side. Al came into the house and smelled the familiar aromas. He ate that night with gratitude and pleasure.

By Thanksgiving, I'd had almost a year to poke around the markets of Port of Spain and find things that were close enough to what we'd known in Boston or learn how to cook what was totally unfamiliar. We weren't going to have turkey, for instance, but I'd gotten a nice capon the day before, all plump and with lots of flesh on its breast even after I'd plucked the feathers. I used breadfruit instead of sweet potatoes. I found a sausage maker, and although the taste wasn't like my uncle Sal's fennel sausage back home, it was still pork and hot. I couldn't make lasagne, like Mama always did for Thanksgiving, because I couldn't find any cheese similar to ricotta. But I bought some cornmeal and made *pastelles* instead, an island dish we had one night in a local tavern and Al liked so much I got the owner's wife to show me how she made it. I used the sausage and a bit of beef I was able to get my hands on, chopped up and browned with onions and garlic and carrots and then simmered in broth and the local spices Imelda, the old lady in the village, supplied me with. At the end of the simmering you toss in olives and raisins. With the cornmeal you make dough with water and shape it into balls that you flatten with your hand. You put a spoonful of the meat mixture in the middle and mold the cornmeal dough around it, then wrap each little pie in banana leaves coated with oil and annatto powder. You tie up the leaves like a package and then steam the packets. Oh, when you unwrap those leaves, those *pastelles* are just bubbling with red juices and that spicy flavor that wafts through every kitchen in Trinidad.

There was a lot of homesickness on the base, and the only way I knew how to dispel those feelings was with food. I invited all the married couples in the compound and the single guys in Al's platoon to Thanksgiving dinner. Each of the girls offered to bring something; several of them had gotten packages from home, so we had a real feast that afternoon. We set up two long tables out in the courtyard between the cottages and covered them with bedsheets. Everyone brought their own chairs and dishes, since nobody had enough to set a table for eighteen.

I think it was the first holiday any of us had spent away from our families. But you know, that day, sitting across the table from one another, we *were* a family.

Despite the heat and the strangeness, I got used to tropical life. I found an office job working for the navy and rode my bike to the base every day, along roads lined with pale blue and yellow shacks with rusty corrugated tin roofs and curious children watching me as their mamas spread laundry out to dry in the sun.

Children. Al and I both wanted a family. Who didn't? But two years went by in Trinidad, two years of lovemaking in the humid night, breezes drifting over us carrying the fragrance of frangipani or the roar of the night rains. Two years of waking up every month to renewed disappointment. I'm not one to dwell on missed opportunity. When the milk spills, I mop it up and refill the pitcher. But as time wore on, as I washed blood out of the sheets for yet another month, I couldn't help myself. I cried. I wondered what was wrong with me.

I didn't think it was the tropics. If anything, the heat seemed to make everything and everyone around me *more* fertile. Two of the girls who lived in our compound had already given birth and three more were pregnant.

One day when I was in the village picking up my eggs and greens from Imelda, I had to wait for her because she had another customer. But instead of filling the young woman's basket with provisions, she pressed a packet wrapped in brown paper into her hands.

"Remember, make a tea, let it steep for five minutes and then drink the whole cup. Every morning."

I watched the young woman take the packet nervously with a shy smile. Imelda patted her belly.

"You'll be carrying something in there in no time."

I felt a sharp longing and a desperation to try anything—even Imelda's potion. I didn't tell Al. I didn't think he'd understand. Besides, I didn't want him to feel inadequate—that somehow, because we hadn't been able to make a baby, I wasn't satisfied with our life.

So I bought the packet of herbs from Imelda in secret that day, along with okra and onions, and made myself a tea of hope.

The next morning the Japanese bombed Pearl Harbor. We'd known we were preparing for war, but the horror of the attack and the chilling reminder of our own vulnerability—on yet another navy base on a tropical island—brought urgency and renewed purpose to the work at Chaguaramas.

For the next three months the construction crew made an intense push to finish. Al worked long hours, coming home at night and collapsing into exhausted slumber after supper. He had no energy for lovemaking, and I was so afraid I was barren it was all I could think of on those few nights when we managed to reach for each other in the bed. I can't say our lovemaking wasn't passionate. But it wasn't the same as the early days when we couldn't get enough of each other. Besides my own worries, which I kept to myself, we had others, as well. My brothers Carmine and Jimmy had both been drafted. And with the completion of the base we realized new orders for Al were coming soon. God only knew where he'd go.

When the orders came, I should've been glad that I'd at least be going home. I hadn't seen my family in two years and the timing meant I'd get to see my brothers before they shipped out. But leaving Chaguaramas also meant leaving Al. I wasn't going with him on his next assignment, because he'd be on a ship heading across the Pacific and into war.

I was so busy packing up I didn't notice that I hadn't gotten my period. I wasn't very regular, anyway, so I didn't give it a thought. The navy flew us out of Trinidad to Florida instead of transporting us by ship. It was my first time in a plane. Al made me sit by the window and—oh my God—what a sight as we lifted off and circled the island. There was Al's work below us, the long, straight landing strip, crisscrossed by two other runways, and a complex of hangars and administrative buildings and barracks. A small city in just two years. I squeezed his hand and then threw up into a waxy bag.

● ● ●

We had two weeks in Boston before Al shipped out. We got there in time for a combined party— welcome home for Al and me, farewell for Carmine and Jimmy. Our mothers cried; the boys got drunk; Cookie, with my two-year-old nephew Vincent and another baby on the way, sat at the table rocking her toddler and trying to hold back her tears.

The next morning Carmine and Jimmy got inducted at the base in South Boston and were on their way to Fort Dix in New Jersey for basic training. Al and I had a chance to talk about where I'd live and what I'd do once he was gone. I told him it didn't make sense for me to rent an apartment just for myself. I'd move back in with my parents and get a job. After two years of working for the navy, I knew I had what it took to make a living. I was going to be okay, I assured him, remembering the haunted look on Cookie's face and vowing I wouldn't be a burden to anyone while Al was away.

We got back some of what we'd lost in those last months of exhaustion and worry on Trinidad. Spring was arriving in Boston and we made excuses to our families and took ourselves outside.

We walked all the way to the Esplanade on the Charles River.

"It's going to be different now, Rose."

"It's always been different for us, Al. And we've been apart before. I didn't forget what you looked like then. Or felt like." I grinned and put my hand on his chest, pushing him gently. I was trying so hard, you know, to let him go without worrying about me.

He grabbed my hand. "I'll never forget what you feel like, either."

I dressed in my best suit, put on stockings and high heels, gloves and a hat the day his ship sailed. I wanted Al's last memory of me to be special. I hadn't worn clothes like that since we'd left Boston two years before. The suit was a little snug, and I thought, That's what married life does to you—rounds you out. I stayed on the dock with the other wives as the ship left port, taking some comfort in our numbers. But I got on the trolley and went home very much alone.

I fought the loneliness by staying busy. I got a job right away at the Shawmut Bank, as a secretary to one of the vice presidents. When I took the typing and shorthand tests, I did the best of all the candidates. I'd learned a lot on Chaguaramas. You make opportunities where you find them. I put my hair up, knew how to address the higher-ups with respect and saw what I needed to do to make my boss look good. It wasn't long before the bank promoted me to office manager. I even had a nameplate on my desk—Mrs. Dante. I was twenty-one years old and felt as if I knew something.

In April I missed my period again and this time I didn't ignore it. But I was afraid to hope. I tried to put it out of my mind, busied myself with work so that I could bear the moment when, as always before, I'd start to bleed. But May arrived and I finally allowed myself to believe I might be pregnant. I kept my suspicions to myself until I saw the doctor, as if confiding in someone else might make it disappear. Generally I'm not a superstitious person. I don't go in for the *mal'occhia* that my mother's generation brought from the old country. But I did break down in Trinidad and let myself fall under the spell that despair sometimes drives us to, and I wasn't willing, just yet, to go back to being a totally rational person.

I found a doctor at Boston Lying-In Hospital. I didn't want to ask Cookie who her doctor was because I knew it would set off a chain reaction that would ripple through the family and only compound my grief if I was mistaken. I had to wait a few days for the answer. I didn't give the doctor my phone number because my mother might have answered. I made sure I was the one to pick up the mail from the box in the vestibule every morning. When the envelope finally came I stuck it in my apron pocket and brought everything else—a letter from Carmine and some bills—to the kitchen. I went to my bedroom, the same room I'd shared with my sister Bella as a girl, and sat down on the narrow bed. All my senses seemed sharper that morning—the feel of the chenille bedspread against my bare legs, the rumble of city traffic on the elevated highway a few blocks away, the aroma of onions and garlic from Mama's cooking, the bitter taste of bile rising in my throat. I opened the letter and held my breath as I read the results of my pregnancy test. And then I cried.

The person I was when I'd left Boston for Trinidad was not the woman who returned. I thought at first that it was my pregnancy, the change in the weather and being without Al that made me feel so different. I heard all kinds of stories from aunts and cousins about the discomforts of carrying a baby, but for me, it wasn't that. My body felt strange—not my own, that was for sure. But the strangeness I felt had more to do with my head than my growing belly.

I was noticing things—about Boston, about life—that I hadn't seen before I'd lived in Trinidad. Now I didn't just stand on the wharf at the edge of my neighborhood staring out at the harbor, wondering what lay beyond the ocean's horizon. I'd sailed that ocean. Been out of sight of land and all that was familiar. Some people— a lot of people in the North End, I discovered— didn't even wonder or ask what lies outside the concrete and brick boundaries of their corner of the city. It was enough for them—the daily routine of waking up in their comfortable bed, drinking a cup of Maxwell House coffee with two sugars and cream, getting on the MTA with a pepper-and-egg sandwich in their lunch pail and keeping the circle of people they knew tight around them, not letting in anyone or anything new.

Maybe that was what Chaguaramas changed about me. I didn't have those routines to fall into. Sometimes on my days off, especially toward the end when Al was working nonstop to finish the air base, I climbed by myself to the top of the plateau past the housing compound. From there I could see the Caribbean and forget myself in the endless vista of sea and sky. Close in, of course, were the battleships and tenders, an ominous reminder that we were at war. The harbor was as busy and congested as Boston. But if I looked up and off to the right, beyond the gray metal hulls and camouflage netting that disguised the glint of guns, I saw only open sea, and it opened up my heart.

I wished the rest of the world could feel this, instead of bombing cities.

There were other things I experienced at Chaguaramas. Imelda and her family, for instance. Her husband, Buddy, who played drums at a club in Port of Spain and delivered ice in his wooden wagon. Their daughters Jane and

Margaret and their children, who ran around Imelda's garden and climbed into her ample lap.

I'd never been around black people before, had never seen them with their families. The first time Imelda offered me a cup of coffee, I have to admit I hesitated. A lot of the merchants in Port of Spain treated the navy people like invaders, intruders. But Imelda, up in her village—after her surprise at my sudden appearance the day I went looking for fresh vegetables—took an interest in me. Maybe I needed some mothering in those early months away from my family and she understood that. She didn't pressure me that first time, when she offered and I made an excuse not to stay and sit with her. But then I felt foolish. What was I afraid of? That someone would see and think I was doing something wrong? I usually don't care what other people think. So the next time she asked, I said yes.

Imelda's coffee was strong and sweet, like Mama's. Black coffee—espresso—was what Mama made for Papa after dinner. One demitasse with a shot of anisette and a twist of lemon peel is how he liked it. But in the afternoons, after she'd finished the laundry, the cleaning and the marketing and before she started dinner, Mama sat with her cup of "American coffee." She learned how to use the grinder at the A&P and brought home a bag that took her a month to use up. Sometimes she sat with her sister and visited.

But more often than not, she enjoyed her coffee alone, listening to the radio.

At Imelda's table I felt like I was in my mother's kitchen. If I'd told anyone back home that, they would've thought I was crazy. Even the girls in the compound never went to the village.

"Rose, honey," Imelda would ask, "have you written to your mama lately? If Margaret or Jane and my grandbabies were so far away from me I don't think I could stand it." She fanned herself with an old catalog while she poured us both a cup.

Mama never learned to read, but I wrote her a letter every week. My brother Jimmy read them to her. She sent me photographs each month holding up one of my letters.

Her not being able to read made me realize how cut off she must've been from her own family when she left Italy. At least I knew we weren't going to be in Trinidad forever. But I wondered if I could've done what she did—leave everything and build a new life from nothing.

# Motherhood

ALBERT DANTE, JR., was born on Thanksgiving Day at Boston Lying-In Hospital. It was Patsy, my maid of honor, who got me there, calling a taxi when my water broke and pain ripped through me. It hadn't been an easy pregnancy. I threw up for five months; I gained forty pounds and spent the last six weeks propped up at night with pillows because the heartburn was so bad. But I wrote none of that to Al. I wrote instead about the first time I felt the baby move, a flutter that felt like he was pushing off the inside of my belly as if it were the end of a swimming pool. I wrote about the shower the girls at the office gave me, the bassinet I'd found at Jordan Marsh that just fit in my room, the blanket Al's mother had crocheted. I didn't write about how terrified I was to give birth. Al had plenty of his own to be terrified about.

He was on a ship in the Pacific carrying marines. Like me, I think Al was holding back on describing the daily terrors of his life. I saw enough in the newsreels, read enough in the *Herald,* to know he was keeping the worst from me. And he was never one who liked to write a lot, so for him to fill one of those thin blue sheets every week with any news at all was a big deal.

He was bursting, of course, when I wrote him about my pregnancy, which I sat down and did minutes after I'd read the results of the pregnancy test. He worried that he wouldn't be with me when my time came. Honestly, I wrote him back, what man *was* when his wife was giving birth? He could pace the deck of his destroyer just as well as he could pace the waiting room of the maternity ward. He made me promise to send a telegram as soon as the baby was born.

I wasn't the only woman to have a baby alone while her husband was at war. But that doesn't help you much, I discovered, when you're scared and in pain and then in so much joy that no one else can share with you except your baby's father. I wanted Al with me so badly that first moment when the nurse put our son in my arms. I wanted to see Al's face light up; I wanted to watch him stroke the fine swirl of hair on his baby's head and kiss his cheek.

I wanted him to take us both in his arms.

Instead, I asked Patsy to take a photograph. She fixed my hair and made me put on some rouge and lipstick, and then presented me with a box wrapped in lilac paper.

"For the new mother. A little something to remind you that you're still a woman."

I opened it while she held the baby. Inside,

buried in layers of tissue paper, was a peach-colored peignoir with a matching quilted silk jacket.

"You put this on, *then* we take the picture for Al. What better for a guy at war than a photo of his son in the arms of a woman worthy of being a pinup?"

So I changed and sat in the chair by the window, wrapped Al Jr. in the crocheted blanket from his grandmother and beamed at the camera.

Later, when the nurse took Al Jr. back to the nursery, my parents arrived with Thanksgiving dinner. With Carmine and Jimmy overseas, my sisters and my brother Sal spending the holiday with their in-laws, and Cookie and her babies with her parents, Mama needed someone to feed, and I was it.

She made a turkey that she stuffed like a veal roast, with parsley, bread crumbs, sausage and hard-boiled eggs. She even put some *alice*—anchovies—in the stuffing, which she knew I liked but weren't a favorite with anyone else in the family. She had manicotti in her basket, as well, filled with her own ricotta. And she brought me a stuffed artichoke, overflowing with garlic and Parmigiano.

I leaned back and let her slice the meat and pile my plate with more than enough food. Papa, dressed in his Sunday suit, walked down the hall to peer at his new grandson and returned smiling.

"He looks like me. He's gonna be a good boy."

"Hah!" said Mama and handed him a plate of food.

It wasn't Al sitting there with me. God only knew when he'd see his son. But after I'd eaten the meal my mother had prepared for me, I was able to sleep. I wasn't alone.

When Al Jr. was four months old, my boss at Shawmut called. My replacement hadn't worked out; they wanted me back, if I was willing. With so many men called up in the war, the government was encouraging women, even mothers, to go to work. Because Mama offered to take care of Al Jr., I went back.

Mama had done piecework at home when we were kids. So the idea of a mother earning money, working at something outside the family, wasn't an issue for me. But I hadn't thought about what I'd do. I was so intent on giving birth, getting through what scared me the most, that anything afterward was still a dream. All during my pregnancy I prayed that the war would be over by the time the baby came, because I couldn't imagine being a family, being a mother, without Al.

But the war didn't end, and I brought Al Jr. home to the back bedroom in my parents' apartment. I sat on the edge of the bed and held him, and the fear I'd overcome by giving birth was replaced by the fear of having to be both mother and father to him. Once I had him in my arms, heard his cry, felt his heartbeat, I understood what I'd seen in Cookie's eyes the night before Carmine left. Because she was already a mother, she knew. The fierce need to protect our children, keep them safe from harm. It was such a monumental task. I asked myself how I was going to do it without Al, and knew I had to find a way.

The job—being able to provide for us—was part of how I survived the fear. I aired out my suits from the mothballs I'd stored them in, put on my stockings and heels and went back to work.

With so many men gone, there was too much for my boss to handle, and he turned to me. He gave me small jobs at first, but gradually he realized he could trust me with more. I took to numbers quickly. I liked the certainty; I liked the satisfaction of balancing debits and credits. I liked figuring out the worth of something and judging whether someone asking for a loan had the capacity to pay it back. Not just the dollars and cents, but the honor to make good on a promise.

I couldn't define the quality I was looking for when applicants came into the office. Maybe I was simply measuring them against Al, whom I knew to be true to his word, a man who'd face a challenge and meet it, despite the obstacles.

In the afternoons, when I got back from the bank, I changed into my housedress and fed Al Jr. his supper, stacked blocks with him, nuzzled and tickled him until he giggled and kicked his chubby legs. When I put him to bed, we kissed the photo of Al I kept on the dresser.

"Kiss Daddy good-night, sweetheart," I told him, long before he knew what a daddy was.

After he was asleep, I described everything he did in letters to Al. "Al Jr. took his first step today. Your mother held out a *biscott'* and he let go of the chair he was clutching and raced across the room to grab it." "He said 'Da-Da' tonight and pointed to your picture!" "He's out of diapers!" "He climbed the jungle gym in the park on Prince Street for the first time."

It never occurred to me that Al Jr. would be a little boy before he met his father.

I was helping Mama cook for Thanksgiving. We had celebrated Al Jr.'s second birthday on Sunday with his cousins, and Al had managed to send him a birthday card that arrived in time. Al was in the South Pacific. That was all I knew. The newsreels were full of images of planes dropping bombs and exploding battleships. All I could do was pray that one of them wasn't his.

I was up to my elbows in pastry dough for the pies. I'd convinced Mama that we should serve an American apple pie in addition to the sweet ricotta pie with ten eggs and grated orange peel she always made for the holidays—not only Thanksgiving, but Christmas and Easter, as well. I wanted Al Jr. to grow up an American. He spent the week with grandparents who only spoke Italian to him. But his father was an American serviceman, fighting for his country. The least we could do was teach Al Jr. to eat apple pie, sweet potatoes and cranberry sauce.

"You spend too much time with those Americans at the bank. What's wrong with what I cook for the holidays?"

"Nothing's wrong, Mama. It's delicious. But we're Americans, too! It's not such a bad thing. You and Papa chose to come here."

"I don't know how to make apple pie and I'm too old to learn. If you want your son to have apple pie, then you make it."

Which is why I was kneading dough when the doorbell rang. I wiped my hands on my apron and answered.

"Mrs. Dante?" The Western Union delivery boy stood in the doorway, a thin yellow envelope in one hand, a pen and receipt in the other. I blindly signed the form and took the envelope, my hand trembling and a silent voice screaming inside my head, *No! No! No!*

I sat down at the kitchen table and stared at the envelope, unable to move. Al Jr., who'd been playing with a toy truck on the floor, stopped and came up to me, tugging on my sleeve.

"Mommy, Mommy, what's that?"

Mama came in carrying a stack of shirts to iron.

"Rosa, who was at the door?" Then she saw the envelope, made the sign of the cross and kissed the crucifix that always hung around her neck.

"What does it say? Which one? Who?" she screamed at me.

I hadn't even thought of my brothers, God forgive me. But the envelope was addressed to me, not my parents. It could only be Al. But I couldn't answer. I was frozen.

Frantic, she grabbed the envelope and tore it open. She thrust it in front of my face.

"Read it to me!"

I didn't want to. Couldn't.

"Rosa, read it to me *now*. We have to know."

She spoke with the firmness of voice I'd learned to use with Al Jr., and I listened.

" 'Mrs. Dante—We regret to inform you that your husband, Petty Officer Albert Fiore Dante, has been wounded in action in the Philippine Sea. The extent of his injuries is serious and he is awaiting transport to a hospital ship.' "

"Oh, my God, he's alive! He's coming home." And I collapsed in tears in my mother's arms.

# Reunion

TWO MONTHS LATER, in January 1945, Al arrived at the navy hospital in Bethesda, Maryland. I got a few days off from the bank and took the train from South Station to Washington. It had been nearly three years since I'd seen him. When I walked into the ward on that gray day in January I scanned the line of beds looking for my husband and did not recognize him until the nurse pointed him out.

The tanned, robust man who'd left in the spring of 1942 had been replaced by a gaunt, pale shadow. In the intervening months since the telegram arrived, I'd learned that his back, leg and arm had been broken by the impact of an explosion. His body was riddled with shrapnel. Although many of the external scars had healed, he was still in a body cast and faced months of rehabilitation. The navy had informed me that his Seabee career was over. More than likely, he'd never work in construction again.

But he was alive, I repeated to myself. He was alive.

I moved to his bedside. I'd taken the time, when I got to Union Station, to change and put on some makeup. I was wearing his favorite perfume, and as I bent toward him I saw the flicker of recognition at my scent.

"Hey, baby," I murmured and kissed him on the lips.

"Hey, baby," he replied and, with his good arm, pulled me as close as I could get against his rigid cast. I exhaled. We were going to make it.

It would be another month before Al was transferred to the VA hospital in Boston. I couldn't stay with him in Bethesda—because of Al Jr., because of my job—but that first week. I barely left his side.

I fed him. I gave him ice chips to suck on and wiped his forehead when he got the sweats. I bathed the parts of his body not covered in plaster.

At first, he didn't want me to. Out of shame.

"C'mon, Al. I've touched every inch of your body. You think there's something I haven't seen? What did you do, get a tattoo with some other woman's name on it?"

I teased him.

"It's not the same," he protested. "I'm not the same."

"Neither am I. I wasn't a mother before you left. I have a few scars, too."

But it was more than our bodies, I knew, that we were thinking about. We weren't kids anymore. The war had seen to that. And we were strangers to each other. I'd kept so much from him in my letters, not wanting to trouble him with what he could do nothing about. He didn't know about the nights I'd spent walking the floor with Al Jr. when he had the croup and I was afraid it would turn into pneumonia. Or the fight I had with Mama about how to treat it—she with her witches' remedies and me wanting to take him to the doctor. He didn't know that I'd looked for an apartment during my lunch hour after that fight, ready to pack my bags and take my baby. Maybe I'd gotten too used to being on my own in Trinidad. Too much of me had been shaped into something Mama would never understand. There were nights I'd blamed Al for how I felt. If he'd been with me, not fighting the war, we'd have been a normal family with a place of our own. I never talked about this to anyone. I was so ashamed—how unpatriotic, when so many families were sacrificing even more.

I don't know how many times over the past three years I'd imagined Al's homecoming and what it would mean for us. He'd been gone longer than we'd been together and, in the grim, cold winters of Boston, with a sick baby and empty bed, I began to forget who he was. Our life together at Chaguaramas seemed like a fairy tale, a story that had happened to someone else, not Al and me. I wondered if we could ever be those two people again. I could only guess at the secrets Al kept from me during those years apart. Horror. Loneliness. Fear.

Don't get me wrong. Having him back, even broken as he was, was all I wanted. But I was scared. And I knew he was, too. It felt as though we'd have to start all over again, but this time with a child who didn't know his father, and parents—both his and mine—watching every move, listening to every word.

I wanted to scream.

Instead, I got back on the train to Boston at the end of the week, pulled a scrap of paper out of my purse and made a list of every positive aspect of our situation. There were so many women who didn't have half of what I had—no husbands, strangers or otherwise, to welcome back into their beds, no fathers to introduce to their children. They wouldn't even have graves to visit.

"Be grateful," I told myself. "God gave us a second chance."

As the train pulled into South Station late that night I'd calmed down. Al was in no condition to have me go all mopey. He needed me to be stronger now than all the years he'd been away. There'd be time for me to lean on him later.

Al spent two more months in the hospital, but once he was back in Boston, I could visit him every weekend and his mother learned how to take the trolley out to Jamaica Plain on

Wednesdays so she could bring him food. We decided to wait until he was out of his cast before I brought Al Jr. to the hospital. It was the end of March by then and Al was able to sit up in a wheelchair. He was in the hospital solarium when we arrived. He'd shaved and gotten a haircut for the occasion and had even put on some weight since he'd been taken to Bethesda. I convinced myself that he looked close enough to the photograph Al Jr. knew as "Daddy" that he wouldn't be a total stranger to his son.

The whole ride out to the VA hospital I rehearsed with Al Jr. His little legs dangled over the edge of the trolley seat and he swung them back and forth. I'd shined his shoes the night before and pressed his pants and shirt. He looked well-cared for, content. I smiled at how much he was starting to resemble Al as he lost his baby face. I wondered if Al would see himself in his son's eyes.

"Remember, sweetie, we're going to see Daddy, the man in the picture. Just like Papa is my daddy, you have a daddy, too."

"Why doesn't he live with us, like Papa does?"

"Because he's been fighting far away. But he got hurt and now he's getting better so he can come home to us. But he misses you very much and wants to see you."

Al Jr. clung to my hand as we climbed the steps of the hospital, stealing glances along the hallway at bandaged men and briskly moving nurses. He squeezed my hand tighter. Maybe this wasn't such a good idea, I thought. Too much for a little boy to take in. But Al wanted so much not only to see his son, but to hold him, feel the weight of him in his arms.

At the end of the long hallway I bent down in front of the door to the solarium. I took Al Jr.'s face in my hands and kissed him. "Your daddy is waiting for you and he loves you very much. I'm going to be right here with you."

Al was looking out the window when I opened the door. He turned, smiled first at me, then moved his gaze down to his son. His hands gripped the arms of his wheelchair and he pushed himself up onto his feet.

"Hello, son," he whispered. His eyes filled up.

Al Jr. grabbed my leg and hid behind me.

"He's not my daddy," he mumbled into my thigh.

A cloud moved over Al's face. He heaved himself back into the wheelchair.

I put my arm around Al Jr.

"It's okay, sweetie. He *is* your daddy. He just looks a little different from his picture. Remember the baby photo Aunt Patsy took of you the day you were born? You don't look like that anymore, do you?"

He shook his head, still keeping it hidden against me. "No. I'm growed up now."

"Right. And so is your daddy. He's grown up now, too."

He peeked out from his hiding place.

"What's his name?"

"Al. Just like yours. Can you say hi to him?"

He shook his head again.

I saw the disappointment in Al's eyes. And the hunger.

*Give him time,* I mouthed to Al.

"Well, Mommy's going to say hi, so you can stay here or come with me while I give him a kiss."

"Don't go!"

"I'm only going to Daddy. Not far."

I moved deliberately across the room to Al, but Al Jr. still clung to me, hiding behind me as I reached Al and leaned in to kiss him.

"Hi," I said, meeting his lips and lightly brushing his cheek, wet with tears.

"He's beautiful," he murmured.

"Like you," I answered.

"And stubborn."

"Also like you." I smiled, trying to ease his hurt with a little ribbing.

It was at that moment that Al Jr. let go of me and raced out the door.

I pulled back from Al and felt him stiffen.

"I have to go after him," I said, as if I needed to explain.

Then I followed Al Jr. down the hall, his legs

pumping and his arms flailing as if he was running from a nightmare.

And I felt as if I was in the middle of one.

Stern nurses cast me disapproving looks as I chased after Al Jr., my high heels clicking against the linoleum. At the end of the hall an orderly saw him coming and scooped him up. He was sobbing and kicking by the time I got to him.

I thanked the orderly, apologized for my son's outburst with a very red face and took the tangle of beating arms and legs into my own arms.

"We're going outside, young man, while you calm down. Don't you *ever* run away from me again!"

I struggled between the words of a mother who wants to put the fear of God into a child to keep him safe and the words of a mother who understands her child's confusion and anger. I never for even a second felt like running away from Al but, sure as hell, there were moments I wanted to run away from how hard it was to see him the way he was now.

I took Al Jr. outside to a bench and held him on my lap until he stopped sobbing. I got out my handkerchief and wiped his face and made him blow his nose. I figured out I wasn't going to be able to explain to a two-and-a-half-year-old that in time he'd get to know the strange man in the wheelchair and understand how much that man loved him. But I wasn't above bribery and guilt.

"Daddy's feeling very sad because you ran away," I said. "I think we need to go back up and say, 'I'm sorry.'"

Al Jr. shook his head vehemently. "No! I don't want to go back."

"Well, if we go back and say, 'I'm sorry,' then we'd be able to stop at La Venezia on the way home and get a lemon ice."

When we returned to the solarium, Al was still there, thank God. I worried that he might have wheeled himself back to his room, and I couldn't bring myself to take Al Jr. in there. But the solarium overlooked the bench where Al Jr. and I had been sitting, and Al had watched us the whole time.

I carried our son into the room and sat on a chair with him on my lap, his head facing away from Al. I prompted him. "Al Jr. has something he wants to tell you."

It took him a few minutes, but the promise of a treat was enough to get the words out.

"Sorry I runned away."

"Okay, son. But don't ever do that again. Your mom and I want you to be safe. Hey. Now that you're here, do you want to see some pictures of my ship?"

Al pulled a small scrapbook out of the back of his chair and started turning the pages. At first, Al Jr. was wary, but his curiosity soon overcame his need to cling to me. He edged closer to Al and the photos—snapshots taken on the deck of his destroyer. But then he turned a page and Al Jr. recognized something.

"That's me!" He pointed to the photo Patsy had taken of the two of us the day he was born.

"Your mom sent that to me and I've always had it with me, right here." Al touched the pocket over his heart.

"I have a picture of you," Al Jr. said. "But you don't look like in the picture."

Al and I exchanged glances over his head.

"Pretty soon you won't need a picture of me. I'll be right there, home with you and your mom."

## Homecoming

AL CAME HOME at the beginning of May, just before VE Day. He was on crutches and hobbled up the steps to my parents' apartment, his face as white as one of my aunt Carmella's bleached sheets that hung out on the line every Monday. The sweat was pouring from his face as he slumped into a chair in the living room.

I was glad we'd put off his welcome-home party until the following Sunday. I didn't want the rest of the family to see him like this—to take pity on him. And I sensed that he didn't want to be seen—by his brothers, his cousins—as less than the man who had left Boston so long ago. If I knew Al, it would only make him angry to have people feeling sorry for him.

And he was angry enough already. At the hand the war had dealt him; at the pain; at the gaping hole that was his future. What was he going to do with his life now that he couldn't build? Of course, he didn't tell me these things. I had to figure it out myself, lying alone in the middle of the night.

We didn't have room in my bedroom for a double bed, and Al was still recuperating, so he slept on a hospital bed we'd rented and put in the living room, and I stayed with Al Jr. in the bedroom. I was at my wits' end, longing for a moment alone with my husband. Not even to make love, mind you—I understood that was still months away. No, all I wanted was a blessed hour or two to eat a meal that I'd cooked and just the two of us ate, sitting across the table and talking to each other.

But my mother did all the cooking, with me still working at the bank—and thank God for that! Dinnertime was like a movie set for a Frank Capra extravaganza, with a cast of thousands. Al's parents came at least once a week, resentful that we weren't living with them, and we had to go to them on Sundays for dinner. Everybody wanted to see Al, wish him well, exult in the fact that he was alive.

I couldn't blame them. Just seeing him at the table in the kitchen reading the *Herald* when I came home from work was a comfort to me. A sign of normalcy.

But it wasn't enough. Not for me. And I knew that, soon, it wouldn't be enough for Al, either. I understood that we weren't going to have what we'd been blessed to experience on Trinidad at the beginning of our marriage. I'd accepted it. You can't go backward in life, not after you get hit with something as big as World War II. And not after you have kids.

But that doesn't mean you give up on having a decent life. I knew if we stayed too long with my parents, with Al out of work and sleeping in the living room, we'd slip into a pattern that would be too hard to pull away from.

That's why, on my way home from work one summer evening, I stopped in my tracks as I was walking down Salem Street. My feet were killing me; the heat had made them swell up and my pumps were too tight. All I wanted to do was get home and out of those shoes and my suit. I was rushing. And then I saw the sign in the window of Nardone's. It was a small pizza place on the corner of Salem and Stillman. They made a decent Neapolitan pizza and had a few basic dishes—meatballs, eggplant parmigiano—on the menu. I'd heard that old man Nardone had passed away in April.

The sign that made me stop said For Sale.

I stood on the sidewalk for a few minutes. The place was open and a few people were seated at tables. One of the things I'd learned in my time at the bank was the importance of location to a business, especially a business that served the public. I crossed the street and pretended to be looking into the Lu Ann dress shop, but I was actually watching the reflection in the shop-window—watching the number of people walking past Nardone's.

Satisfied, I crossed back and pushed open the door to the restaurant. I sat down, ordered a cup of coffee and chatted with the waitress. I'd seen her now and then in the neighborhood. She'd been a few years ahead of me in high school, although I have to say she looked worn-out. Waitressing is the kind of job that can do that to you, on your feet all day, lifting heavy trays. Despite my too-tight pumps, I was grateful I'd had the training and the skills to get my job at the bank.

"Hey, Milly, I saw the sign in the window. How come the Nardones are selling the place?" I stirred my coffee as if I was just making idle conversation, not seriously interested.

"Anthony's convinced his mother to go to Miami with him. He wants to 'start a new life' and none of the other brothers care about the restaurant. He's champing at the bit to get outta Boston, but far as I know, nobody's biting. All I care is that whoever buys the place keeps me on. Hey, I hear Al's back. How's he doing? My brother was asking about him. Tell him Sonny said hi."

"Thanks, I'll do that."

When I got up, I left her a nice tip. She smiled and waved at me through the window when she went to clear the table.

The next day on my lunch hour I did some research on restaurant sales in the city. Not much was moving, since so many places got passed down to the next generation. I didn't know much about running a restaurant, but I knew food. I hadn't known anything about banking, either, when I'd started three years ago, and I'd learned fast enough. That night after I got Al Jr. settled in bed and Al was listening to the Red Sox game out on the stoop with his cousin, I sat down at the dining room table with my savings account book and my ledger. Al and I probably couldn't buy Nardone's on our own, but if my parents took a share and the bank was willing to give us a loan, we might be able to make an offer. I knew the Nardones owned the building, not just the restaurant, and there were three apartments above it. That meant Al and I could have a home of our own again, and we'd have the rent from the other apartments to help pay off the loan.

I went to bed with a sense of hope that night for the first time since Al had been wounded. I was pretty sure I could talk my boss into the loan—provided I promised to keep working for him and assured him I'd be handling the business end of the restaurant. And I was equally sure Mama and Papa would be willing to invest in and work at the restaurant. It was Al I needed to convince, Al I needed to inoculate with my hope.

I thought back to our early days, especially in our cottage at Chaguaramas, when we'd had nothing under that tin roof except each other, and I knew that, somehow, I had to find our way back there.

To get there, I lied.

I lied first to my boss. "I need to take Wednesday off, Mr. Coffin. An appointment for my husband's treatment, and I have to accompany him."

Next, I lied to Al. "I got a call from the hospital. They've scheduled a checkup for you, but not at the VA. They gave me an address in Marblehead."

"Marblehead? How'm I supposed to get there with these?" He waved his crutches at me. He was getting pretty good at using them as extensions of his emotions, but not so great at moving around with them.

"There's a bus that runs up 1A. I checked. And I'll go with you."

"You don't have to babysit me. What about your job?"

"I'm *supposed* to go with you. I think it's about some new treatment, and they want to teach me how to do it, be part of your recovery."

The thing is, I didn't feel I was lying with the words I was saying. I believed that the reason I was taking Al to Marblehead *was* going to help him recover.

I even lied to Mama.

"I'm not going to work on Wednesday, Mama, but I still need you to watch Al Jr. I can't take him with us to this appointment. It's too much for me with Al still on crutches."

The night before, I stayed up cooking. I made Al's favorite foods, not just Calabrese dishes, but one of the island specialties I'd learned to cook on Trinidad, fried bananas in a sweet rum sauce. I packed everything in a picnic basket the next morning and tucked our bathing suits and beach towels underneath the food. And I wore one of the sundresses I'd made that first year on Trinidad. It still fit, I'm pleased to say.

"You going to the doctor dressed like that?" my mother asked.

Mama let nothing escape her.

"It's a long bus ride, Mama, and it's hot. I've got a shawl to put over my shoulders when we get there."

"I think she looks great, Mama. The doctor will

be jealous." Al was standing in the doorway. The look of appreciation on his face was the first spark of life I'd seen since he'd come home.

I twirled around in front of him, letting him catch a whiff of my perfume.

"You smell like you did on the island," he murmured.

I wanted to pull him into my bedroom right then and there. But with Mama standing in the kitchen, hands on her hips, and Al Jr. dawdling with his farina at the breakfast table, I knew that was a surefire way to extinguish the longing I'd just heard in Al's voice.

One step at a time, I told myself.

"Let's get going. We don't want to miss the bus." I grabbed the basket and brushed Al's hand to follow me.

I'd given us plenty of time to get to Haymarket Square and the bus stop. I didn't want Al to exhaust himself before we'd even started the trip. Our route took us past Nardone's. The For Sale sign was still in the window, but I didn't do anything as obvious as point it out.

Al was wearing his uniform, and everyone we passed made mention of it.

"Welcome home, son."

"God bless you."

"Thank you for your sacrifice."

I could see that Al was embarrassed by the attention.

"It's just their way of showing appreciation." I smiled at him, proud to be at his side.

"Yeah, but so many guys were braver than I was, and they're not here anymore."

"But your being alive doesn't make their sacrifice—or yours—any less." I stroked the side of his cheek.

"I know. But it's hard for me to believe that."

I fought the tears that were welling up in my eyes. I didn't want Al to think the conversation was upsetting me when, in fact, it was exactly what I'd wished for. Just the two of us, talking about things that were important.

We got on the bus and found seats near the front. Al stowed his crutches and the picnic basket in the rack above us and settled stiffly into the aisle seat with his leg stretched out. I saw the by-now familiar wince cross his face and heard the sharp intake of breath that was the only signal he allowed himself to indicate that he was in pain.

He would never have ventured this far, or been willing to risk the pain, if I'd told him where we were going. He would have refused and locked himself back in his empty silence in the living room.

But the twinge appeared to be fleeting this time, which I think surprised him. His face relaxed and I shifted my weight so that my thigh was pressed against his good leg through the thin yellow cotton of my dress. It was the closest we'd been physically since he'd returned, except when I was taking care of him, which didn't really count.

Little droplets of sweat were forming on my upper lip and also dripping down under my arms. I wasn't sure if it was the heat or my own nervousness. If I'd wanted to recreate the atmosphere on Trinidad, I'd gotten off to a good start. It was always hot there, and anytime Al and I had been close our bodies were slick with sweat.

Al reached up and wiped the sweat from my lip with his thumb.

"So where are we really going, Rose? Your mother was right. This dress is no outfit to wear to a VA doctor's office. I'd have to fight guys off with my crutches the minute anybody got a look at you!"

My face turned bright red.

"You knew? Are you angry with me?"

"I'm here on this crazy excursion, ain't I?"

"Well, then. We're going to the beach. Not Revere, where half the world knows us. I wanted us to get completely away. And Marblehead has a bus that goes directly to the water. You won't have to walk very far."

"Why the beach? Why not a picnic on the Common?"

"Because I wanted us to remember Chaguaramas."

At that point, I couldn't hold my tears back. I wanted so much for him to remember.

"I remember Chaguaramas," he said softly. "I remember a beautiful woman in my bed, who made love to me in the rainy season, who swept away scorpions as if they were specks of dust, who kept my dinner warm and waited up for me."

"Oh, Al. I want that for us again."

"Me, too, Rose."

He put his arm around me and kissed me hard. And then he held me all the way to Marblehead.

When we got to the beach we found a spot that wasn't too far along the sand but also wasn't on top of other people. That's why I'd picked Wednesday, hoping it wouldn't be too crowded, like Revere on the weekends—which is fine when you're high school kids hanging out with your friends, but not when you're a couple of lost and lonely adults trying to find their way back to each other.

I spread the blanket on the sand near the shoreline. It wasn't the azure blue of the Caribbean, but the sun caught the water at just the right angle and broke up into thousands of pinpoints of light. It was as if my brother Jimmy's girlfriend, Marie, the Sicilian, had snagged one of her gaudy dresses and all the sequins had spilled across the ocean.

Al pulled me down next to him, and I swear, I

would've done anything with him at that moment. But he whispered to me.

"I just want to hold you, Rose. Rest your head on my chest so I can breathe in your perfume."

We lay like that for a while, quiet, listening to one another breathe. I felt the weight of his arm draped over me and knew with certainty that's where I wanted to be.

When both our stomachs started growling, I stirred.

"How about some lunch?" I murmured.

"As long as you promise to lie down with me again after we eat."

I set out the dishes I'd prepared the night before: chicken salmi that had absorbed the flavors of wine vinegar and garlic and oregano overnight and that we ate with our fingers, the olive oil slick on our chins; string beans and potatoes with some chopped-up tomatoes from Uncle Annio's garden; and the fried bananas now soaked through with rum and brown sugar. I'd even managed to put a couple of bottles of beer in the basket.

"I used to dream of your cooking when I was sitting below deck opening up a can of C rations. Some of the guys in my unit swooned about their girls' hips or legs, the way they danced or kissed. But none of them could brag about the way their girls cooked, because you always had them beat."

"You talked about my food and not my looks? What, is *that* what you remembered about me?" I slapped him playfully, but hard, on the arm.

He laughed. "I kept those memories to myself. I didn't want to share with anybody else what you looked like coming out of the shower or stretched out next to me in bed. I could close my eyes and picture you asleep. Did you know I used to just watch you sleeping? Especially early in the morning when I left for work. Sometimes I sat on the edge of the bed and looked at your face. I couldn't believe someone as beautiful as you was my wife. I still don't."

I choked up a little at that. For a guy who'd been moping on the couch for two months without showing much interest in married life, he'd been holding back *a lot*.

"I'm glad you made us get away, Rose. The sun, the water. It's a little like old times."

"Let's go for a swim." I pulled at his hand. At first, he resisted. I don't think he wanted me or anyone else to see his scarred body. But it really was pretty deserted where we were. I made him hold a towel around me so I could change into my swimsuit, a two-piece from Port of Spain.

"I remember that suit. You still fill it out in all the right places."

He patted my backside. A good sign, I thought. I turned around and began to unbutton his shirt. He stopped my hand and shook his head.

"You go, and I'll admire you from the shore."

"I don't want to swim alone. Besides, it's just us on this part of the beach. I bet your doc would tell you swimming's great exercise. And if you swim, we don't have to lie about getting physical therapy today."

Reluctantly he agreed. But only if I'd glance away while he undressed and also walked ahead of him into the water.

"I don't care what your body looks like, Al. I just want to feel it close to mine."

But I plunged into the water and waited with my back to him until I felt his arms around me. I pressed myself against him and then wriggled free.

"Come on, swim with me."

I dived down under the water and took off. I hadn't been able to swim like this since we'd left Trinidad. The few times I'd taken Al Jr. to Revere Beach, I'd waded in the shallows while he splashed around.

I moved through the water, propelling myself with strong kicks and loving the sensation of slipping through the waves. I looked over my shoulder to see if Al was having as much fun as I was. He was behind me, stroking slowly and carefully, as if he was testing how far he could push himself before he started hurting. But his face was serene, not tight with pain or with the color drained out of him like he got when he hoisted himself up the stairs on his crutches. I think he was surprised.

I turned onto my back and floated, waiting for him to catch up.

When he swam up next to me, I threw my arms over his shoulders and wrapped my legs around him. Out of the water he could never have held me like this. But he cradled me and pulled me close, kissing me as the water lapped around us.

It's a good thing my face was wet and salty already, because it hid the tears.

We swam for about fifteen more minutes, then stretched out to dry on the blanket. Al put on his undershirt when we got out of the water. I turned away so he wasn't embarrassed. But I could see what six months in a body cast had done to the muscles in his chest. I bit my tongue to keep from saying anything, from letting him hear any pity in my voice.

We slept for a little while, relaxed from the swim and the sun in ways that the daily grind didn't allow us. When I felt him stirring, I chose my moment.

"Al?"

"Mmm?"

"Thank you for coming with me today."

"I wouldn't have missed it for the world."

"Me, neither. It's what I dreamed we'd have, all through the time you were away. It's what I dream we'll always have. I've got another dream, Al. A new one. You want to hear about it?"

He turned his body to me, so that we were facing each other.

"Fire away."

I told him about the restaurant for sale, the apartment above it. What I thought we could do with the place. A home of our own. Our own business. I started to get excited, describing the potential I saw on that street.

"Whoa, Rose." He raised his hand to stop my babbling. "How are we going to pay for this?"

He was well aware that I knew to the penny how much money we had in the bank and coming in every month from my paycheck and his navy pension. His question wasn't a challenging or incredulous one. I felt like he believed in me, believed that what I was describing wasn't a pipe dream but was really within our reach.

I sat up, enumerating on my fingers each of the sources I'd thought of. He listened to me.

"Have you talked to your folks yet, or the bank?"

"No, of course not! Not until I'd talked to you. I want this to be *our* future. But only if you want it, too."

"Aw, Rose. What do I know about running a restaurant? My ma did the cooking. All I know is how to hammer a nail and level a two-by-four. And now I can't even do that."

He started to slip back into his shell and I had to grab him before all the goodness from this day in the sun got wiped out by the darkness of his self-pity.

"Al Dante! I've never known you to give up, so don't go giving up on yourself right now. There was a time in your life when you didn't know what a two-by-four *was,* and you learned. You're a smart guy and a brave guy. And I can't believe you'd turn away from something just because you didn't know how to do it. If you have no *interest* in running a restaurant, or think it's a bad decision, then I'll listen to you. But if you're going to say no to every idea I present you with because you feel like you *can't* do it, then you're not the Al I love!"

"I need to take care of my family. I don't want you to feel you have to do it all."

"That's why I got excited when I saw the sign in Nardone's window. I thought we could do it together. And live right above the shop, so I wouldn't have to go off to work every day and be away from you and Al Jr. I want us to have a chance, Al. Whether it's the restaurant or something else."

"You really didn't talk to anyone else about this?"

"No. And I won't until you give me the go-ahead. This is between you and me, Al. I know other girls bring their families into the middle of things, pit themselves against their husbands sometimes. But you and I had a different start than other couples because of Chaguaramas. We only had each other. And all the time you were away and I was living alone with my folks, I never once forgot that I was your wife first. I'm still your wife first, a daughter second. I believe in you, Al. I believe in us—that we have a future together. We're luckier than most. I know you look at yourself and don't see that yet. But you will. Believe in us, Al."

I hadn't intended to get so worked up. I'd meant to be rational and businesslike, to show Al what good sense it made for us to buy the restaurant. Instead, I was becoming dramatic. I had his hands in mine and held them tight, as if to transfer to him all the faith I had that we would make it.

Maybe it was the difference between men and women, or maybe it was the difference between being in the middle of battle and being on the homefront. I'd had fears, but bombs weren't exploding next to my bed; nobody'd pointed a gun at my head or at my baby. If that's what it was, we were always going to have that gulf between us—our separate experience of the past three years. And I'd have to be the one who fought for us to have faith in ourselves and our future.

That's what I grasped that afternoon on the

beach, and why I poured my heart and soul into convincing Al that we had to have the courage to take the next step in our lives—even if that step seemed to be off the side of a cliff. I needed to let him know that I was holding the release cord on the parachute and I wouldn't let us fall.

"You really want this, don't you, Rose?"

"Yeah, I do. But not for me. For *us*—you, me and Al Jr."

"Then I'm okay with it."

It was all I could ask for right then—that he was okay with the idea. I understood he was still too scared and too tired to imagine himself strong enough to take on anything more than getting himself up the stairs on his own. But I didn't ever want him to think he wasn't strong enough to take care of his family.

I threw my arms around him. "Oh, thank you, Al!"

I kissed him hard and he pulled me close.

That night, Al came to my bed after my parents had gone to sleep.

"I need to hold you. I can't give you anything else right now. But lying next to you on the beach I realized how much I miss having you in my arms."

I lifted the sheet in welcome and he slid his sunburned body next to mine. I nestled my behind against his belly; he wrapped his arms around me and we settled into the best night's sleep either of us had had in years.

# Paradiso

A MONTH LATER, the Japanese surrendered. The war was over. And the Dante and Vitale families bought a restaurant.

After Al had agreed to my idea on the beach at Marblehead, we sat down with my parents and asked them to put money into the restaurant. And as I'd expected, they said yes—not only to the money, but to helping us out, Papa with the renovations, Mama in the kitchen.

It took us three months to clean the place up. No wonder Anthony Nardone's brothers wanted nothing to do with it. It was a pigsty. One of the first things I did was get a cat to take care of the rats.

On nights and weekends I scrubbed and bleached and scoured. Al started tinkering with the equipment, and even though his right arm was too damaged to wield heavy tools, he found he could still do the delicate work with small parts that took a sharp eye and a slow, careful hand. He could've been a surgeon, I told him. Thanks to Al, we didn't have to scrap the stove or the refrigerator.

We hoisted a new sign over the windows just

before Thanksgiving. *Paradiso*. It was red and black with gold leaf around the edges of the letters. Everybody got dressed up and we took a photo out front—Al and me, Al Jr., my parents and Al's parents. Then we went inside and toasted with a bottle of Papa's Chianti.

We held Thanksgiving dinner in the restaurant that year, shortly before we opened to the public. Everybody came. My brothers Carmine and Jimmy had made it back safe from Italy. My sister Bella traveled from Albany with her husband and three kids. My brother Sal, the butcher, who lived up the street, my sister Lillian, who'd moved out to the country when her husband got a job at the General Radio factory, my sister Ida, the nurse, who worked at Mass General, Al's folks, his brothers and their wives—they all trooped down to Salem Street. The first snow had fallen and everyone arrived with red cheeks and cold feet, hungry and looking for warmth and a good meal.

We didn't disappoint. We'd pushed all the tables together to fit the thirty of us. While the three turkeys roasted, Mama and I spent the morning arranging platters of antipasto with her pickled eggplant, olives, fennel, roasted red peppers, vinegar peppers, marinated mushrooms, tuna, provolone, salami, prosciutto and *soprasatto*. After the antipasto, we served escarole soup with little meatballs, then Mama's handmade manicotti and, finally, the turkey along with candied yams and broccoli and cauliflower that we'd battered and fried the way Mama did zucchini flowers in the summer. For dessert, Mama made her sweet ricotta pie and I, of course, baked the apple pies.

We ate for four hours. To have everyone together, especially the boys home from the war, was a gift. But not everyone was happy for us about the restaurant. I put it down to jealousy and lack of imagination. I felt resentment from my brother Sal's wife, who until then had been able to feel like the queen of the manor because her husband owned his own business.

My brother Jimmy worried that Mama and Papa were in over their heads financially. Because I was the baby of the family, he thought my parents were spoiling me, doing for me what the others had to do for themselves.

So there was this undercurrent of tension at dinner. I saw the eyes of appraisal as people came into the dining room. It wasn't fancy, but it wasn't cheap-looking, either. We had curtains on the windows that I'd sewn and cloth tablecloths and napkins. The linoleum on the floor had been stripped and waxed and buffed, so it looked like new.

I knew the value of appearances. You had to look like a winner for people to believe you were a winner. But some of my family thought I was putting on airs, trying to be better than they were.

And they were right. I *did* want to do better. I didn't want to spend the rest of my life in a back bedroom overlooking the alley. I wanted my son and the rest of my children, God willing, to have more than we had growing up in the Depression.

Don't get me wrong. Most of them at the table that day wished us well.

*"Salute,"* they said. *"Buona fortuna!"*

But those with small minds and jealous hearts only knew how to be naysayers, full of doom and gloom.

"What do any of you know about running a restaurant?" they sniffed.

"Do you know how many restaurants go under in the first year?"

"How much in hock are you—and Mama and Papa—for this place?"

At one point, I had to get up from the table and go into the kitchen to keep from shooting my mouth off and throwing the whole family into turmoil.

Al followed and found me furiously slicing bread, tears ruining my makeup.

"Hey, babe," he said quietly, putting his arms around me. "I miss you out there."

"They make me so mad! I was afraid I'd say something I'd regret and upset Mama."

"They can all go to hell. Especially after we show them what a success this place will be. Just ignore them. Let them stuff their bellies with your delicious food and then go home, mad that they didn't think of it themselves."

He kissed me on the neck. I wiped my face and brought the basket of bread to the table with my head held high.

I worked at the bank another whole year while we got on our feet with Paradiso. Al and I moved with Al Jr. into the space directly above the restaurant; we'd kept the tenants in the other two apartments—the Boscos, who had no children, in the smaller one on the top floor, and the Agostinos, who'd been in America about three years, right below them. Both families were good people who paid the rent on time and were happy with the change in landlords.

Paradiso survived that first year with all of us working hard. When I came home at three o'clock, I changed into my cooking clothes and headed downstairs to help Mama and Al. We served pizza and sandwiches—meatball, sausage and peppers, cold cuts—for lunch. At five o'clock we started serving dinner. We kept Milly on as a waitress, and when it got busy, I waited tables, as well. Al had been cautious in the kitchen when we first opened, deferring to Mama and doing whatever she instructed him to do, which wasn't much beyond adding ingredients to pots she'd already started. But when our volume began building, he saw for himself that he needed to take on more. He conquered pizza, mastered a kneading technique that only required one hand, and worked out a smooth assembly process that got the pies in the oven in record time. From there, he started taking on other dishes with gusto, watching Mama downstairs at Paradiso or me on Sundays in the kitchen upstairs. He'd slip his arms around my waist and, in between nuzzling my neck, watch and sniff as the garlic and basil hit the olive oil in the pan.

"I figured it out the other night, Rose. Cooking in a restaurant kitchen and building bridges on a South Pacific island in the middle of conflict are a lot alike."

The business grew. At the end of our first year we'd more than kept up with our loan payments. When I finished doing the books in November 1946, just before Thanksgiving and Al Jr.'s fourth birthday, I got up from the kitchen table and found Al downstairs in the cellar taking inventory. He was counting jars of tomatoes that Mama and I had put up in August.

I leaned against the shelf and studied him. He wasn't as washed out and scrawny as he'd been the summer before, and the haunted look that had been his constant expression only broke through now and then when he wasn't busy. When you saw him from his left side, as I was doing, you didn't notice how withered his right arm was. It was more than having filled out on good Italian cooking. He looked sturdy and purposeful, a man who knew he was doing useful work. The more confident he became, the more he'd taken on in the kitchen. Pretty soon he'd moved from being Mama's apprentice to becoming our primary chef. I smiled to myself. He was still handsome.

"What?" He'd finished counting, wrote the total on his clipboard, then glanced at me with curiosity.

"Can't a girl admire her man once in a while, especially in a dark corner when no one else is watching?"

"You didn't come down here to flirt. What's up? Did you find a problem with the books?"

"Just the opposite. We've cleared enough in the past three months to cover my salary at the bank. I wanted to talk to you about my quitting and working full-time at the restaurant."

"You sure that's what you want? Your job at the bank's important to you. You're so smart. Is this going to be enough?"

He was really asking, *Am I going to be enough?* Sometimes the man could be so blind to how much I loved him and it drove me crazy that he thought my job was more important than him and our life together. . . . So I played it out a little to show him how ridiculous that was.

"Maybe you're right. Maybe I should forget about the restaurant altogether and stick with banking. I'll become a businesswoman and give up everything—my child, the man I love—for my almighty career. On my deathbed I'll pat the pile of money I've accumulated, 'cause that'll be all I've got, and tell myself it was worth it."

I stuck my tongue out at him. "Jeez, Al. I don't know where you get these ideas."

He put down the clipboard and took me in his arms.

"If you want to quit the bank and you think we can manage, then go ahead."

# ROSE
## 1947–55

# Miami

I HANDED IN my resignation on the Monday after Thanksgiving and by Christmas had packed up my desk in a Hood milk crate and headed out the door. Mr. Coffin was a gentleman about it, but we both knew there were five guys back from the war waiting in line to take my job.

I was also two months pregnant, which I found out on New Year's Eve. I hadn't experienced any of the throwing up or exhaustion I'd had with Al Jr., so it was a surprise. But not an "Oh, no, what am I going to do now?" surprise. I'd seen some women react like that, women with too many mouths to feed and a husband still trying to put the war behind him and get on with life.

Ours was a joyful surprise. You'd have thought Al had played the numbers and won big when I told him. He whooped and danced me around the restaurant. Later that night in bed, he lifted my nightgown and kissed my belly.

Our son Michael was born in July of 1947 and spent his infancy in a bassinet in the restaurant kitchen, falling asleep to the Frank Sinatra records we played and the sizzle of bracciola frying in olive oil. Our daughter was born in

1950. We followed tradition and named her after Al's mother, Antonella, but like many things my generation was doing differently from our parents, we called her Toni. That wasn't on her baptismal certificate, of course, but I don't think I ever called her Antonella. Even when I was yelling at her and stringing together all her names for effect, I always said, "Toni Marie Dante! You stop that right now."

My generation was different from our parents when it came to having kids. I don't know how my mother managed with seven. Yes, I do. She depended on the older ones to watch out for the younger ones; she laid down the law, expecting us to abide by it, and she pretty much left us to amuse ourselves while she cooked, cleaned, washed clothes and did piecework. She didn't worry the way I did about my kids.

By the time I had three, I was done in. One Saturday night in 1952, right after I'd nursed all three kids through two weeks of the measles, we cooked for a private party for an engaged couple—five courses, one hundred people and enough wine to give them all headaches the next day. I finished up in the kitchen, sent the extra help home with their pay and their tips and locked up. I crawled upstairs, checked on the kids asleep in their beds and collapsed in my own. It was more than physical fatigue. I was over the edge. I'd yelled all day: "Where was the extra wine we'd ordered?" "Who took delivery on the veal, because there wasn't enough?" "Why aren't the tables set?" "Do I have to do everything myself?" You get the idea. I'd been so wrapped up in making sure my kids didn't go blind from the measles or—God forbid—die from it, that I'd neglected the details downstairs and paid for it in a massive case of *agita.*

I must have slept for almost twenty hours after that. We closed the restaurant on Sundays back then, so my mind simply shut down. Al made the kids some pastina with beaten egg and let them play. They were just well enough to feel bored with being cooped up in dark rooms for two weeks and were getting on one another's nerves. How Al kept them away from me, I don't know, but he did.

When I finally woke up on Sunday evening, groggy and with my mouth as dry as my aunt Zita's almond cookies, Al already had the kids bathed and in bed.

"You need a rest, Rose. And I mean more than a long sleep like you just had. Why don't we close the restaurant for a couple of weeks after Christmas, ask Carmine and Cookie to watch the kids, and you and I drive to Miami?"

"How can I do that? What if they get sick again?"

"Then we come back. But you should've seen them today. They're full of energy. If you don't take some time off, you'll be the one to get sick, and then where'll we be?"

And that's how we started going to Florida every winter. It was a mixed blessing. Something I don't talk about, because Florida was how Al met Estella.

Despite my reluctance and reservations about leaving the kids, Florida was just what I needed that year. We stayed in Miami Beach at the Casablanca; after 1954, it was always the Fontainebleau, which was right on the ocean. Al, who always had a good eye for what looked good on me, had put a stack of boxes under the tree at Christmas, each one holding a beautiful outfit for me to wear in Miami: cocktail dresses in aqua-blue lace and wine-red satin; jersey halter dresses with plunging necklines and cinched waists to show off the figure I'd gotten back after Toni's birth; two Jantzen bathing suits, one a maillot and one a two-piece floral print that reminded me of the suit I'd worn years before on the beach at Marblehead; silk and cashmere wraps for the evenings. At the top of the stack was a tiny box with a pair of diamond earrings.

We had a ball. We went out dancing every evening, at the Copa or the Napoleon Ballroom at the Deauville Beach. Then we slept till noon, ate lunch on the pool patio and walked on the beach in the afternoon. I swam laps in the pool or bodysurfed in the waves.

One afternoon at lunch Al slipped an envelope across the table.

"What's this?"

"Two Pan Am tickets."

"Are we going to fly home? Has something happened to one of the kids?" I could feel my heart start to race.

Al grinned. "Everybody's fine, Rose. This is a little surprise. One of the guys I played cards with the other afternoon recommended a side trip to Havana—the casino, the nightlife. I thought we should give it a try, spend a night. It'll be like the old days, the island life."

So the next day we flew on a little puddle jumper to Havana, along with men my banking experience told me had a lot of cash to throw around. I made Al promise me he'd only take one hundred dollars in chips at the casino, and when that was gone, we'd spend the rest of the time dancing.

Havana was really something in those days, at least the Havana that we saw. Cadillac convertibles cruising the streets, pastel buildings filled with shops and restaurants, the casino ablaze with crystal chandeliers and open all night long. If Fidel Castro and Che Guevara were up in the hills then, nobody at the roulette table was giving it a second thought. Like most gamblers, they assumed their winning streak would last forever.

And the women at the casino were gorgeous.

Elegant and sophisticated. You could tell that most of them were mistresses, not wives. The jewelry was too ostentatious—the consolation prizes for not having the diamond and the wedding band the wives back in the States were wearing. And I imagine that some of those beautiful women were sitting by the sides of men they might not have come with but hoped to leave with.

It was an experience. I wore the burgundy strapless number Al had given me for Christmas and I'd had my hair and nails done in the hotel salon. I'd pulled my hair back from my face so you could see the diamonds in my ears.

While I was getting dressed, Al kissed my neck.

"If I win big tonight, I'll buy you a necklace to match the earrings."

"If you win big tonight, we're putting the money in the bank for the kids, but I'll always remember you wanted to give me a necklace," I told him with a kiss.

I knew Al was proud of me when we walked into the casino. He had his arm around my waist like a caress. I spent the evening perched on a stool next to him at the blackjack table, my leg pressed against his through the satin. Every now and then he'd gently squeeze my thigh.

"You bring me luck, Rose. Throughout my life."

When he hit a thousand dollars, I leaned over and whispered in his ear. "Let's finish this stroke of good fortune in the bedroom."

With a smile, he gathered up his chips, cashed them in and followed me to our hotel room. Through the louvered shutters on the windows I could hear the waves and the music of Sinatra wafting from somebody's radio.

Two winters later, Al's cousin Mario and his wife, Vera, were down in Miami at the same time. Mario had heard Al go on about Havana and wanted to fly over for a couple of days at the casino. Vera didn't want to go. She was deathly afraid of flying and begged me to stay with her and keep her company while Al and Mario went. Against my better instincts, I agreed.

Al and Mario were gone longer than they planned. Like a fool, I initially assumed it was because they were winning. Al wasn't much of a gambler, but he liked to go to the track now and then. He must've been winning big. I pictured him tapping the cards with his good left hand and keeping his right arm resting on his lap. I'd tailored the white jacket of his tux to fit him. By the time he and Mario went to Havana he already had a nice tan. I could understand that in Havana's high-stakes, booming culture, a guy could get caught up in the excitement. With his slicked-back dark hair and penetrating eyes, I'm sure he was on every unattached woman's radar the minute he strolled into the casino.

There's a heat to the Caribbean that we both knew—a heat that has nothing to do with the temperature. It's in the music, the dancing, the way people—especially women—just walk down the street. When you're near someone, you see the sweat glistening on her skin and you smell her perfume mingled with her own distinctive fragrance.

My imagination was taking me places I really didn't want to go. By the end of three days of playing canasta with Vera and drinking too many daiquiris at the bar before dinner, I was ready to get on a plane myself and drag Al back. He hadn't even called.

He and Mario finally showed up on the fourth day, rumpled, unshaven, but with wide grins, big cigars and a lot of cash. Vera and I were on the patio having coffee and Danishes, so I wasn't going to make a scene in public, but I was seething.

They went upstairs to shower and sleep.

Vera shrugged. "Boys will be boys."

"Al's not a boy," I said sharply. "He's got three kids and a wife who loves him. He should know better."

I let Al sleep it off for a few hours. I considered going through his pockets, but decided not to stoop so low. Instead, I took a long walk on the beach without Vera, who was really annoying me. In my head I enumerated all the reasons I should give Al the benefit of the doubt. He'd always been faithful, never even looked at another woman. He took tender care of me; suggesting that we spend time in Florida at all had been for my benefit. He adored the kids. He worked hard. So what if he spent an extra couple of days throwing money around? He'd come back, hadn't he? I thought I could forgive him. But I promised myself I'd go to Havana with him from now on.

When I got back to the hotel room Al was getting dressed. You could see why a woman would be drawn to him.

I sat down on the edge of the bed. "You want to talk about why you stayed in Havana so long without even a phone call? For all I knew, someone had rolled you and left you in an alley somewhere."

"I'm sorry, Rose. We were playing so hard we lost track of time. We got into a card game—you don't just walk away down there."

"Since when do you gamble like that, Al? I've never known you to be so obsessed." Maybe it wasn't a woman.

"I'm not. But Mario, he's reckless. I felt I needed to keep an eye on him. My mother and my aunt Philomena would never forgive me if I let him get in over his head. Like I said, I'm sorry."

I stared hard at him, trying to see the truth in his eyes. It scared me that I doubted him. He'd never let me down. I decided I needed to give him this one. And I didn't ask him if he'd been with a woman.

"Okay," I said.

He lifted me from the bed and kissed me. He smelled of the hotel's fancy soap, Prell shampoo and his Old Spice aftershave.

But Cuba still clung to him.

I tried to shake the scent—and the suspicion. I didn't want to be weighed down with it. I didn't want to ruin our last night in Florida.

I put a smile on my face, changed into my sexiest dress and went down to dinner with Al. But it was still there in the far-off look in his eyes every now and then, as if he'd remembered something. It was still there in my own watchfulness.

That night in bed we didn't reach out for one another—me because I couldn't bring myself to touch him, Al because he fell into a profound sleep minutes after hitting the pillow.

# A Piece Missing

WE STARTED THE DRIVE back to Boston the next day and didn't speak about Havana again. By the time we arrived in the North End, to kids who'd missed us despite having a ball with their cousins, and a restaurant stove that needed to be fired up again, I was too busy to deal with whatever Al had done in Cuba.

Oh, my wariness was still there. I felt like I had antennae constantly rotating, trying to pick up a signal: an unexplained phone call, a letter with a Havana postmark, a receipt for a piece of jewelry that wasn't sitting in *my* jewelry box or a dress that wasn't hanging in *my* closet. I was on pins and needles. I didn't know what I'd do if I found any of those signs—after crying my eyes out, that is. I didn't find anything, nor did I want to. But I realized that didn't prove that nothing had happened.

As you can imagine, I was on edge those first weeks back. Florida was supposed to be our R & R, and instead, it had turned me into a bundle of nerves. On top of that, Al Jr. was having trouble in school. There was a note from Reverend Mother, asking me to come in for a meeting as soon as we were back.

I've never done well with nuns. The ones I'd had to deal with growing up always made me feel like a tramp. My skirt was too short or my sweater was too tight or I had on too much makeup. I took pains when I kept my appointment with Reverend Mother to wear a suit and not one of the outfits Al had bought for me. But I was still nervous.

When I walked into the school I could feel my stomach churn. The smell of whatever they used on the floors—disinfectant, wax—lurched me right back to when I'd been in seventh grade at St. John's, heading down the hall to be chastised for talking back to Sister Alphonsus when she'd wrongly accused Vinny Tosi, an immigrant boy who'd arrived from Avellino only a few months before. She always assumed the worst of the Italian kids, especially the boys.

Reverend Mother's office was stuffy and dark, with the blinds drawn instead of open to the playground where the children were at recess. Hanging behind her desk was a large crucifix with Christ in agony.

"Thank you for coming, Mrs. Dante. I was surprised when you didn't respond to my note, but Albert told me you and your husband were in Miami. We don't see many parents taking a vacation in the wintertime and leaving their children."

"My children were with their aunt and uncle

while we were away." This woman was already making me bristle.

"Yes, well. Perhaps it was because you were gone that Albert thought he could get away with his behavior."

"Exactly what did he do?"

"He's disrespectful, Mrs. Dante. A back talker. We also have reason to believe he's being influenced by older, public-school boys. I brought you in to let you know that we don't tolerate insolence at St. John's. If you don't put a tighter rein on him, we may ask him to leave."

"I'll talk to him about his mouth and what he's picking up from the older boys. I don't expect to have to come back."

I got up and held my back straight the whole way down that highly polished corridor. But instead of turning for home, I went in the opposite direction toward the waterfront. Some of the piers weren't the best place for a woman to walk, even in broad daylight, but there was a short stretch near Lewis Wharf where I could sit on a stone wall and see and smell the ocean. It was where I went when I needed to collect my thoughts.

I hated the way I felt just then. Small. A failure as a mother. Oh, I'd have my words with Al Jr. when he got home from school, especially about the older boys he was supposedly spending time with. The neighborhood was changing, not that there hadn't always been tough guys hanging out on the corners. But it wasn't what I intended for my own kids.

I felt as if my hold on Al Jr. was slipping, loosening far sooner than I knew a mother ought to let go. It wasn't just that Al and I had gone to Florida for a couple of weeks. I was being pulled in too many directions—the kids, the restaurant, the strain between Al and me since Havana—and I wasn't giving enough attention to any of them.

I was falling apart. I felt like I had a piece missing, something important that the people I loved needed from me and that I couldn't give. That I didn't have. Which was why Al had gone looking for it elsewhere in Havana, and Al Jr. had tried to find it by seeking out boys he thought were big shots in the neighborhood.

The wind off the harbor and my tears stung my cheeks. I felt frozen to the stone wall, unable to move, not knowing how I was going to fill this empty space inside me. But the afternoon was wearing on. Soon enough, Mike and Al Jr. would be home from school and Toni would wake from her nap. Mama and Al were already in the kitchen prepping for the evening meal. They were all expecting me.

But I didn't move. It scared me that I wasn't picking myself up and getting on with what I recognized as my responsibilities. I didn't think a conversation with a nun—even a Reverend

Mother—could push me over the edge like this. But I knew it wasn't just the judgment that I was a poor mother.

I knew I'd bottled up my anger and kept my mouth shut about Havana because to all outward appearances nothing had happened there. I had grown up watching women of my mother's generation look the other way when their husbands had an *amante*—a mistress—on the side, as long as he put food on the table and kept up the appearance of a marriage. I just had never understood the cost.

Al had slipped back into our Boston routines without a hitch. But he'd never said to me, "I swear, Rose, I wasn't with another woman." Because I'd never asked him. What I realized now, sitting on this cold rock and shivering as the sun set behind me, was that I needed to ask him. I wouldn't be able to let go of the doubts that were eating away at my insides. And if he said yes, I needed to know why he'd been unfaithful.

Sometimes it's hard to look at yourself and face the truth. I really wanted to bury in some remote corner of my heart whatever Al had done in Havana. But no matter how many layers I tried to muffle it with, I could still feel it—like the pounding of the telltale heart in Poe's story. Well, I wasn't going to let this make me crazy.

Wrapping my coat tightly around me, I stood. The streetlights had come on. My feet were frozen, but I got the circulation back in them as I started walking. About halfway down Atlantic Avenue I saw a figure coming toward me. It was Al. I could see the white edges of his chef's jacket flapping beneath the hem of his old navy peacoat.

"Rose! Rose! Where the hell have you been all afternoon? I called Cookie and Patsy. Nobody had seen you. When it got dark, I thought maybe you had an accident! I couldn't stay in the restaurant not knowing where you were. I was pacing like a madman. First, I was furious with you for not showing up or even calling, then I was just worried. The kids are upset. What happened to you?"

"I got lost, Al. In my thoughts. I was upset after meeting with Reverend Mother about Al Jr. and we need to talk about that, but later. I went down to the water to think."

"How long does it take to think?"

I could sense Al's frustration and anger. Maybe this wasn't the best time and place to have this conversation, but I'd spent the last month finding too many reasons not to have it at all.

"Long enough to consider not coming home at all."

"What are you talking about, Rose? What did the nun say that would make you not come home? What did Al Jr. do?"

"It's not Al Jr. But what happened at my

meeting made me ask myself how I was living my life, and the answer is that I've been avoiding the truth."

"What are you talking about?"

"I've been hiding my anger. From you. From myself."

"Anger about what?"

I took a deep breath. "Havana."

I thought he'd start again about babysitting his cousin in the casino. But he didn't.

"What do you want to know, Rose?"

"I want to know if you had an affair in Havana."

The cold moisture that had been blowing in off the harbor all afternoon was turning to an icy rain. But the discomfort I saw in Al's face had nothing to do with the weather.

"I don't want to hurt you with my answer."

"You'll hurt me more if you lie."

"Her name was Estella. I spent one night with her. That's all. I swear to God. I'm sorry, Rose."

I felt a different kind of chill than what I'd been sitting through all afternoon on the pier. It spread from inside me, filling my belly with such pain that I thought I wouldn't be able to walk. Was this really better than the gnawing doubt?

"Why, Al?" I could barely say the words. "Am I not enough anymore?"

"It's nothing you did or didn't do. I was a jerk. Caught up in the high-rolling, anything-goes atmosphere of the casino. Telling myself that after all I went through in the war, all the struggle to recover from my wounds, all the work to make the business a success, I deserved it. It was . . . like I was outside my life, and that whatever I did wouldn't touch you or the kids. But after that I could tell something was wrong between us. You may think I don't notice but, Rose, I know—maybe sometimes even before you do—when something's bothering you. That's why I came looking for you tonight, when I realized you weren't with anybody and hadn't told us where you were. I knew I had to find you. I knew I didn't want to lose you. What I did was stupid and selfish."

I didn't want to lose him, either. But the pain of his betrayal was too fresh. The knowledge I had now had ended my doubts. I certainly didn't have to wonder anymore. But what I knew didn't give me any comfort. It didn't show me what to do next.

"I have no idea what to say to you right now, Al. I can't even think, I hurt so much. Let's just go home. If the kids are upset I need to be there."

We trudged silently. When we started to cross Hanover Street he took my elbow protectively and I flinched.

I had never felt so alone, not even when he was overseas.

When we got back to Salem Street, Al headed

to the kitchen door of the restaurant and I went straight upstairs. Papa was with the kids. I could see from the dishes in the sink that they'd eaten macaroni.

Al Jr. was in the bedroom he shared with Mike and didn't come out. He knew I'd gone to see Reverend Mother and had probably put two and two together. Toni was lying on the couch fingering her blanket next to Papa, whose idea of babysitting is to read *Il Progresso*. He figures that as long as he's in the apartment, the kids can find him if they need him. Mike was sitting at the kitchen table with newspapers spread out, gluing together a model of a navy destroyer.

When I came in, Papa put the newspaper down. *"Dove eri tu?"*

His English is passable, but if he doesn't want the kids to know what he's talking about, he uses Italian.

"I had things to take care of. Important things. Thank you for watching the kids."

He shrugged, folded the paper and got up to leave.

"They need their mother," he mumbled.

Toni scrambled into my arms. "Where were you, Mommy? I woked up and you weren't there."

"I had a meeting, baby. But I'm home now. Let's go have a bath."

I stuck my head in the kitchen. "Mike, do you have any homework?"

He looked up sheepishly from his model.

"Just some arithmetic. I have to memorize the nine times table."

"Come and sit by the bathroom door while I give Toni her bath and go over them with me."

It was eight o'clock before I got Toni to bed and Mike had recited his multiplication table often enough to have it stick. I let him go back to his model and then went in to talk to Al Jr. Al was still downstairs in the restaurant but at that moment I didn't want him with me.

Those first couple of years of Al Jr.'s life, when we only had each other, we grew close. I could read in his face, without his saying anything, if something was wrong.

The lights were out and he was in bed. Now, this was a kid who thought he was too old for a regular bedtime, a kid who considered himself beyond the rules I set for his little brother and sister.

I flicked on the light and sat on the edge of his bed. "I know you're not asleep, A.J. Sit up, because I need to talk to you."

He turned his back to me and pulled the covers over his head. I had no patience for this tonight.

"Sit up right now, young man. Unless you want to have this conversation with the back of my hand."

That got him upright.

"Reverend Mother tells me you're being disrespectful at school and acting like those smart alecks down on Prince Street who do nothing but hang out on corners and smoke cigarettes. Is this true?"

It seemed to me I was asking for a lot of truth from the men in my life that day.

"They gave me a quarter for running errands for them."

"What kind of errands?"

"I got their cigarettes."

Oh, my God. Fireworks were going off in my brain. "You didn't *steal* those cigarettes, did you?"

"*No!* They gave me the cash and I ran down to the news store to get them."

"So, you're their errand boy, and for that privilege they let you hang around with them?"

"I'm the only one they talk to. The other guys in my class are such babies. I'm not a baby anymore."

He was going to be twelve in six months. Now, in my book, that's not a baby, but it's not a man, either. He was all arms and legs, not even peach fuzz over his lip.

"No, you're not a baby. You're a boy. Who ought to know better than to answer back or treat a teacher without respect. No matter what those morons on the corner do or say. Did it ever occur to you that the reason they're hanging out is because they have nothing in their heads? No dreams to strive for. No respect for themselves, let alone their teachers or parents. I don't want you running any more errands for them. If you're looking for more work and more quarters, I've got plenty for you to do downstairs. And I want nothing but 'Yes, Sister' from you at school. I never want to be called into Reverend Mother's office again. Do you understand?"

"Yes, Mom."

I hoped that would be the end of it. He had two more years to get through at St. John's, and I didn't need more of Reverend Mother's withering judgment or, God forbid, Al Jr. getting into trouble outside school with mischief that crossed the line into petty crime.

I was exhausted. I yelled at Mike to clean up the mess on the kitchen table and get to bed. I couldn't even give him a hug when I saw the tears well up in his eyes. What had he done wrong? It was his brother who'd gotten into trouble and his mother who'd been gone all afternoon.

I left the dirty dishes in the sink and went to bed, but I couldn't sleep. Too many pieces of my life were falling apart. I'd always felt rock-solid, been the one to make decisions and carry them out. For the first time, I didn't know what to do.

I couldn't stay in bed tossing and turning alone. Maybe it would've been worse if Al had been there, maybe not. I wasn't sure I could stand having him beside me, knowing he'd shared a bed with the Cuban. But I wasn't sure if I could stand *never* having him in my bed again, either.

I got up, put on my robe and slippers and went to the kitchen to heat myself some milk and a little brandy. I washed the dishes, figuring I'd only have a hardened crust of tomatoes to deal with in the morning if I left them.

The next morning was St. Joseph's Day. I'd forgotten. A day to invite people in off the street to a feast at the St. Joseph Table. A couple of years ago we'd begun to invite the neighborhood charitable societies for a free lunch in the restaurant.

Usually I spent the day before St. Joseph's baking cream puffs. I hurried out to the back landing off the kitchen where we keep our extra refrigerator. Inside it were the eggs and fresh ricotta I'd had delivered in the morning, which meant Mama hadn't gone ahead and made the puffs when I didn't come back this afternoon.

I lugged everything out of the refrigerator, rolled up my sleeves and put on my apron. I have to admit, furiously beating the eggs into the flour to make the cream puff dough was a lot better use of my *agita* than struggling to fall asleep.

By the time Al came upstairs from the restaurant I had three racks cooling on the kitchen table, another two dozen puffs in the oven and I was whipping sugar into the ricotta for the filling.

He didn't say anything. I could feel the muscles of my back stiffen, and my fingers clenched the whisk in my hand. But I kept my hand moving. I heard a sigh that sounded like relief to me. That I hadn't packed my bags—or his. That I was standing in my nightgown in the kitchen with a smudge of flour on my cheek, doing what I always did on the day before the feast of St. Joseph.

He went to the drawer and pulled out a knife and a pastry bag and started slitting the cooling puff shells. I finished preparing the ricotta cream and removed the last of the shells from the oven. He filled the pastry bag with the ricotta and began piping it into the puffs.

After that, I placed them on trays, wrapped them and set them in the refrigerator.

Neither of us had said a word.

Al was filling the sink with soapy water as I closed the refrigerator door on the last tray of cream puffs. He washed; I dried.

When we had nothing left to do in the kitchen, the thread that had been holding us together snapped. In the kitchen, we'd done what we'd always done; we hadn't had to make any choices or ask any questions.

But now, faced with moving from kitchen to bedroom, one question loomed over us.

It was Al who broke the silence.

"Do you want me to sleep on the couch?" he asked, standing in front of the linen closet.

Did I want him out of our bed? No. But the way I saw it, he'd taken himself out of it by his own action.

"Yes," I said. I handed him bedding from the closet. I went into our bedroom and shut the door. No night I'd spent without him during the war was lonelier or harder than that night.

In the morning, despite how late we'd been up making the cream puffs, he was awake before the kids and had put away the sheets. He had a pot of coffee going and was reading the *Globe* in the kitchen when the boys stumbled to the table. Like the night before, we slipped into a wordless routine. He poured milk into cereal bowls I filled with Rice Krispies. I signed school papers while he made sure the boys put on their hats and mittens.

We lived like this for a week, speaking to each other only the bare essentials, sleeping separately, working side by side without even an accidental brushing of hands. We both had darkening circles under our eyes. I was barely eating.

Mama, who never misses anything, commented on what was hanging on my clothesline the morning I did the laundry.

"You got too many sheets this week. You got

company? Or is somebody in your house acting like a stranger?"

I didn't want to listen to her simplistic advice about not going to bed angry, and I definitely didn't want to discuss why Al was sleeping on the couch.

"It's nothing, Ma. Al's back was bothering him so he tried sleeping on a different bed."

That week was when the gift arrived. Oh, I'm not talking about anything lavish. I didn't feel as if he was trying to buy his way back into my bed. But one afternoon after I'd put Toni down for a nap I walked into the bedroom and found a single stem of Chaconia in a vase. It was the flower that grew all around our bungalow in Trinidad. I don't know how he'd managed to find one in Boston, in March. Propped up against the vase was a snapshot of me in a sundress leaning against our porch railing with one of the deep crimson flowers tucked behind my ear. I was smiling.

You know, it caught me off guard. The memory of that time in our lives—before the war, before Al's injuries, before *this* tearing us apart.

I took the flower out of the vase, put it in my hair and went downstairs to the restaurant. When Al saw me, I watched the light come back into his eyes.

After we closed the restaurant that night and Al came upstairs, he retrieved the sheets for the couch as usual. But I put them back in the closet.

He stood in the bedroom doorway.

"Do you forgive me, Rose?"

I looked at him and saw the pain and longing in his face. I also saw the man who'd had fought to get back on his feet after the war, the man who was the father of my beautiful children, who adored those children and who worked sixteen hours a day to make sure they had what they needed.

And I saw a man I knew loved me.

He'd made a mistake. But I wasn't going to force him—or all of us—to pay for it the rest of his life. I'd seen marriages like that. The North End is like a small town; everybody knows everybody else's business. I knew women filled with bitterness. They had the things their husbands provided but they didn't have love. They never let go of whatever pain had been inflicted on them thirty years ago. I didn't want to be one of those women.

"I forgive you, Al."

And I took him back into our bed.

It wasn't like our wedding night, or the night after the war when he was finally whole again. But it was new. I don't know how to explain it. We were like strangers and old lovers at the same time. We had added new layers over the core of knowledge we had about each other. My layer was something I'd learned about myself; I understood the price of honesty in a marriage and knew I was willing to pay it. Al's layer was taking responsibility for what he did.

We came to each other with a twinge of sadness and a great hunger. The coldness and loneliness of the past weeks needed to be put behind us. And I was the one who'd raised the barriers with my silence. I just had to be sure I was taking Al back for the right reasons. Al seemed to understand that, by being so patient and by putting up with that lumpy couch as if it were penance Father Lombardi had doled out after confession.

I never asked Al if he'd confessed to the priest about Estella. It was none of my business. He had confessed to me, and that was all that mattered. And I never questioned him again about her, never wanted to know any more than he'd already told me.

"I've missed holding you," he murmured to me as he wrapped himself around me that first night back in our bed. And then his hands moved over my body as if he were learning it for the first time.

# ROSE
## 1961–66

# The Last Full Table

THE WOUNDS INFLICTED by Cuba healed, and like the physical scars Al bore from the Pacific and I from childbirth, we were stronger because of it. Forgiveness is a balm, for the one doing the forgiving as well as the forgiven. We were both released from the burden of mistrust and able to lean on each other again, for ourselves and for our family. God knows, they needed our attention.

Al Jr. was a smart boy. Thank God Reverend Mother had picked up on the bad influences when he was still in sixth grade; after that, I watched him like a hawk. Straight home after school—homework, then chores in the restaurant. He got a scholarship to Boston College High and the Jesuits took over riding his tail to keep him out of trouble. They also taught him how to use that smart-aleck mouth of his for good and put him on the debate team. I wasn't pleased at first that he was going all the way to Dorchester for high school, which took him so far from the neighborhood and its watchful eyes. But when he kept bringing home good report cards, I couldn't complain.

One thing Al regretted was that he'd never taken advantage of the G.I. Bill after the war and gotten an education. He was certainly intelligent enough. But it wasn't something Italian men of his generation did. There was no question for him about Al Jr. going to college. He was going. Period. We expected him to graduate from BC High and go right on to Boston College, even though there were a lot of O'Reillys and Kellys and not many names from our part of the city.

But Al Jr. had other plans. Oh, he still intended to go to college, but when he told us where, I could see Al's mouth get that tight line . . .

Pennsylvania. He wanted to go to Villanova. At least it was Catholic. But for both Al and me, it was like he was going to the moon. This was a first for our family. Cookie and Carmine's sons, Vincent and Anthony, hadn't gone to college; and Bella's kids were at St. Rose of Lima in Albany, where they lived.

I couldn't imagine Al Jr. not home every night and not at the table every Sunday afternoon for dinner. But I also understood his wanting to get away from the neighborhood, and I gently reminded Al that we'd done the same thing at his age when we left for Trinidad. So grudgingly, in the fall of 1961, Al and I packed up the Ford station wagon and drove Al Jr. to Pennsylvania.

It was a time of change, not only for us, but for the country. The year before, a Catholic had been elected president. Even though he was Irish, we considered John F. Kennedy one of our own. His mother, Rose, had been born in the North End a few blocks away from Paradiso. Al Jr., after reading Kennedy's *Profiles in Courage* during high school, had worked on his campaign, knocking on doors in the neighborhood to distribute flyers. It was the highlight of Al Jr.'s adolescence when Kennedy stopped by the campaign headquarters on Hanover Street to shake hands and thank the kids who were working so hard to get him elected. Kennedy's inspiring words had set Al Jr. on the path he was following—to leadership, to accomplish something important in his life.

Like anyone who's old enough to remember, I can tell you exactly where I was that afternoon in November of 1963 when Kennedy was assassinated. The lunch crowd in Paradiso was thinning out and I was reviewing the reservations for that night, a Friday. The radio was on and I was only half listening. But when the words had sunk in, I went into the kitchen and found Al. We held on to each other in disbelief. Outside on the street, normally hectic as the weekend approached, all was still. All I could think to do was pray, so I put on my hat and coat and walked down to St. Leonard's. I wasn't alone. The church filled up with Catholics and non-Catholics alike, all seeking some solace for the incomprehensible.

That night, Al Jr. called us from Villanova. He was going to Washington for the funeral. We were all stunned, of course. But for young people like Al Jr., Kennedy's assassination was an anguished turning point. Some of his college friends reacted by becoming cynical and bitter. But not our son. If anything, he became more committed to the challenge Kennedy had thrown out to that generation with his inaugural speech. We were so proud of him. He joined the navy ROTC, which couldn't have made Al any prouder. Senior year he came home for Thanksgiving in uniform; when he walked into the restaurant, every head turned. He looked so much like Al.

I hold on to the memory of that Thanksgiving as though it's etched in stone. That was the first time Al Jr. had ever brought a girl home. It wasn't like in the old days when Al and I were keeping company and you couldn't even go to the movies without the boy coming into the house to meet your parents. With him in Pennsylvania during the school year, who knew if he was even dating, let alone who the girl was. In the summers, when he came home and helped out in the restaurant, there'd never been anyone special. If it hadn't been for ROTC, I'd have thought he was headed for the seminary.

So it was a big deal that he invited Marianne, a girl from New Jersey who went to Rosemont, the girls' college down the road from Villanova. I liked her right away. She came into the kitchen, told me it smelled just like her mother's and asked what she could do to help.

I put her to work peeling and chopping garlic for the stuffed mushrooms and artichokes and then had her rolling prosciutto and salami for the antipasto. I liked the way she joked with Al Jr. and took some of the wind out of his sails when he started talking like a senator instead of a college boy. And she was nice to Toni, who at fourteen was still a kid who looked up to her big brother.

I watched as Al Jr. brushed her fingertips when he passed her the breadbasket at the table, or put his hand on the small of her back when he slid past her in the kitchen. Just like his father.

When I had him alone for a few minutes behind the bar opening wine bottles for me, I asked him straight out. "So, is she the one?"

"The one what?" He was keeping his eyes on the corkscrew, not looking at me.

"You know what I mean."

The cork slid out of the bottle of Ruffino—not Papa's wine anymore. The younger generation, even though they'd grown up on his Chianti, mixed with water, wanted imported wine from Martignetti's at the corner instead of our own cellar.

"I guess that's up to her."

"And you want her to say yes?"

"What is this, Ma, the Spanish Inquisition?"

I lifted my hands. "I won't ask any more questions. But if she *is* the one, you've made a good choice."

I kissed him and went back to the thirty-four people sitting around the table, a wine bottle in each hand and a smile on my face.

What can I say? For a mother to see her son grown into a handsome, thoughtful young man in love with a woman she likes and approves of—what more could I ask?

I could ask that they be allowed to enjoy a life together, like Al and me. I could ask that a war on the other side of the world not cast its bombs and flames in the middle of my restaurant and my family. But I didn't know that then.

By the fall of 1964, with Al Jr.'s graduation only a few months away in the spring, the nightly news was sprinkled with reports from Vietnam. We had a TV in the bar now, and you couldn't avoid hearing Walter Cronkite every night. But I didn't understand until Al Jr. mentioned his commission at the dinner table that Thanksgiving.

"Looks like I'll get my papers in July, about a month after I graduate."

It wasn't like it had been for Al and me, when the whole country mobilized after Pearl Harbor. Unless you had a son in the service, Vietnam wasn't on your mind.

I thought of all the times I'd let Al Jr. go, some-times sooner than I was ready for. I can still remember the ache in my heart when he stepped into his kindergarten class that first day, and certainly the moment Al and I drove away from Villanova in his freshman year. I cried the whole length of the Jersey Turnpike.

But I never dreamed I'd ever have to watch my son go to war. Not after the war his father had fought. Not when he had a life of promise ahead of him.

Until November 1964, only a handful of Americans had been killed in Vietnam—advisers to the South Vietnamese army, pilots flying bomb-ing missions. But just before Election Day an air base near Saigon had been shelled and seventy-six young Americans were wounded. I heard that as I was making a batch of meatballs. I stood there in the kitchen, my hands deep in one of our big stainless-steel bowls. I mix the meatballs by hand, and I use dried bread that I've softened in water and squeezed out—again by hand—instead of bread crumbs like some of the bigger places in the neighborhood do. I don't skimp when it comes to the quality of the food I serve. I also use ground round, not chuck, for my meatballs. They're tender and moist, not dense or heavy. That night, listening to the news as I cooked, I completely lost track of what I was doing. My hands came to a standstill and no meatballs took shape.

I thought of Al and all he'd suffered and could not believe we were once again putting our young men in harm's way. But it wasn't until Thanksgiving dinner, with Al Jr. sitting there in his uniform next to Marianne, that I began to understand what was at risk. My son. My first-born.

The food and wine were as abundant as they'd always been at our table. You wouldn't have known we were at war. We still had everyone there, with us. My parents and Al's, in their places of honor, their bodies shrunken and wrinkled but their minds and tongues still sharp. My sister-in-law Cookie balancing her youngest grandchild on her lap while she ate.

"I don't want to let her go," she protested when her son Vincent offered to hold the baby so she could eat her soup.

My son Mike, a senior in high school, freshly showered after his football game, basking in the aftermath of a victory he'd secured with his field-goal kick and devouring every course—piling his plate high with manicotti after the antipasto and the escarole soup, followed by two servings of turkey and sweet potatoes. Al, his face flushed from the morning in the kitchen and then two hours on the football field, but his back straight and his eyes clear as he took in the scene. Even Toni, taking tiny bites because her braces hurt—how stupid of the orthodontist to put them in right before Thanksgiving—was making an effort to enjoy the meal and the family.

I describe them all now because it's important to me to remember that meal and that moment when we were all together and didn't yet know what was ahead for our family, for our country. Because by the next Thanksgiving, two places at the table would be empty.

## Loss

MAMA WENT FIRST. She was seventy-seven, coping with the diabetes that Dr. Tucci had diagnosed the year before. I had learned how to give her insulin shots and went over to my parents' place every morning after Mike and Toni left for school. Usually she was sitting at the kitchen table waiting for me. Like most of the old women I knew, she was up at the crack of dawn, had the apartment cleaned and the laundry hung on the line by the time the rest of the world was turning off the alarm clock.

But one morning in January, when I let myself in the apartment, she wasn't in her chair. The coffeepot was empty instead of perking gently. I walked down the hall to her bedroom and peeked in the half-open door. Papa was on his back, snoring loudly, which was no surprise. He often slept late. But it wasn't like Mama to still be in bed, and it also wasn't good for her blood sugar if she had her shot late. I tiptoed into the room and reached for her.

As soon as I touched her I knew she wasn't going to open her eyes. I couldn't find a pulse. Still, I called to her, the daughter in me, the wishful thinker, not wanting to accept what my hand on her cold and stiffening cheek was telling me.

My cry of "Mama! Mama!" woke Papa.

*"Que fa?"* he asked, confused, his eyes cloudy with cataracts, his brain registering the unusual situation—me in their bedroom, his wife not yet up—but he hadn't quite connected what it all meant.

"It's okay, Papa," I found the strength to say to him, then slipped out of the room. They didn't have a phone in the bedroom, which was just as well. I didn't want him to hear what I was going to be saying, or how upset I was.

My hand and my voice were shaking as I dialed the operator and asked for an ambulance. I tried to explain, without breaking down, but it was all I could do not to wail.

I phoned Al and asked him to call my brothers and sisters. Then I went back to Papa.

He was sitting on the side of the bed next to Mama, stroking her hair and rocking back and forth, muttering a low litany.

The ambulance came just as Al and Carmine ran up the steps. Helplessly, we watched the futile efforts of the emergency crew.

"I'm sorry," one of them said, turning to me. "From the state of rigor mortis, she probably passed away during the night."

The remaining hours of that day were a blur, as the rest of my family arrived, the doctor came to sign the death certificate and we called my father's cousin Severino, the undertaker.

Somehow I held myself together, the way I always do in a crisis. I was most worried about Papa, who seemed paralyzed. I made him eat something, but I practically had to spoon it into him, as if he were a baby. He finally pushed the spoon away and just sat in his chair, staring out the window.

We closed the restaurant for the week and hung black bunting on the windows. Al Jr. took the train up from Philadelphia to attend the wake and the funeral. I thought about keeping Toni away from the funeral parlor. I didn't know if she'd be ready for an open casket. I had bad memories of when I was a kid and the wakes were held at home, with the body in the living room, and didn't want to inflict that on my baby. But she made a fuss, as only a teenager can, about *not* being a baby anymore. If her brothers were going to the wake, then she was, too. Frankly I was too exhausted to argue with her. I'd slept, badly, at

Papa's the first night, not wanting to leave him alone. I don't know, maybe I was afraid I'd wake up to find him gone, too. I'd heard that sometimes happened—people dying of a broken heart when their wife or husband passes away. Mostly it was in dramatic stories from the old country— the kind of superstitious fable you had to take with a grain of salt. I remember one that Mama and my aunt Cecilia used to bring up about a distant cousin, Lucia, who had been barren. She'd once turned down a proposal of marriage because she had fallen in love with someone else. The mother of the rejected suitor had gone into the village piazza, bared her breasts and cursed Lucia, calling down upon her "a life full of misery." Given the sad state of Lucia's existence after that, Mama and Aunt Cecilia were convinced the curse had been the reason.

"Watch out who you harm with your choices" had been their warning.

As far as I knew, no one had placed a curse on either of my parents. But nevertheless, I made sure Papa took his blood pressure medicine and I checked on him several times during the night.

My sisters-in-law, God bless them, took over the kitchen at Paradiso during the week of the wake and the funeral and had a meal ready for us at five o'clock every day between the afternoon and evening calling hours. Cookie knew best what the family needed, especially Papa, and had pots of soup and some simple chicken—nothing heavy—simmering on the back burner as we came back from Severino's to take a break. Everybody was numb. Such a shock, we all said. One minute Mama was there—with her wisdom and her energy and her cut-through-the-bullshit observations—and then she was gone, without warning or a chance to say goodbye.

It was hardest on my sisters Bella and Lillian, who no longer lived close enough to see her every day, the way those of us still in the neighborhood had. They hadn't seen her since Christmas, and who knows what their last words with her had been. Everyone has regrets, the "woulda, shoulda, coulda, if I'd only known" kind of thoughts. It's why I still hug and kiss my kids, my Al, every time they walk out the door.

For me, besides the shock of finding her that morning, the pain was the empty place in the kitchen. The knives hanging unused instead of wielded by gnarled fingers chopping two dozen cloves of garlic or five bunches of parsley. The dwindling supply of mason jars on my cellar shelves that wouldn't be replenished come August when the tomatoes and eggplants were ripe and she, churning with industry, would've been canning for the winter.

We buried her in the lilac dress we'd bought for her to wear to my nephew Vincent's wedding. It broke my heart that she didn't live to see Al Jr.

graduate from Villanova, but he stood with his cousins as pallbearer alongside her coffin at St. Leonard's. When he hoisted that box on his shoulder, with his white gloves and navy uniform—that's when I finally fell apart. Al held on to me as we followed behind the casket.

But Mama's funeral was a dress rehearsal for what was to follow.

## *Broken Glass*

AL JR. GRADUATED from Villanova with honors in June of 1965. We retraced the journey we'd made four years earlier, this time with Mike, Toni and Papa along. After Mama's funeral, my brothers and sisters and I had realized that leaving Papa to live alone wasn't a good idea. He was eighty years old and had worked hard all his life shaping rough stone from Vermont quarries into the polished granite blocks of Boston's churches and banks and office buildings. But he could barely boil an egg and had probably never turned on the washing machine. More than his unfamiliarity with housework was our fear that he'd slide into a depression so deep he wouldn't come back out. As it was, he'd barely spoken or eaten since the morning of Mama's death.

I'd like to tell you I was the noble one in the family discussion, immediately offering to take him into my home. After all, I lived just down the street, and Mama had been working at the restaurant with us for twenty years. But I didn't. I held back. It's not that we didn't have the room. With Al Jr. about to go into the navy and Mike heading off to Holy Cross in September, we could've easily taken Papa in. But a piece of me selfishly thought it was time for Al and me to have a break—from responsibility and worry. But that wasn't going to happen. My brothers and sisters elected me, for all the right reasons, and I didn't argue.

We moved Papa in during the two weeks we would normally have gone to Florida. I fixed up a back room in the apartment for him with his favorite chair and his own TV. It was on the quiet side of the building, away from the bustle of Salem Street.

I made sure he got out to his social club, the St. Anthony Society, to play cards twice a week. In the evenings, sometimes, he'd sit downstairs at the bar in the restaurant. One night, when we were really busy, I asked him to pour a few drinks. He got behind the bar and surprised me. Despite his grumbling that nobody knew how to make a good Bellini, it was the first time since Mama died that he'd done anything with enthusiasm. It may have been the women waiting for their table who were enjoying his gusto in putting the cocktails together. He was good enough with his fractured English banter to get them to order a second round.

The next evening, I saw him put on a clean shirt and shave before he came downstairs.

"You want some help at the bar tonight?" he said to me after he finished his pasta fazool.

"Sure, Papa. That would be a big help."

By the time we all drove down to Pennsylvania for Al Jr.'s graduation, Papa was getting up in the morning like a man with a purpose. He even had a group of regulars who came in every evening to debate the latest news in *Il Progresso* and have a glass of grappa after their dish of spaghetti.

The graduation at Villanova was interesting. I didn't want us to look like a group of *cavonne* coming down from the tenements to the ritzy Philadelphia Main Line. I'd seen both *The Philadelphia Story* and *High Society,* so I knew what we might find here. I was no Grace Kelly, but I know how to shop to look classy. I put my hair in a French twist, wore the rose-colored mock Chanel suit I'd found at Filene's Basement and a double strand of cultured pearls. I made both Al and Mike get new suits, to much grumbling. Toni was more difficult to outfit. At fifteen, she was beautiful but not in a conventional way, so she didn't see it yet. I prayed that someday she'd come to recognize how attractive she was, but at that moment it was all I could do to keep myself from marching her in front of a mirror and yelling, "Look at yourself! You're gorgeous!"

But we were at that stage in the mother-daughter dance when nothing I said was considered worthy of attention. I still bought her clothes, however, and I combed through the junior sections in both Filene's and Jordan Marsh to find her something she'd wear without making all of us suffer because she hated it or thought it made her look ugly. I settled on an adorable yellow pique sheath with a bolero jacket that had daisy buttons. When she put it on, she could've been one of those *High Society* wedding guests. "Okay," she muttered, examining herself from side to side in the mirror. "Can I get yellow heels to go with it?"

So there we were that morning in Villanova, PA, trying not to look or sound like the urban version of *The Beverly Hillbillies*. I adjusted Mike's tie and, as we got out of the car, tucked a stray curl of Toni's hair—as black as Al's—behind her ear. She wore the tiny gold studs I'd finally allowed her to pierce her ears with. I smoothed Al's collar and kissed him on the lips.

"Big day," I said.

"You look like Elizabeth Taylor," he said.

"I was trying for Jackie Kennedy."

"You're much prettier. And you've got a better ass."

I didn't like him to talk like that in front of the kids, but they were ahead of us, and I shot him a look of mock disapproval mixed with appreciation. I was forty-four, with a teenage daughter who was driving me crazy and two sons stepping into new stages of their lives.

Every time one of my kids passed a milestone—first day of school, first communion, confirmation, graduation—it was like giving birth all over again. I felt as though life was changing for me, too. *When this day is over,* I thought to myself, *I'll be the mother of a college graduate and a navy ensign.* How did I get here so fast? One minute I'm sewing myself maternity clothes and the next I'm sitting on a folding chair in the sun, watching a tall, handsome young man march past. I was on the aisle. As he moved by me, he squeezed me on the shoulder. Just like Al. Letting me know it was going to be all right.

When we got back to Boston, we held a family party for him at the restaurant. It was a big deal, a college graduate in the North End. Most of his buddies from St. John's were working in the trades. Some of them were no doubt as smart as Al Jr., but nobody had expected as much from them as I had from him. I didn't regret for a minute that I pushed him hard. I'd always had ambitions. Seeing to it that my kids got educated was one of them.

What a party! We received permission from the city to use the vacant lot behind the building. We strung Christmas lights and hired a band to play live music. Al's cousin welded some oil drums together and made us big grills to cook the sausage and peppers. We had all of Al Jr.'s favorite foods—lasagne, eggplant parm, *sfogliatelle,* even big tubs of lemon ice from Mike's Pastry Shop. You'd have thought it was one of the feast days, except there was no Madonna on a wagon draped with ribbons pinned with dollar bills.

The kids danced. My aunts sat on their plastic beach chairs, fanning themselves and pinching Al Jr.'s cheeks as if he were still a little boy. Papa and my uncles sat at a back table playing pinochle.

*"Come sei buono!"* How good you are!

"God bless."

My friend Patsy came over and put her arm around me. "You did a good job. I remember the day he was born, and you scared to death about raising him alone. Be proud of him, but be proud of yourself, too."

We toasted him many times and teased him about running for mayor, finally giving us an Italian in the new city hall just on the other side of the expressway. He laughed, but I could tell it wasn't such a far-fetched idea to him. It was 2:00 a.m. before we doused the lights and folded up the tables and chairs.

And then he was gone.

He took the train to Virginia, where he trained as a medic. By October he was in Vietnam. I never questioned for a minute that he should do his duty. But sending a son to war was the hardest thing I'd ever done.

Because he'd joined ROTC at Villanova, Al Jr. had volunteered, not been drafted. It was still early in the draft, so not too many boys from the North End had been called up yet, although they would be soon enough, especially since so few of them were in college. There were no other women to share my fears with—in the family or in the neighborhood—facing the day as I did every morning, turning on the *Today Show* the minute I got out of bed, watching Walter Cronkite every evening as I cooked in the restaurant.

"You're making yourself crazy, listening to this garbage every day, Rose," Al said to me one night, flicking off the TV as a draft dodger burned his draft card in front of a courthouse.

"I *need* the news, Al. I need to see what he's seeing."

"He's on an aircraft carrier, Rose. He sees planes taking off and landing. And when someone in one of those planes comes off on a stretcher, he's ready with an IV and bandages. He's going to be fine, Rose."

Al and I each found separate ways to get through the day. Al's was to believe that Vietnam wasn't the navy's war, and that Al Jr. wasn't reliving his father's nightmare of twenty years before. But every now and then he'd come up against the war in unexpected places, despite his deliberate refusal to watch the evening news.

One afternoon he ran over to Haymarket when we were short on our order of broccoli rabe. He knew a couple of guys with stalls who were willing to give him a wholesale price.

An antiwar rally was going on in City Hall Plaza, a shallow sloping bowl of paved brick built to mimic Siena's Piazza del Campo. Two of Al's cousins were masons who had worked on it.

Al could hear the loudspeakers and the chants of the crowd and wandered over to the fringes with his shopping bags full of greens. What he saw and heard disgusted him.

"Goddamn freaks," he said as he slammed the bags on the stainless-steel counter in the kitchen. "Bunch of unwashed cowards. And the police just stood on the sidelines, letting them rant and rave!"

"This is America, Pop. They're allowed to rant and rave." Mike was helping out on a weekend home from Holy Cross.

"Is that what your Jesuits are teaching you?

133

What about your brother, fighting so these morons can spout their disrespectful drivel."

"He'd be the first to tell you they've got the right."

"Are you turning into one of these antiwar nuts?"

Mike shut up. There was no point arguing with Al when he was so single-minded.

I don't know how I would've felt if I'd been face-to-face with the protesters as Al had been. If they were dishonoring my son and his sacrifice, I'd probably have slapped them across their mouths. It was one thing to question whether the government had made the wrong decision, but another to blame the young men laying down their lives.

It had been so different when Al and I were young. The country was united. We knew we were doing the right thing. A family had been proud to hang a blue star in the window when they had a son in the service.

Nowadays there were no stars. Maybe people were afraid their windows would be broken. I felt lonely as the mother of a serviceman. Al poured his concern for Al Jr. into anger at the war protesters. I had no comfort there—not from Al and not from my own mixed feelings.

Thanksgiving 1965 was a quiet one, our first without Mama, of course, but Al Jr. was eating his turkey on a ship in the South Vietnam Sea.

I'd sent a package of canned goods—anchovies, roasted peppers, marinated mushrooms and olives—and I double-baked the peppery hard biscuits Papa liked to dip in his wine. I figured they'd keep in transit. I put in hard salami and a round of provolone coated with wax. It wasn't lasagne or fresh mozzarella and bruschetta, but I knew he'd appreciate the taste of home. We got a letter just before the holidays and I read parts of it out loud at dinner so everyone could hear his voice coming through in that smart way he had with words.

"Give everyone around the table my love and remind them how good life is. The guys in my battalion, when I describe our Thanksgiving to them, can't believe what goes into it. I'll be thinking of you all. I'll imagine the aroma of the turkey wafting up the stairs; the lasagne bubbling as it comes out of the oven; the artistry of the antipasto platter that I'm sure Toni has arranged so the colors are as vivid as the taste; Mom bursting with pride when everything's finally on the table; Dad standing like a samurai with his carving knife ready to slice. I miss you all. God bless."

We didn't know that he'd been transferred from the carrier to a river operation. The navy had started building up its inland forces with small boat patrols. But the nightly news wasn't carrying stories about them. Like Al, I began to be lulled by the thought that since he wasn't a pilot and wasn't in the infantry, he was safer than most. But we were mistaken.

When the two navy officers walked into the restaurant one night in April, I assumed they were customers. Toni offered to seat them, and then I saw the puzzled look on her face. She came to the kitchen door. "Mom, Daddy, the captain is asking for you." Al took off his chef's cap and wiped his hands. We exchanged a look and he grasped my hand as we went out to them.

"Is there a private place we can speak with you?" They glanced around at the busy dining room. People were starting to notice them. I was beginning to shake. Al had the presence of mind to lead them to the office. I heard a glass break in the stillness that had descended on the usually hectic kitchen.

Al closed the door and held me as we listened to the report of our son's death, the medal he would receive posthumously, the date we could expect the plane carrying his body home.

A pain pierced my heart at that moment, leaving a hole that has never been filled.

I lost two children that night and I almost lost Al. Toni, reeling from a world gone suddenly and horribly wrong, needed a mother who could be a refuge and a role model. Someone who could show her how to put one foot in front of the other even when she didn't know where she was headed or why.

But I failed her. The tension between us that had been simmering in her early teens exploded after Al Jr. died. She was sixteen and we could barely speak to each other without yelling and tears. She pulled away from me, one small step after another, and in my own grief I didn't realize that until it was too late.

I felt I was the last person in the world she wanted to be like. I was someone to be ashamed of, someone who couldn't possibly understand her.

She'd always been artistic as a kid. She'd keep busy for hours in the restaurant during the early days, as long as you gave her a stack of paper and some crayons. You'd think she'd been given a pot of gold the day she got a box of 96 Crayolas.

Before the funeral she grabbed the photo albums I'd been keeping for each of the kids and picked out several pictures of Al Jr. She spent hours alone in her room listening to Joan Baez.

I didn't make her go to school that week. I could hardly get out of bed myself. Cookie made sure we had food in the kitchen, but who could eat?

One night, Al peeked in Toni's room after

she'd fallen asleep. Taped all around the walls were big sheets of black paper with pastel portraits of her brother—as a little boy, a teen-ager, a navy officer. The last one was sketched from a photo taken the night of his graduation party. She'd captured each moment with excru-ciating accuracy.

Al made me get out of bed to see what she'd done. Her fingertips were smudged with the colored chalk, and the dark circles under her eyes looked as if she'd drawn them herself. What she'd created was as much a shrine as Mama's painting of St. Anthony that she'd kept on her dresser with a flickering red votive candle.

I sat on the floor for a couple of hours, sur-rounded by the images, rocking myself and crying silently. I didn't want to wake Toni. I crept out around midnight.

Al coaxed Toni into letting us frame the sketches and hang them at the wake. He'd explained to her that we wouldn't have an open casket like we did for Mama. Those drawings brought people to a standstill, like they were at St. Peter's in Rome in front of Michelangelo's *Pietà*.

Throughout the wake Toni sat in one of Severino's wing chairs in a black suit that looked too old for her. I hadn't wanted her to wear black at Mama's funeral and I couldn't bring myself to shop with her for this one. Patsy had taken her downtown and let her pick out something at Ann Taylor. She looked like a career girl, not my baby, but I kept my mouth shut for a change. Not out of common sense or understanding that my daughter was growing up, especially after a tragedy like Al Jr.'s death. I was just too locked inside my own pain to care.

And maybe that's what happened to Toni and me. She thought I didn't care about what she did or who she was anymore, so she stopped trying to tell me.

Somehow we got through the funeral. St. Leonard's was full to overflowing. Family, Al Jr.'s classmates from BC High and Villanova, friends of Mike's and Toni's, people from the neighborhood. Al Jr. was the first boy from the North End to be killed in Vietnam, so even the politicians showed up. Marianne, the girl Al Jr. had brought to Thanksgiving dinner in 1964, had driven from New Jersey. She'd sat with me at the wake for a while the night before, both of us in silence. There was nothing we could say to each other, but she held my hand —the hand that should have blessed them on their wedding day and held their babies.

I thought I'd already emptied myself of tears, but I cried through the whole Mass. At the cemetery, when the young navy officer handed me the flag that had been draped over Al Jr.'s coffin, I hugged it like an infant.

This isn't supposed to happen, that a child goes before a parent. It's unnatural. We are left not knowing how to go on.

Al and I faced our son's death in totally different ways. Al was still angry, but he turned his anger into activity. He started renovating the restaurant, throwing himself into a marathon every day so he wouldn't have time to think about his lost son. And me, I thought about A.J. constantly and stopped living. I sat at the kitchen table in the mornings after Toni had gone to school and didn't move, my coffee grown cold in its cup, the plain toast I thought I could stomach lying uneaten and dried out on my plate.

At noontime Papa would come in and ask, "Where's lunch?" and I'd make him some peppers and eggs or open up a can of Progresso soup. Al grabbed himself some cheese and prosciutto in the restaurant kitchen and didn't bother coming upstairs.

After I fed Papa, I went to bed. I was usually sleeping when Toni got home from school. She did her homework and went downstairs to wait tables for the supper crowd. Al let me disappear like that for a couple of weeks. He crawled into bed around 1:00 a.m. and fell asleep from exhaustion. And because I'd been sleeping all day, that's when I woke up. I tried to stay in bed with him, but I tossed and turned and eventually gave up. I wandered around the apartment.

Sometimes I sat in the bedroom Al Jr. and Mike had shared, still full of books and sports equipment and LP albums. I smoothed the bedspread. I opened the closet and tried to breathe in the scent of my boy, but like a good housewife, I'd hung mothballs to protect the unused coats and jackets that he'd hung there before he left.

"Rose, you need to see a doctor," Al said to me one morning. "You can't continue like this. *We* can't continue like this."

But the doctor didn't solve my problem. He gave me Valium, which numbed the pain and let me get some sleep at night, but made me care even less about everything falling apart around me.

Al was spending too much money on fixing up the restaurant at a time when business in the neighborhood was turning bad. We'd managed to weather the ups and downs over the years because I'd watched our costs, and kept our waste to a minimum. Like Mama, I'd learned to make do in times of scarcity and put by in times of abundance. But now I just wasn't there. Al wasn't paying attention to that part of the business because he'd never had to. The financial end of things had always been my responsibility. At the same time, Toni was hiding in her room whenever she was in the apartment. She didn't seem to have any friends. She was a bookworm, like Al Jr., and when she wasn't reading she was drawing. I was relieved, frankly, that she didn't have a boyfriend at sixteen, as I had when I started dating Al. She was going to Sacred Heart, an all-girl Catholic school, so she didn't have much opportunity to get herself involved. God only knows what might have happened if there'd been boys around. We had nieces on both sides of the family who'd gotten pregnant as teenagers. Oh, the boys married them, but what a way to begin a life together.

One night Al came upstairs with mail that had accumulated in the mailbox. I was so out of it I wasn't going downstairs more than once or twice a week.

"When's the last time you paid the bills or did the books?" he demanded, slamming a pile of overdue notices on the dining room table.

I looked at him blankly.

"Rose, wake up! You can't keep living like this, ignoring everything around you. Including me. Don't you care anymore?"

How do you say to the man who's been by your side for almost thirty years, who'd overcome incredible pain and survived, who adored you, that you didn't care about anything? I was speechless. The pills made me so weepy that all I could do was cry.

Al stomped into the bedroom and grabbed the pill bottle off the dresser, then pulled me into the bathroom.

"I want you to watch." And he dumped every last pill down the toilet. "I'm calling the drugstore and the doctor and telling them not to renew your prescription."

I was scared and horrified. I didn't think I could face what I knew was coming if I didn't have the Valium to take away the pain.

"We need you, Rose. All of us, but especially me. You're the life of this family, and without you we're dying, just as surely as Al Jr. died.

"Take care of yourself, Rose. Take care of us. And pay the damned bills!"

He went back downstairs, where he'd been spending most of his time.

I fought the urge to find something to replace the pills—a glass of Scotch on the rocks, anything. I looked in the bathroom mirror. I was a mess. My hair was like a rat's nest, pulled back with a rubber band. My skin was rough and without any makeup. My neck was dirty. I didn't recognize myself.

I turned on the shower, hoping to drown my tears and wash away the scum I felt had accumulated all over me. I scrubbed and scrubbed. When I finished, I spent half an hour combing the tangles out of my hair. I filed my nails, which were chipped. I put on a clean pair of slacks and a blouse. I admitted there might be some wisdom in the busywork of my mother's generation. If you kept moving, working, you might not have time to feel the pain.

So I cleaned the house, starting with the bathroom. I pulled down curtains, gathered up the throw rug and the toilet seat cover and got everything in the washing machine. I dusted and polished and vacuumed. When I reached the dining room I saw the pile of bills and remembered.

I put away my dust rags and mop. I found my checkbook and sat down. I was overwhelmed by what I saw—charges for work I had no idea was going on; prices from our suppliers that I didn't remember negotiating; orders for items that were well beyond what the receipts showed we needed.

I sorted through everything, trying to decide what to pay first, what to question Al about. When I added it all up, my stomach was churning. For the first time since Al Jr.'s death, I was feeling something other than emptiness. I was angry, and I was staring at our survival—as a business, as a family.

It was past midnight when I finished organizing everything and knew exactly how much we owed and how much we didn't have. I'd made a list of what I had to do in the morning—who I had to call, orders I needed to reduce, a loan I'd try to arrange to get us back on our feet. I had to put the fire out before I could figure out how to rebuild what was so clearly falling apart.

I was furious with Al, of course, for throwing away money we didn't have. But I was more furious with myself for throwing away what I'd worked so hard for.

When he came upstairs, it was with the usual expectations—a wife somewhere in la-la land, dirty dishes in the sink, a daughter hiding from us. At least I was able to surprise him on the first two counts. He saw that both the house and I were clean. He saw the neat stack of stamped envelopes on the counter. He saw the old Rose in my eyes—not the dull and clouded haze of indifference.

"It's bad, Al. We've got a lot to talk about in the morning. But I'm back."

After a couple of yelling matches—of the "How could you do that?" variety—over the next few weeks, we settled into a partnership that we knew would be our only chance of survival.

We were lucky to be heading into summer. The tourist business picks up, and even though we're not on Hanover Street, we get enough foot traffic to pull people in. But we needed more than a steady stream of customers to stay afloat. I canceled some of the work Al had scheduled for the renovations and I took a hard look at the menu, what people were ordering and what it was costing us to prepare some of those dishes. It was one thing to offer regional specialties that we'd grown up with, but did we have to put *everything* on the menu? I cut back on the variety. And I returned to work in the kitchen so I could keep an eye on the little things, like how much food they were putting on the plate, only to scrape it into the garbage later.

I even managed to get us a loan. Somehow we made it through that year. Our economic survival was paramount, but I also hoped that my renewed energy sent a subtle message to Toni. She never commented on the change, but it was enough for me if she absorbed the lesson that change was possible.

It wasn't easy. I didn't crawl back into my bed, afraid that everything I'd worked for would be gone when I woke up. That fear overshadowed my grief. In that way, I became more like Al, driving everything I was feeling into work.

# ROSE
## 1969

# Emanuel

BY THE WINTER of 1968 we'd turned a corner. We were paying the bills, the dining room was full and we were no longer in the red. Although Al was head chef, I continued to have a hand in the cooking and experimented with dishes I thought we could add to the menu. Business had improved enough for us to add staff that year, as well. In addition to family, we still had Milly, who'd been waitressing for us for more than twenty years. One of the Agostino boys, who lived in the apartment above ours, bussed tables and washed dishes. Over time, we'd had wait-staff come and go. I had high expectations for the people I hired; some of them worked hard to meet my standards and others couldn't be bothered, so I showed them the door.

At Christmas, Al put four plane tickets to Miami under the tree and right after New Year's we took Mike and Toni to the Fontainebleau. It was Toni's last year of high school; Mike had one more year at Holy Cross. Because he was the only surviving son he wasn't going to lose his deferment after he graduated from college if, God forbid, the war was still on.

I hadn't realized how much in his brother's shadow Mike had felt. I'd never had much interest in child psychology books—written by men who had no kids, if you asked me. I let my kids know how much I loved them, I came down on them hard when they messed up and I always forgave them. I also made sure I knew where they were, who they were with and what they liked to eat. They understood that when they felt lousy they could come into Mom's kitchen and get filled up—with attention, with linguine and white clam sauce, torta Milanese, zabaglione . . . whatever they wanted. I'll admit I found it easier with the boys than with Toni.

It was good to take time off with the kids. Toni spent her days at the pool in a two-piece bathing suit slathering herself with baby oil and burying her face in a book. She'd never had a steady boyfriend—or even many dates—and I had mixed feelings about that. I didn't have to worry the way some mothers did about their daughters, but I also regretted that she hadn't had someone special in these past few years of so much loss. I worried, too, that she'd be going off to college with so little experience of men. She was almost too naive. I didn't think she'd even been kissed. Who knew? Maybe she was going to be a nun. I wasn't crazy about that idea; in my opinion, you give up too much as a woman—the love of a man, children, a home. She wanted to go to art school. Mother Bede, the art teacher at Sacred Heart, had allowed her free rein in the studio and she'd produced a mighty portfolio that she'd carted around to art schools in Providence and Boston and Portland, Maine. Two people in her life were not happy with her choices: Mother Bede, who wanted her to go to *Catholic* schools, and Al, who didn't want her to go to art school at all.

"What kind of work can you get with an art degree?" he demanded. "Are you going to wind up decorating store windows at Filene's? Why can't you go to school for nursing or teaching or accounting? Something practical."

Al finally relented when she pointed out that she could always teach art when she finished. All her applications were done by the time we got to Florida, so I expected her to relax and enjoy herself.

"I *am* enjoying myself, Mom," she insisted when I told her she didn't seem to be having a good time, stuck on a chaise lounge while the other young people at the hotel had found one another.

"They're jerks. I'd rather read my book."

So I kept my mouth shut. We'd gone shopping a couple of times, but I couldn't interest her in a haircut or a manicure when I went to the salon. She said she didn't want "old lady" hair. She'd grown hers long and wore it parted in the middle like all the folk singers whose albums she collected. I thought the hairstyle didn't flatter her at all—it made her nose look big. But I could tell her that until I was blue in the face and she'd still wear it that way. What did I know?

"Relax and let her be, Rose." Al didn't get caught up in the struggle. But at least a few times I was able to shrug it off and leave her at the pool. She was almost eighteen, not much younger than I'd been when I married Al. I had to believe she'd figure out what she wanted, even if it was just a quiet afternoon reading a book and getting a tan.

Mike, on the other hand, was out from morning till night with a group of college kids he'd met on the beach. He made it to dinner with us every evening because we insisted, but then he was off to the clubs. He was a little reckless, that one, not the solid citizen of his older brother or the bookworm, dreamy artist of his sister. But I couldn't complain. They were both good kids and they were all I had.

So that vacation was as much of a family trip as you could expect with two nearly grown children. Until it became something else entirely.

Before we'd left Boston, Al had gotten a letter from an old friend of his from the neighborhood, Dominic Morelli. They'd gone to St. John's together as boys, but after high school, when Al went into the navy, Dom had entered the seminary and become a priest. We'd lost touch with him when his order, the Franciscans, sent him to Delaware. But the letter came from Florida. Father Dom was working with Cuban refugees at a parish in Miami's Little Havana. He asked Al to give him a call when we were down so they could get together, but Al let it slip.

Al played cards most afternoons in one of the lounges. When the game was over, the waiter who'd been serving the drinks stopped him.

"Mr. Dante?" Al had signed the check, so the waiter was aware of his name. He was Cuban, one of the refugees who'd come over in the December 1965 airlift, he told Al. And he knew Father Dom.

"Father Dom said to tell you there's something you should know," he said. "Someone you should meet."

Al didn't want to listen to him. But he called Dom that night and asked him what it was all about.

"Let's have breakfast tomorrow. We've got a lot of catching up to do."

The next day, Dom joined Al and me on the patio around ten. Thank God the kids were sleeping late.

He wasn't alone. Antonio, the waiter, was with him, and a boy about thirteen.

"I want you to meet Emanuel," Dom said.

And we looked into the dark, somber eyes of a boy who could've been Al Jr. or Al at that age.

It took my breath away.

I watched Al struggle with himself, ready to leap up from the table and run away from the past—or reach out and touch it.

"Shall we take a walk?" I said. I didn't want this played out in front of strangers.

We went down to the beach, the five of us.

"Antonio and Manny are cousins," Dom went on. "Manny's mother died of emphysema when he was ten. Before she died, she told Antonio about Manny's father and she gave him his name and this photograph." He handed Al a faded Kodachrome that looked like it had been handled many times. It was one of those pictures nightclub camera girls used to take. Al, tanned and handsome in his white dinner jacket, with his arm around a honeyed blonde in an orange chiffon dress.

Al turned to me.

"I didn't know."

"I believe you."

Antonio nodded vigorously. "My aunt never told Mr. Dante. She never saw him again. She wanted me to get Manny to America. When she got so sick, she made me promise to get Manny out of Cuba and find you."

"One evening when I was shooting hoops with the kids," Dom interjected, "I mentioned how I'd played on an asphalt court in my neighborhood in Boston. Antonio heard the word *Boston* and remembered what little his aunt knew about Manny's father. He brought the photograph to me. That's when I wrote you the letter, Al. I had to tell you in person, not long-distance."

All this time Manny stood on the edge of the conversation, saying nothing but not taking his eyes off Al. He was a skinny little thing, not yet grown into his body. I wasn't sure he understood English or, if he did, whether he knew what his sudden presence in Al's life meant for Al—and for me.

I could only imagine what was going through Al's mind. But after the initial shock and disbelief—how could this be? I asked myself—something happened to me that I can't really explain.

Al and I had managed to lock up the whole Cuban episode in some hidden place in our hearts years ago. We never spoke of it after that painful winter, and I never threw it in his face when we fought. The jagged tear in our marriage that his affair with the Cuban had caused had been stitched back together over the years. Sure, if you ran your fingers over it you could tell it was a repair job. But like the fine, tight stitches of Mama's darning, it had held, maybe even more strongly than before.

Until that day on the beach. When I saw the photograph of her and Al, that wound just split wide-open. I didn't think I could bear the evidence that he had loved someone else. But that moment, when I felt as if my insides were spilling into the ocean swirling around my feet, I looked into the eyes of that boy—hungry, haunted—and knew what I had to do.

"What is it you want?" Al was asking Antonio, like he was negotiating with a union steward to prevent a strike. "Money?"

"He doesn't want money," I said to Al. "He wants a father. He needs a father."

"How am I going to do that?" Al glanced from me to Manny.

"I don't know yet. But we'll figure it out. Dom, Al and I need to talk about this. We'd like to take you out to dinner tonight. Can you meet us back at the hotel at six?"

Antonio seemed reluctant to let us go now that he'd found Al. I wondered how long he'd been looking for him.

"Don't worry, we won't disappear." I dug into the straw bag I'd taken with me and pulled out a pen and a scrap of paper.

"Here. This is our restaurant in Boston, so you'll always know where to find us. And Father Dom knows our address, too. But we'll be here tonight. Okay?"

That seemed to calm him down. He nodded and shook Al's hand. Manny put his hand out, as well, and Al pulled him close with a hug. When he released him, I could see the tears in his eyes.

The boys and Dom turned back toward the

hotel. The beach was growing crowded. The early-morning fly fishermen were reeling in their lines as the cabana boys set up lounges and umbrellas.

"You want to walk or you want to sit?" I asked Al, who, despite his tan, looked stricken.

He answered me by heaving himself into one of the beach chairs. He leaned back, eyes closed. I sat at the edge of the chair, facing him, and took his hands in mine.

"Oh, my God! Oh, my God, Rose. I never for a minute even suspected. What am I going to do?"

"You're going to do the right thing, Al, like you always do. The boy is motherless and fatherless at probably the moment in his life when he most needs a parent."

"This must be killing you. After all these years."

"I thought back there that it would. But something happened to me. I saw the boy, not the sin that created the boy. I know this is going to sound like my cousin Nancy who spends too much time lighting candles and saying novenas, but I feel God put that boy in our lives for a reason. Did you notice how much—"

"—he looks like Al Jr." Al finished my sentence in a whisper.

"We can't see him as a replacement, a substitute. We need to love him for himself." I said it out loud to remind both of us.

"Love him? How can you do this, Rose?"

"It's not like you kept a woman on the side for years, Al, taking away from me and the family. It was one night. And it made me mad as hell, don't be mistaken. But that child is a consequence of that one night. And I've never known you to walk away from the consequences of what you do."

"I won't walk away. But I can't ask you to take this on."

"You're not asking. I'm taking it on because I see a child who needs to be fed and loved and guided, and I think I've got a good track record in that department. Particularly with boys."

"You don't have to do this. We could send a check every month, make sure he gets an education."

"Living with a twenty-year-old cousin in a city that's all glitz and booze and fast women? That's like asking Mike to raise a child right now. We can do this, Al. Together."

He leaned toward me and stroked my face.

"You're remarkable, Rose."

"So are you, Al."


We walked back to the hotel arm in arm, working out how much to tell the kids about who Manny was and what we intended to do. In the end, we decided it was too soon to tell them anything at all. We asked Mike to take Toni out to eat and didn't include them at dinner with Dom and Manny and Antonio. The next afternoon, Al asked Dom to help us find a local lawyer.

By the time we flew back to Boston we'd started the paperwork to adopt Manny and get him citizenship papers. Once his adoption was final we'd bring him home. We thought that would give us a chance to prepare the kids and the rest of the family.

We decided that no one, not even Mike and Toni, needed to know that Al was Manny's father. We told everyone we'd heard about some Cuban orphans through Al's priest friend in Miami. It wasn't too much of a lie, since it was through Dom that Antonio had been able to connect with Al. We said to the family that although Mike and Toni were almost grown, we weren't quite ready to give up taking care of kids.

A few eyebrows went up, but most of my women friends understood, especially those who'd recently watched their youngest get married and move out. I didn't want anybody to think I was a saint and put me on a pedestal or, worse, think I was crazy and pathetic for taking my husband's illegitimate child into my home. I wanted them to believe that I was adopting a child to fill my own need as well as the child's. And I was.

In March, Al and I drove back to Miami to complete the adoption and bring Manny home.

When we left Miami he called us Mr. and Mrs. Dante and sat silently in the backseat hunched against the door and staring out the window. We took our time getting back, stopping along the way at South of the Border. Manny and Al played Skee-Ball and tried to grab a stuffed animal with one of those claws. We ate too many fried onions, had our picture taken with huge sombreros on our heads and picked up some fireworks to save for the Fourth of July.

By the time we got to Baltimore, Manny and I had switched places in the car. He sat in front beside Al, joking with him and playing with the radio. When we stopped to eat, Al said, "Manny, we're your family now, your parents. Strangers you call Mr. and Mrs., but your parents are Mom and Dad."

I didn't think it would be difficult for Manny to call Al Dad. After all, he'd been looking for his father ever since he'd arrived in Miami. But I was a different story. I was pretty sure his memories of his mother were strong enough that he'd somehow feel he'd be dishonoring her if he called me Mom.

"You can call me Rose, honey, if it's too hard to say Mom. I understand."

"I never called my mother Mom," he said. "She was Mami. Maybe I could call you Mama Rose."

And that is who I became.

# Good Friday

ONCE BACK IN BOSTON we got Manny settled into seventh grade at St. John's and talked to Father Collins at BC High about enrolling him there for high school when the time came. We wanted him to have the same advantages his older brothers had been given. But we also had the same expectations. He had chores in the restaurant, bussing tables at dinner after he'd done his homework. We discovered he liked baseball, and Mike took him to opening day at Fenway to see the Red Sox play the Yankees, and then found him a Little League team in the neighborhood. Mike even offered to coach a summer team when he finished at Holy Cross.

Both Mike and Toni were more than great about our taking Manny into our family. Both of them got a kick out of having a little brother. And both of them were such do-gooders, always lecturing us about "social justice," that they felt some of their ideas had finally rubbed off on us. They were proud of us. We'd surprised them, they said, by doing something "cool."

"Maybe we should tell Toni and Mike the truth," I said to Al one night soon after we'd gotten back. "I worry about them finding out some other way. And I think it's hard on Manny to ask him to keep a secret like this when he's so young."

"What if the kids turn on me, lose respect for me, because of this? Especially Toni. You've had fourteen years. Remember how you felt when you first found out? I thought you'd never forgive me. Let them get used to Manny before we tell them he really is their brother."

I understood Al's fear. He'd given so much to our kids. But more than their respect, I think he feared losing their love.

"They'll be angrier that we lied to them than that you're taking care of your own son," I countered. "They're also smart, Al. If you and I saw the resemblance the moment we laid eyes on Manny, how long do you suppose it'll take them to wonder why he looks so much like Al Jr.?" I knew I was pushing him, but I was listening to my heart on this one, just as I had that day at the beach.

"Let me think about it."

It took a few more weeks of my gently bringing it up, usually late at night when we were getting ready for bed and I had his undivided attention. Manny was starting to fill out on my cooking and I predicted a growth spurt as I watched him wolf down plates of baked ziti and linguine with stuffed squid. I dug out some of my recipes from

Trinidad, thinking I might hit on a few dishes that were similar to what Manny had grown up with in Cuba. That gesture, plus the attention he was getting from Toni, who joked with him and helped him with his English homework and sat on the bleachers during his baseball games, made him seem more comfortable in his own skin.

He was becoming such a part of us that we'd begun to forget he hadn't always been a member of the family. For me, his taking his place at our table was a blessing, a miracle filling me up.

"Did you see the kids tonight after closing, working together to clean up? They were laughing and fooling around as if they'd being doing it forever. Toni's not going to turn her back on you, Al, for bringing Manny into the family."

"Okay, I hear you. How do you want to do this? Talk to them together when Mike comes home for Easter?"

I put my arms around him and kissed him. "That's a great idea."

On Good Friday we always closed the restaurant. Papa was going to a fish fry at the St. Anthony Society after the Stations of the Cross, so that's when we decided to sit down with the kids to explain why we'd adopted Manny. They'd have a couple of days to absorb what we expected would be a bombshell before the rest of the family descended upon us for Easter Sunday.

163

I made a simple meal: filet of sole baked with garlic, parsley and bread crumbs and an artichoke-heart pie made with mozzarella and Bisquick. Toni sliced some tomatoes and Bermuda onions and I sent Manny down the street to pick up a loaf of Campobasso bread.

Mike caught the early bus from Worcester and arrived just as we were setting the table.

When everybody was seated, I rested my hand on Al's.

"Daddy and I want to talk to you all about something important, something that needs to stay in this house."

Toni and Mike looked across the table at each other.

"What's wrong? Is one of you sick?" Toni's voice was agitated. She'd always been the worrier in the family.

"Nothing's wrong. It's just something we want to keep in the family."

Everyone waited. I squeezed Al's hand. This had to be his show, not mine. He cleared his throat.

"A long time ago, I made a mistake and hurt your mother. She had the goodness to forgive me then, and we thought we'd put it behind us."

Even with that limited information, I could see the understanding of what his father meant spread across Mike's face. I prayed he'd keep his mouth shut and let Al finish.

"We found out this winter that my mistake had greater consequences than the pain I caused your mother. The woman I'd been with—yes, Toni, that's what I'm talking about—had a child. My child. I didn't know that till Father Dom told me in Miami."

Al stopped for a minute. He'd kept his eyes down and his voice was almost a whisper.

Toni started to speak, but Al held up his hand.

"Not only did I find out I had a child, a son," he went on. "I also learned that he'd lost his mother. He was an orphan."

I put my arm around Manny, who was sitting next to me, as Toni and Mike understood what Al was telling them.

"Your mother, God bless her, knew before I did what we needed to do for this boy, and that's why we adopted him. We want you to know that Manny isn't just your adopted brother. He's your *brother*. I'm his father."

The table was silent.

Toni's face crumpled as she tried to suppress tears. I could read her like a book even though she thought I didn't understand her, and I knew she was fighting back disbelief that her daddy could have done what he'd just described. I held my breath, praying that she'd weigh the evidence of all that she knew of her father's goodness against this one fall from grace, as I had done. But she couldn't see beyond the betrayal. She threw down her napkin, pushed back her chair and bolted from the room. We heard her door slam.

Mike turned to Manny, who was shaken by Toni's departure.

"Hey, squirt. I *knew* there was a reason you were such a good athlete! Welcome again to the family." And he high-fived him.

"Do you want me to talk to her?" I asked Al.

"No. I've got to do it myself. I was afraid of this." He stood from the table, squeezing Manny's shoulder as he left the room. He was not a happy man.

"I'm sorry, Mama Rose. I shouldn't have come to Boston."

"No, honey. You don't have to say you're sorry. You belong here. Toni knows that. She just needs time to forgive her dad for not being perfect."

Nobody seemed interested in eating anymore. It was as though everything had been sucked out of the room—appetite, oxygen, conversation. I got up and began clearing the table, and Mike and Manny went into busboy mode, whisking all the dishes into the kitchen in record time. We all stayed busy, the boys rinsing and loading the dishwasher, me putting leftovers away.

At least Toni hadn't locked her door and had let Al in. I was afraid she was so hurt and angry that she'd refuse to speak to him. But from the low murmur coming from behind her door, I could tell she'd allowed him to say what he needed to say to her.

"Let's watch TV." Mike pulled Manny into the living room when the kitchen was back in order. I was relieved that Mike wasn't leaving to have a beer with his buddies the way he usually did on a Friday evening when he was home from Holy Cross. He seemed to understand that we needed to circle the wagons and pull ourselves together that night.

I went and sat with the boys while they watched *The Wild, Wild West,* but I was too distracted to follow the show. Had I been wrong? *Should* we have protected Toni with our lies? And what was going through Mike's head? He'd been kind to reach out to Manny, who was the innocent in all this, but would he do the same for his father?

My heart ached for Al, trying to do right by all his kids. And I worried that I had urged him to be honest. Maybe there were good reasons the old generation had handled things like this by sweeping everything under the rug, hiding the truth.

My head was pounding by the time Al came out of Toni's room. I got up and met him in the kitchen.

"How'd it go?" I bit my lip.

"She's pretty angry. I asked her if she would've wanted us to abandon Manny when we found out about him. And she said, no, she was glad we'd brought him home and into the family. So I asked her, should we have continued to lie about who he was, and again, she said no, that she needed to know he was really her brother. She said sometimes she sees flickers of Al Jr. in his eyes and his smile, and now she knows why."

"Those are all positive things."

"Yeah. But her disappointment in me, that's what I can't shake. 'How could you, Daddy?' is what she kept saying to me. I'm no longer my little girl's hero. I'm the bad guy. And I gotta tell you, Rose, it's killing me."

"Give her time, Al. Just like you gave me. She's too young to understand that everybody makes mistakes in their lives, does things they regret. She'll come to understand that what you're trying to do now is make it right again, not make it worse. What's she doing now?"

"She said she wants to be left alone. But I told her Manny could use a hug from her, and soon."

That's when we heard her door open and her footsteps go down the hall. I looked through the dining room and saw her slip down to the floor where Manny was sitting and throw her arms around him.

I thought that would be it, a quick squeeze and then back to her hiding place. But she stuck around and watched the rest of the show with her brothers.

I made Al and me cups of black coffee and put a shot of anisette and a strip of lemon peel in them.

"I'm proud of you, Al. You did a hard thing today, a brave thing. It's the end of innocence for Toni, but maybe that's not so bad. Someday she's going to look back on today and realize how important it was. And she's going to be grateful to you for telling her yourself. I'm glad she didn't hear it from some mean-spirited person who'd only be doing it to hurt our family."

"You're a dreamer, Rose. But I agree—in the long run, it was the right thing to do. But, man, it hurts like hell to see that look in her eyes. I wish I could rewind my life and do it over again."

"We all do, Al. But there's one thing I wouldn't change even if I got to relive my life."

"What's that?"

"Marrying you."

After that Easter, we settled into the ups and downs of family life with three kids. Manny, after his honeymoon period of welcome to the family, got himself into a few scrapes that required some strong words. He was a little too quick to use his fists on the playground and more than once came home with a bloody nose and a note from Reverend Mother—not the same one who'd been head of the school when Al Jr. was there, thank God.

We had two graduations that spring, Toni's from Sacred Heart and Mike's from Holy Cross. Manny got his first suit; he'd grown four inches since January. Toni was accepted into art schools in Portland, Maine, and Boston, and we told her we wanted her to stay in Boston and live at home. I didn't think she was ready to be on her own, especially in Boston in the late 1960s, where every time you turned around there was another demonstration against the war or, worse yet, a love-in in Franklin Park with girls dancing around wearing flowers in their ratty hair and next to nothing on while everyone smoked pot. And with Toni at art school, it was going to be hard enough for her to hold on to the way she'd been brought up without also having to fend off the pressures and temptations that come with living on your own. I'd already had too many of my cousins tell me about the birth control pills they'd found in their daughters' underwear drawers when they were putting laundry away. Maybe that was better than finding out your daughter was pregnant, but if you ask me, it was the fear of getting pregnant that kept most of my generation on the straight and narrow. Toni was still an innocent, too inexperienced and a prime target for getting hurt by the kind of freedom that was screaming at her from every corner and every television set.

She didn't like our decision one bit and cried

and pleaded with us to let her rent an apartment down by the Museum School on Huntington Avenue. But we stood firm and lived through the silent treatment for a few weeks until she realized what a good deal she had—her own room, great food that she didn't have to shop for or cook and parents who thought she was doing wonderful work.

Mike came home from Worcester after graduation and got a job at the New England Merchants Bank. When we gathered for Thanksgiving that year we were a full house again. I added black beans and rice to the menu and learned how to make a mole sauce for the turkey.

# ROSE
## 1972–80

# The Wedding

I SHOULD'VE BEEN a better judge of Bobby Templeton when I first met him. It wasn't at our home, where he should've come to meet us when he started going out with Toni. Instead, they'd meet at her art studio after school. I didn't even know about him until I ran into the two of them downtown. They were holding hands. After all my worries about her not having any experience with men, I was too thrilled to see she had a boyfriend. I just wished she'd felt comfortable enough to introduce him to us at home.

They were coming up out of the Park Street T station as I was on my way to go shopping.

"Hey, Mom! We're headed to Mike's Pastry to pick up some cannoli. This is Bobby. Bobby, my mother, Rose Dante."

He let go of Toni long enough to shake my hand.

"Hi, Mrs. Dante. Nice to meet you."

"Good to meet you, too, Bobby. Stop by the restaurant with Toni sometime and have dinner with us. In fact, if you two are going to the neighborhood, join us tonight."

"Can't, Mom. Sorry. My print class is throwing

a birthday party for our instructor. I'm bringing the pastries."

"Are you in Toni's class, Bobby?"

"Who, me? No, I'm not an artist. I'm an engineer."

"Where do you go to school, then?"

"I'm out of school. I work over in Kendall Square in Cambridge."

"Shouldn't you be at work now?"

"I'm on my lunch break. Just volunteered to help Toni pick everything up. She seems to think the only place worthy of her patronage is on Hanover Street."

He shot her a wide grin, obviously humoring her. I don't know who I expected Toni to fall in love with, but in my wildest dreams, it wasn't somebody like Bobby Templeton. He was, let me put it bluntly, not like us. To begin with, he stood well over six feet, with blond hair and blue eyes. At least he wasn't one of those long-haired, guitar-playing, skinny artists sprawled all over the steps at the Museum School when we went to see Toni's exhibits. He was clean-cut; he had a job. He wasn't Italian, which was probably going to be a little difficult for Al. But the world was changing and, of all of us, Toni was the one out in front, finding her place in it.

I had mixed feelings, of course. On the one hand, I was excited to see her starting to figure out how talented she was. She'd begun to really blossom at the Museum School, bursting out of the narrow ideas the nuns had about art. I was no expert. Most of what I knew on the subject came from a book on Italian masterpieces Toni had given me one Christmas. But I did know that what she was painting came right out of her heart and stopped you dead in your tracks. The summer after her second year in art school, she'd painted a mural of the Bay of Naples on a wall in the restaurant. One of her classmates had sent her a postcard with a view from a hillside over-looking the harbor with Vesuvius in the distance. She studied that photograph and turned it into a work of love that brought tears to the eyes of the old-timers in the neighborhood. They'd probably stood on that very hillside—maybe just before they left Italy forever. I watched people at her exhibits at the Museum School get lost in her portraits, faces staring back at you and pulling you into their secrets.

I regretted that we'd sent her to Catholic high school. It was different for the boys with the Jesuits. They taught them to think on their own. But the nuns at Sacred Heart cared more about the length of the girls' skirts than the depth of their ideas. I hadn't realized how tightly they'd contained Toni until she started to paint in college. Also, putting her in an all-girl school meant she hadn't had a chance to get to know boys.

I think Bobby Templeton was the first boy to

pay attention to her, and he swept her off her feet. He was the kind of person everyone stared at when he walked into a room. He commanded attention. Part of it was those all-American good looks. Not to my taste, mind you, but he had a quality like James Dean or Steve McQueen that made people, especially women, notice. So I guess Toni was flattered that somebody who was wanted by everyone else wanted *her*.

At first, like any mother, I worried that he'd hurt her. She was so crazy about him, although she wouldn't admit that to me for a minute.

Between her studio classes and the academic courses she was taking to get the teaching degree Al and I had insisted on, she wasn't home much. It made me nervous that she was often out late, but she spent every night at home. Other than school, Bobby Templeton was her whole life.

One night, I decided we needed to talk. They'd been going out for about a year. Their generation was starting to disregard the taboos ours had respected about sex. Couples were moving in with each other, setting up house, without a ring and the blessing of the priest. In my opinion, that was a recipe for disaster, especially for the girl. I didn't want that for my daughter.

So when I heard her key in the door, I was waiting in the kitchen with a pot of tea, which is what she's always liked to drink.

"Toni, have a cup with me. I don't get to see

you enough, and this seems like the only time we're both home."

She set down her knapsack. I could see she was about to protest, beg off because she was tired. We'd never done well at this mother-daughter thing. Somehow, no matter how much I loved her, no matter how thrilled I was with the wonderful woman I saw her becoming, I managed to garble the message. She must have seen something in my face—a longing or a resistance to being put off—and she thought better of saying no.

She slipped reluctantly into a seat at the kitchen table and I poured her a cup of tea. We got through the "how was your day?" part of the conversation pretty quickly. Then I said what was on my mind.

"Toni, I know you and Bobby are getting serious—at least, that's how it appears to me. I need to talk to you, woman to woman. You know I'm not an openly religious person. I don't make a big show of going to Mass every day or lighting banks of candles. But I have to tell you, every night I pray to Jesus, Mary and Joseph that you are not having an affair with Bobby Templeton."

She almost spit out the tea she'd just sipped.

"Ma! An affair? An *affair* is something your generation has, something between two people who shouldn't be together—usually because one of them's married to someone else. It's sordid and secretive and bound to hurt somebody. I'm *not* having an affair." She didn't have to say out loud that her definition of an affair came straight out of her father's life.

"Well, *my* definition of an affair is sleeping with someone who isn't your husband. I don't care what the rest of the world is doing right now, casually jumping into bed with one another. You give up something precious, a part of yourself, when you make love to a man—and I'm not talking about your virginity. If you find out later he's not the man you want to marry—or he decides he's had what he wanted and moves on—you're setting yourself up for a terrible loss. I don't want you hurt, Toni."

She was bristling. But she pulled back whatever argument she'd planned to throw in my face.

"I know you want to protect me. Look, I'm twenty-one years old. I'm not going to do anything stupid. I'm not going to get myself pregnant, if that's what you're worried about."

"Oh, that's only part of it. I'm thinking more about you, not the family's reputation. I trusted your father, body and soul, when I put myself in his arms. I just want you to be sure that you can trust Bobby in the same way."

"I do, Ma, no less than you did when you placed your trust in Daddy."

I should've known that when she fell in love, she'd measure her experience against her memory of her father's betrayal.

"We're all imperfect, Toni. But I knew, because of what we'd been through together, that even when he stumbled, your father was a good man. If you can ask yourself and know in your heart that at the core of Bobby's imperfections, he's a good man, that's all I want for you. It's your life, honey, and I want you to have a happy one."

I didn't ask her straight out, *Are you sleeping with Bobby?* Because what was I going to do if she said yes? She'd move in with him if I tried to stop her. I wanted her to understand what the consequences were. Not to say "I told you so" if she got hurt in the end. Just to make her think about it and maybe get through the next part of her life with a little wisdom.

"Be careful," I said softly.

When Bobby asked her to meet his mother over Thanksgiving, I sensed it wouldn't be long before I wouldn't have to worry anymore about her having sex outside of marriage. And I was right.

She came into the restaurant kitchen one night just before Easter, breathless with laughter, Bobby at her side.

"Mom! Dad! Bobby asked me to marry him!"

She took her left hand out of her coat pocket and showed us the ring.

Al came up beside me and slid his arm around my waist.

We hugged and kissed her and let her bask in the excitement. Her face was flushed, not just from the heat of the stove but also from the emotion. I don't think I'd ever seen her in such an agitated state.

"I can't believe this is happening to me," she said as she whirled from one station to the next, receiving the congratulations of one after another of us. Manny teased her, humming the wedding march. Papa retrieved a bottle of champagne and poured glasses all around.

Then Al, pulling Toni and Bobby with him, went into the dining room, turned off the music and made an announcement to the guests sitting over various stages of their dinners. For a few minutes, forks went down and veal scallopine, chicken francese and spinach fettuccine with porcini sat idle.

"Ladies and gentlemen, please share in the good news with my family. My daughter, my princess, has just gotten engaged. Drinks all around, on the house!"

Glasses went up and *"Salute!"* echoed across the room. People clapped, and someone tapped a spoon against a water glass. Toni, even more red-faced than before, uttered in exasperation, "Daddy!"

Bobby looked like a deer in the headlights,

standing in the doorway and facing the raucous tumult.

"They're waiting for you to kiss her," I murmured to him, and he finally got the message.

A roar went up when he took her in his arms. Then Manny, as if to rescue his sister, put the Frank Sinatra album back on and people returned to their dinners.

"You should make the rounds," I told her. "A lot of people here tonight will want to congratulate you."

She took Bobby by the hand and moved from table to table, initiating him into the family business. He needed to know he was going to be on display for a few months, at least until the wedding was over.

The wedding, even I have to say, was an extravaganza. The restaurant was fine for an engagement party, which we threw for them a month after their announcement. The wedding itself we held elsewhere.

But we almost didn't make it to the wedding at all, or not in the way we'd expected.

I was surprised by Al's exuberance that night in the restaurant. The little time we'd spent with Bobby up to that point hadn't given us much comfort that we knew who our future son-in-law was. Later that night in bed, Al and I talked about it.

"You got carried away with your announcement tonight. What got into you?"

"It's been a long time since I've seen her so happy. If marrying this guy is what she wants, and it can lift her so high, then I *do* feel like celebrating. We're only going to get to do this once, so why not shout it from the rooftops—or at least from the kitchen door? Why? Did I embarrass you or something?"

"No, of course not! I think it's sweet that you got so excited for her. Some fathers might feel they were about to lose their daughters. It was kind of like the old days, watching you order drinks all around and make such a big deal. It's been ages since we've had reason to celebrate. I feel I've been too skeptical. You did the right thing tonight, Al. Thank you!"

"You know, it's a pretty important moment in our lives, too—the first of our kids to get married. It made me remember that Christmas I proposed to you."

"I thought of that, too. What kids we were! What did we know? I wanted to marry you so much."

"We've done okay, Rose, despite how blindly we went into it." He drew me close and kissed me.

"I only hope Toni and Bobby are as blessed as we were."

"You don't sound too sure."

"Oh, Al, I'm not trying to put a damper on things. I may just be reading into the situation something that isn't there."

"Like what? What am I missing?"

"He's not like you, Al. I want to know she's with someone who loves her for who she is, not who she might be someday. Someone who'll stand by her when they hit bumps in the road."

"You worry too much, Rose. We have to trust her that this is the guy who makes her happy. Did you see her looking at him tonight? The light in her eyes?"

"You're right. I should know by now we can't be sure of anything in this life. We have to take a leap of faith sometimes."

The next few weeks—as Toni and Bobby planned their wedding—tested both of us. Even Al, convinced as he was of Toni's happiness, had to fight with himself to accept some things he'd never imagined.

We knew we were on unfamiliar territory because Bobby wasn't Italian. Toni was the first of the cousins to marry someone who hadn't grown up with the same traditions, the same sense of family. When Bobby's mother, a widow, came east from Indiana for the engagement party, she put her best face on a situation we could see was not to her liking.

From what Toni had told me of her visit at Thanksgiving, Bobby lived in a fancy suburb.

They were country-club people, who kept crystal decanters of bourbon and Scotch on a tray in the living room and served cocktails every evening before dinner. For all I knew, they had a black maid in a uniform who did the cooking and cleaning. Hazel Templeton struck me as the kind of woman who wasn't used to getting down on her hands and knees and scrubbing her own floors.

I'm proud of my home. I keep it spotless myself, just like I learned from Mama. And everything in it Al and I worked for. I suppose we could've moved the family to a house up the North Shore, to Lynn or Swampscott, but it would've meant running the business differently if we didn't live above the restaurant the way we always have. So, even after we were successful, we stayed put. Close to family. Close to the business. My kids never suffered for living in an old section of the city. They got good educations, understood the value of hard work to get where you wanted in life and looked out for one another and those who had less than they did.

But Hazel Templeton was clearly pained when she set foot in my home, wondering what her son was marrying into. She barely ate anything, drank only martinis and asked pointed questions of Toni about how she planned to decorate the home she and Bobby were buying.

That was actually the first time Al and I heard they were going to buy a house. Bobby had a new job out in Concord, so, without discussing it with us, they decided to look in the suburbs for a place to live rather than stay in Bobby's apartment in Cambridge. Instead of a fifteen-minute T ride from the North End, they'd be almost an hour away by car.

I know—Al and I went all the way to Trinidad when we got married. But we came back, as we always knew we would. Toni wasn't coming back. Along with the Templeton name she was going to be taking on a whole lot of other ideas that felt at odds with who we were.

It hurt. I can't deny it. And Al couldn't understand why they hadn't told us.

"Is she ashamed of us, of the home she grew up in, that she's taking off for Bedford without even telling us?" This was after Bobby and Hazel had left and we were getting ready for bed.

"I think she's seeing us through Bobby's eyes, not her own," I said, saddened that she was putting such distance between us.

The house was only the beginning. When they started talking about where they were going to be married, both Al and I hit the roof. Arlington Street Church. So many things about that choice felt like a slap in the face to us. To begin with, it wasn't Catholic. It wasn't even in the neighborhood. Back Bay instead of the North End. You have to understand, the North End is not simply a collection of streets. It's a village, just like all the ones our parents came from in Italy. And on top of everything, the Arlington Street Church was at the heart of the antiwar protests. A few years before, it was where young men had burned their draft cards.

I didn't think Al would even set foot in that church.

"What the hell is going on, Rose? Why can't they be married at St. Leonard's—where we got married, where she was baptized and made her first communion?"

We felt we had to get everything out in the open with them. No more surprises. I told Toni we would all sit down across the table and have dinner together on Sunday. Command performance. No excuses.

I did what I always do when we have something important to discuss. I put care into what we were going to eat. For the pasta course I made orecchiette with peas and ham in a cream sauce. It was one of Toni's favorites. For the main course I did a rolled breast of turkey, stuffing it with spinach and ricotta, and on the side, artichoke hearts sautéed with garlic and then baked with bread crumbs and Parmigiano. For dessert, I whipped up a frothy *zabaione*.

I wanted Bobby to see that Italian food is more than smothering everything in tomato sauce and melted mozzarella.

A wedding's supposed to be a time of joy for a

family, not a reason for *agita*. Every day it seemed Al and I were tossing on a very stormy sea in a gondola designed to float on the Venice canals. Some days he had the oars, some days I did. We were taking turns calming each other down and trying to find our way.

"I want her to be happy, you know I do, Rose. But has she lost her mind? That night in the restaurant when she came bursting in with the ring, I breathed such a sigh of relief. She's always been a loner and an intellectual, and I worried she'd never find the kind of love you and I were lucky enough to have. I know she's different, not like her cousins. But not to get married in the Catholic church? That's going too far for me. As far as I'm concerned, they can call the wedding off. I'm *not* walking her down the aisle of a Protestant church."

"You know if you tell her that, they'll just go off and have their wedding without us. Neither of us wants that. We need a compromise."

I was asking a lot of Al to try to meet Toni halfway. When he seizes on something, he doesn't often let go. Most of the time, that's been a good thing. His passion for me, for instance, hasn't cooled in all these years, and he never once wanted to throw in the towel on the restaurant, even in those early years when he was learning to do things he hadn't imagined would ever be part of his life.

"We can figure this out, Al, because we love her and want her to be happy. I'm not going to have her start her married life estranged from us."

Before the Sunday of that dinner arrived, Al decided to get help from Father Dom. Since bringing Manny to us he'd spent a few more years in Miami before being transferred back to Boston. He was working at a Spanish parish in the South End. Al invited him to lunch at the restaurant and we told him about Toni's decision.

"She said she and Bobby had considered St. Leonard's out of respect for us and had gone to Father Cavallo to talk about the wedding. But he'd berated them because Bobby isn't Catholic. She said he's opposed to mixed marriages and won't perform the ceremony. She was furious. I can't blame her. But I still want her to be married in the Church. Is there a way?"

"Some parish priests are more conservative than the orders. Let me talk to Toni and Bobby. If I'm satisfied that they're entering into marriage as a sacred act, I'd be happy to marry them. And as far as a church, what about the chapel at Boston College? With all your boys educated at BC High, you've got a connection. I can make the call."

Al and I looked at each other across the table.

"This works for me," he said. "Let's just hope it works for them. Dom, do us one more favor and come to dinner with them on Sunday. She'll listen to you directly better than hearing this from us. She's ready to leave the Church entirely."

After Father Dom left, I threw my arms around Al. "I know it's not over yet because we still have to talk to them, but thank you for coming up with a way to solve this. You're the best!"

He kissed me hard. "I want this to work as much as you do, Rose. Married life is complicated enough without a problem like this casting its shadow on a couple."

Toni had always loved Father Dom, especially as she got older and understood the work he did with the poor. I knew she'd hear him out. What I didn't know was if Bobby had any idea how important it was to us—and if he loved her enough to give us this.

I tried to broach the subject as she and I set the table for Sunday dinner. We were using the good dishes, the silver and the embroidered tablecloth my aunt Cecilia had brought back from Italy as a twenty-fifth anniversary gift.

"Why are you going to so much trouble when it's just family? I mean, Bobby's part of the family now."

"I'm setting a nice table *because* it's family. I want this meal to be memorable for us all. A day we can look back on in years to come and say, 'We got it right.' "

"What do you mean? What's going on?"

"Your father and I are trying to give you the wedding you've dreamed of, but we also want you and Bobby to understand what's important to us. A wedding isn't just about the bride and groom. It's about joining two families. You hope the families agree that what matters is the happiness of their children and that everybody works together to start the couple off right."

"Do you think we're *not* working together?"

"I didn't say that. I just want to make sure that you and Bobby—especially Bobby—are open to listening to what your father and I have to say. We invited Father Dom to come, too."

"What's Father Dom got to do with it?"

"He wants to help us find a solution."

"If that solution involves St. Leonard's, I'm not interested."

"Don't worry. Daddy and I actually agree with you about St. Leonard's. It breaks my heart that you won't be married in the same church Daddy and I were, but that's not important in the bigger scheme of things."

"What *is* the bigger scheme?"

"I want you and Bobby to be willing to listen to our side today. Can you ask him to do that?"

"Of course."

At two o'clock I pulled Manny and Mike away from the TV and the Red Sox game. Bobby and Father Dom had arrived in front of the building at the same time and had walked upstairs together—Bobby in his tailored, handmade suit towering over Father Dom in the brown robe and sandals of the Franciscans.

Father Dom said grace; Mike poured everyone a glass of Asti Spumante and we made a toast to Toni and Bobby's future. Toni then surprised us by making another toast.

"To Mom and Daddy, for all they do for us and for bringing us together today. *Salute.*"

The first part of the meal was all small talk—Father Dom asking Manny about BC High, where he was already a junior and playing varsity baseball; Bobby complimenting me on the pasta and taking a second helping; Papa deciding to go have a nap after the salad.

When we'd finally cleared the table of the dinner dishes and were sitting with our coffee and biscotti, Father Dom turned to Toni and Bobby.

"I understand you're having some challenges finding a church that everyone's happy with?"

"No offense, Father, but if it weren't for the close mindedness of the priest at St. Leonard's, we wouldn't even be having this conversation. Did he never hear of Vatican II?"

"Walking away from St. Leonard's doesn't have to mean walking away from the Church. I'm not one to promote cafeteria-style Catholicism, where you pick and choose what you want to believe.

But there are some parts of the city where you might find a more welcoming reception."

"That's why we chose the Arlington Street Church," Bobby interjected.

I could see the color rising in Al's face and was about to jump into the conversation to steer it away from talking too soon about the one thing that could make him explode. But Father Dom turned to Bobby and spoke to him calmly but firmly.

"Bobby, the Arlington Street Church is a wonderful institution and has been a beacon of light and wisdom not only in the history of Boston but also of this country. I know the pastor well and he's carrying on the traditions that were established in the nineteenth century. Al and Rose have great respect for the Arlington Street Church. *But it's not their church.* The Dantes are Catholic. And unless I've missed something, Toni is still a Catholic."

He looked at Toni and she nodded, almost imperceptibly.

"The Dantes want you and Toni to start your marriage off well, and to them, that means treating it as a sacrament and being married by a priest. They aren't insisting on St. Leonard's, even though the family's history is tied to it. Toni and Bobby, I'd like you to consider being married by me, in a place that also has meaning for the family. The chapel at Boston College."

Toni, who'd been watchful and tense throughout the meal and now this conversation, seemed to relax a little, as if we weren't asking for more than she could give.

She turned to Bobby. "What do you think? This would work for me, if you'd be comfortable with it."

I held my breath and waited to see what Bobby would do. It was a test of how much he cared for my daughter and how willing he was to bend. In my eyes, you needed to be flexible to make a marriage work.

"I thought you had your heart set on Arlington Street—the Tiffany windows, the hand-rung bells."

"The beauty of the church is one thing, but if it causes my parents pain to have us marry there, I'm willing to go to BC."

Bobby shrugged. "Then I guess it's fine with me. However we do it, whatever prayers get said over our heads, it doesn't matter to me. What do we need to do to make it happen?"

"I'll want to spend a few moments talking to just the two of you. I'm still bound by the rules of the Church, but let's say I have a more open interpretation of Vatican II than Father Cavallo does."

Al and I and the boys left the three of them in the dining room and cleaned up in the kitchen with the door closed.

"God bless Dom. I think he's saved this family a lot of grief," I said to Al.

"Let's hope this is the end of it. The world's changing too fast for me."

He smiled at the boys. "Do us all a favor and marry Catholic girls when the time comes. I don't want to have to go through this again."

"Don't worry, Pop. I've already got one picked out." Manny grinned.

"And who might that be? That cute girl who always sits over by third base at your ball games?" Mike started in on him.

"You're just jealous 'cause nobody comes to watch you when you're sitting on a bar stool at the Rusty Scupper."

The two of them went at it, teasing each other while they dried the pots, and Al and I felt that life was getting back to normal.

With the decision about the church behind us, I felt like I could put my heart into making a beautiful wedding for Toni. She asked me to handle the details for her.

"I have so much to do between now and the end of school, Mom. If you'd organize everything, it would take such a load off me."

I was happy—no, overjoyed—to do it. She asked if she could wear my wedding dress; it needed hardly any alterations. She and Bobby picked out an invitation and I took care of getting them printed and addressed. The invitation list was huge—three hundred people. That's why we couldn't hold the reception at the restaurant. We wound up at Al's cousin's golf course in Chestnut Hill, near Boston College. I told him I didn't want any skimping on the meal, only the best, and he came through for us.

The ceremony itself, which we had struggled so much with, seemed to fulfill everyone's expectations. St. Mary's Chapel at Boston College didn't have the Italian flair of St. Leonard's, but the stained-glass window of the Madonna and the white marble altar made us feel right at home, and I could tell that the unadorned stone walls fit Toni's idea of beauty. They didn't have Mass or Holy Communion, but the service and the prayers were straight out of the Catholic missal. Bobby followed along without stumbling; Toni appreciated Dom's simplicity in the homily; Al and I were grateful for the familiar words of the blessing and for the dear friend who was raising his hand in the sign of the cross over their heads.

Like Toni, the ceremony had a quiet grace. The reception, on the other hand, was the kind of party Al and I know how to throw when we have something important to celebrate.

During the cocktail reception it took your breath away—two huge carved ice swans with their necks entwined like lovebirds. Hollowed out between their wings were jumbo shrimp, chunks of lobster, and clams and oysters on the half shell. The dinner was three courses. Pear and arugula salad with balsamic dressing; for the pasta course, spinach tortellini with pesto sauce; and for the entrée, filet mignon with green beans and roasted rosemary potatoes. The wedding cake came from La Venezia on Hanover Street.

Of the three hundred guests about two dozen came from Bobby's side. He had no family at all except his mother, his sister, Sandra, and her husband. Both his parents were only children, so no aunts or uncles, no cousins. I felt bad that, compared to them, we had so much in the way of family and tried to welcome them. Some of Hazel's friends made the trip from Indiana, and they seemed stunned by the celebration. I guess weddings in the Midwest were more subdued than the parties we were used to giving.

You should've seen the dining room just before we threw open the doors. I did everything in gold—the tablecloths and napkins, the cutlery and the rim around the cream-colored dishes. With all the candles lit, the room shimmered.

I watched Al on the dance floor with Toni as the band played "Daddy's Little Girl," and I remembered a handsome soldier who'd put his arm around my waist more than thirty years before as he led me in our first dance as a married couple.

I said a little prayer that my daughter was stepping into a marriage that would be as solid and as deeply loving as ours. I wished I could shake the feeling in my heart that, despite the gaiety and lightness surrounding her, she and Bobby had a long way to go and a lot to learn if they were going to make it.

I was starting to feel like my mother, God rest her soul, who saw things the rest of us missed or overlooked in our rush through life. She could cut through appearances and find the core of truth in a situation. My fear for Toni was that she'd wrapped herself in a gauze of illusions. Like my wedding veil, which had disintegrated in its box in the closet when we took it out, I was afraid her dreams for this marriage would crumble.

I hoped I was wrong.

## Raising Sons

I BECAME A GRANDMOTHER a little under a year later, when Toni gave birth to her son, Joseph Albert. I was both thrilled and relieved. I had no idea how overwhelmed I'd feel when I first took that baby in my arms. I understood then why my mother would hold up each of her grandchildren when they were presented to her and utter, *"Il mio sangue."* My blood.

You begin to feel immortal when you have a grandchild, like you'll live on in them.

I was relieved for two reasons. The first was that she had been married longer than nine months before Joey made his appearance. I didn't have to endure any more raised eyebrows or suspicions that she'd been pregnant when she walked down the aisle. As soon as she'd announced she was pregnant back in September, tongues had started to wag that one of Rose's "perfect" children wasn't so perfect. As it was, the family had wondered why they were in such a hurry to get married, only a few months after he gave her the ring. "Because they're in love," I told everybody. "Just like Al and me. Remember, we got married a *week* after he popped the question." Joe was born a full eleven months after the wedding, and that shut everyone up.

I was also relieved that she'd been able to get pregnant so quickly, instead of suffering as I had with doubts that I was barren. I wasn't sure she would've kept trying if it had been difficult for her—not because she gives up easily but because I'd worried that she might not want kids at all. Or rather, that Bobby might not want kids and Toni would go along with his decision.

Who knows? Maybe the pregnancy was an accident, a glitch in the carefully orchestrated life they'd laid out for themselves. But Toni adapted with grace. She had Joe close to the end of the school year, so she had the whole summer with him before she went back to teaching art at Bedford High School in September. If they'd lived closer I would have watched Joe for her, just as Mama had done for me after Al Jr. was born. But I couldn't leave the day-to-day needs of the restaurant or Papa, who, at eighty-nine and nearly blind, needed almost as much attention as an infant. And Toni felt it was too far to drive the baby to me in the city every morning before she went to school.

So she hired somebody, a stranger, to take care of her child. Oh, she had her interview checklists and talked to everybody's references before she made her decision. But to me, it was yet another sign of how far apart her generation and mine were. I accepted that times were changing. It was harder for Al.

"I don't understand why she can't take a few years off and stay home with her baby."

"Al! I worked when the kids were babies."

"Yeah, but that's because I was away at war and then in a VA hospital for a year. Her husband's an able-bodied guy with an engineering degree."

"She wants to work, Al. It's why she got an education, why we *paid* for that education."

"I knew if they moved out to Bedford it was

going to be too easy for her to forget about her family."

As much as it hurt me that I didn't have them close, I'd learned long ago not to question the decisions made by my daughter and her husband.

While Toni was starting her life as a mother, I still had my own two boys at home to deal with. In Manny's junior year of high school, our bright student and star athlete slid into a funk after he broke his arm one afternoon horsing around stupidly with his buddies at the playground. One of them came running into the restaurant yelling, "Mrs. D! Mrs. D! Come quick. Manny's hurt himself."

Both Al and I raced down the street. Manny was writhing on the asphalt, badly scratched up, with his arm at an alarming angle and the bone sticking out.

Al blanched, terrible memories of his own damaged arm flooding back. I sent him home to call the ambulance while I stayed with Manny.

If only it had been a simple broken bone. But it was so badly shattered the orthopedist didn't think Manny would be able to pitch again, and certainly not with the skill and strength he'd shown. His dreams of getting a baseball scholarship to college and aiming for the major leagues began to unravel. He lost interest in everything— his schoolwork, the team, even helping out in the restaurant. We'd excused him from his regular duties downstairs for a couple of weeks to give his arm a chance to heal. The doctor at Mass General had told us no lifting, no unnecessary motion. The arm had to rest. But that inactivity cost Manny. He'd been such an active kid, always on the move. He had practically danced on the ball field. And when he was a base runner, the other team had to watch him constantly or he'd steal a base. He didn't know what to do with himself, cooped up in the apartment with Papa, who slept most of the afternoon. He was angry with himself and with his buddies and couldn't bring himself to suit up and sit on the bench to cheer his teammates on. I didn't realize soon enough exactly what was bothering him. By the time I did, he was locked in his room with headphones on, listening to the Grateful Dead and getting Fs on his papers because he wasn't handing them in.

When we got his midterm grades it was our turn to be angry. Al was beside himself.

"Do you think a broken arm is an excuse to become a bum? Where do you think I'd be if I let what happened to *this* determine my whole life." He pointed to his own arm.

"You don't understand." Manny pushed back. "Without baseball, I have nothing. I am nothing."

Later that night, after a fruitless discussion with Manny that resulted only in frayed tempers,

Al and I tried to come up with a way to get through to him.

"Al, if anyone can reach him, you can. Put aside who you are now and remember the young man who was released from the VA hospital and could barely make it up the stairs. You'd lost hope. Everything you thought you'd do or be felt out of reach. If you can let Manny know that you've been where he is now, maybe it'll help."

"But, Rose, I managed to climb out of that hole because I had you. You showed me how. Made me believe I could be somebody despite my broken body."

"And now Manny has both of us, Al. But he's not going to listen to me. He assumes I won't understand what it means to him not to play baseball."

The next day we told Manny we expected him to return to work in the restaurant. He wouldn't be able to bus tables with one arm immobilized, so we put him on a salad station, arranging plates of ingredients that had already been cut. It was close to Al, who could keep an eye on him, but who also was going about the complex work of cooking. Manny couldn't help seeing Al's swift movements, adapted over the years to compensate for his weak arm. Al said nothing for a couple of days, other than to let Manny know what needed to go on the plates, depending on what salad a diner had ordered.

"You can arrange the plate any way you want," he told Manny.

At first, it was all he could do to throw a handful of romaine, some sliced onions and a couple of carrot slices on a plate just to keep up with the orders. He was frustrated, but he was at least *doing* something instead of lying on his bed.

Most of the time as a busboy he'd been moving in and out of the kitchen so quickly he hadn't paid much attention to what was being created there. The plates he'd seen were the ones he was clearing off the tables, either wiped clean by a piece of bread to soak up the last bit of gravy or, worse, filled with picked-over remnants a diner had pushed around with a fork but not savored or enjoyed.

We wanted to keep him busy and have him absorb the silent message of Al's success. But we got something unexpected.

After a few days, Al noticed that when the kitchen was slow, the salads were looking less like a pile of greens dumped on the plate and more like the artist's palettes Toni had used at the Museum School. Manny was fanning the tomato or pear slices. Placing olives strategically like punctuation marks. Still, Al said nothing.

You can't force a message on someone who's not ready to hear it.

One night during a lull between the turnover

period, when the early diners were eating their cannoli and tiramisu and before the next wave had arrived, Manny was on a break. He was rubbing his shoulder on the broken arm. I fought back the urge to let him off early. I knew he'd done his homework in the afternoon, so if I sent him upstairs, he'd retreat into his headphones. Not a good place, as far as I was concerned. He stood around, watching Al at the stove finishing off some rabbit with olives that had been simmering in wine.

"Dad, how'd you learn how to cook?"

"Mostly by doing and by watching Mama Rose and her mother."

"Was it what you always wanted to do?"

"Me? Nah. I was a builder before the war. I figured cooking was women's work. When I got out of the VA hospital I thought my life was over because I couldn't work at what I'd been trained to do. You can ask Mama Rose. I was one angry guy. Here, stir this a minute while I check on the lamb in the oven."

He handed Manny the wooden spoon and left him at the stove. I watched Manny plunge the spoon in the pot and imitate the scraping motion Al had been using to loosen bits of meat and onions from the bottom. He wasn't great at it, but he shoved the spoon around enough to keep the meat from sticking.

Al came back with an order slip in his hand.

"Manny, we just got two orders for the rabbit. Plate them up with some potatoes and broccoli rabe." And then he walked away.

Manny took two plates from the warmer and spooned out a couple of pieces of rabbit onto each. One at a time he carried them over to the vegetable trays and arranged the potatoes and rabe, then put them under the infrared lamp for the waitstaff to pick up.

"You want me to plate anything else, Dad?" he called over to Al.

"Keep an eye on the orders as they come in. I've gotta go down to the cellar for some olive oil."

Now, I knew very well there were at least two gallons of oil in the cabinet. Al was deliberately leaving Manny on his own. I saw Manny straighten his shoulders. Whatever ache had bothered him earlier seemed to have disappeared. He pulled order slips off the shelf as they came in from the dining room and started arranging plates of linguine with shrimp scampi and eggplant parmigiano. By the time Al came back upstairs he'd plated six different orders.

He was fast and sometimes a little careless, but he looked as if he was enjoying what he was doing.

I nodded to Al as he came back into the kitchen. "I think you unlocked a tiger from his cage," I whispered.

Al smiled. "I can live with a few screwed-up orders if the kid finds himself."

Over the next few weeks Al kept giving Manny more responsibility in the kitchen. It wasn't always easy. Al could overlook a dropped plate of chicken piccata or a forgotten side of string beans, but he blasted Manny if he got lazy or didn't clean up any messes he made. Al wanted to do well by this boy to make up for all the years he hadn't known about him. But he wasn't going to spoil him or let him get away with anything.

Manny, for his part, would go into a sulk whenever Al caught him slacking off; he'd scowl and slam heads of lettuce on the counter until he cooled off. But little by little I could see Manny trying harder, picking up little tips Al gave him, taking on extra work when we got really busy.

You know, even though all three of our other kids had worked in the restaurant as teenagers, none of them had shown the slightest interest in the back of the house. They'd waited tables or bussed, did setup, ran the cash register. The other boys had been helpful with unloading deliveries. But nobody had ever stuck a spoon in a pot except to grab a taste of something for themselves.

I guess we should've seen it coming the day Manny said to us, "I don't want to go to college."

"What is this, you think college was just a place for you to play baseball? Of course you're going to college." As far as Al was concerned, there was no discussion.

"You're a smart boy, Manny. You got your grades back on track. Dad's right. Colleges are interested in your mind, not just your pitching arm."

"But you always said to us how important work is. Mike and Toni, they're doing jobs they needed to go to college for. The work I want to do, I don't need a college education."

"What do you want to do?" Al asked him, but we already knew the answer to that.

"Work in the business with you."

There was probably nothing that could have made Al prouder than to have his son say he wanted to join the business. But we both realized the world had changed since we'd started out. You needed a lot more than hard work and street smarts to survive in our business these days.

"You need an education, Manny." Al's voice was firm, but I knew Manny could hear the love underneath his gruff tone.

"Why not let him go to a college that offers restaurant management?" That was Mike's suggestion, trying to bridge the gulf between Manny and us. "He doesn't have to study medieval art or philosophy to get a college degree."

"He wants to cook."

"Then check out places that'll let him do both. He knows by now it's a business, not just a place for making a delicious veal scallopine. Let me look into it, ask around. I'll see if I can find out what the good schools are."

It was a big help to have Mike step in. Because he was still living with us, he understood his brother. He knew what baseball had meant to Manny. If Manny was willing to replace that dream with being a chef, we didn't want him to be disappointed a second time. But not going to college was out of the question. To Al and me, it was like treating him as a second-class citizen compared to his siblings.

What if, God forbid, the restaurant failed? We'd survived our mistakes in the past, but who was to say the place would still be thriving for Manny to take over? No, he had to have something to fall back on. But you can't tell a seventeen-year-old, even one who'd made it out of Cuba, that you need to be prepared for anything life threw at you.

Al still wanted him to go to Villanova.

"You can't ask him to replace Al Jr.," I said to him. "We agreed when we adopted Manny that he's not a substitute for what we lost. He's having a hard enough time measuring up to his own dreams. Don't saddle him with that, as well."

By Thanksgiving of his senior year in high school, Manny's arm had healed sufficiently to let him prepare simple dishes in the restaurant, not just plating entrées and putting salads together. He cooked on Saturdays and was often downstairs before either Al or me, chopping onions and garlic and taking deliveries. He'd have trays of lasagne assembled and waiting in the refrigerator before Al and I had finished our first cup of coffee.

He worked side by side with Al and me that year to prepare the Thanksgiving meal for the family. The crowd had grown, with so many of my nieces and nephews getting married. We invited Hazel to join us. I didn't want to have Toni gone a second year in a row, but I felt bad if that meant Hazel would be alone for the holiday; Bobby's sister, Sandra, was going to her in-laws' with her husband. I thought she might say no, since she'd never seemed very comfortable at our place, but I guess the pull of being with Bobby and Toni, now that Toni was pregnant, was strong enough to give her a reason to accept. She was older than Al and me, in her sixties. She'd married and had her children late in life. So the prospect of a grandchild was one she'd waited for a long time.

But I knew even she had questioned whether Bobby and Toni had rushed into marriage because Toni was pregnant. I guess she was looking for reasons her son had married someone as "unexpected" as Toni. I could never shake the feeling that Hazel thought Bobby had married into a family that was beneath him.

I'd hoped that Toni would get to the restaurant early to arrange the antipasto platters like she always did. But apparently Hazel had prepared one of Bobby's favorite breakfasts—pork tenderloin in cream gravy and cheese grits—and it was almost noon by the time they'd finished.

They walked in the door of the restaurant just before 2:00 p.m., Toni arriving like a guest instead of one of the family who contributes to putting the meal together.

"What's the matter, Rose?" Al had asked me when I realized Toni wasn't coming to assemble the antipasto. It wasn't that I resented the extra work. Most of the dishes had been prepared in the days before—cannellini beans marinated with garlic and parsley, tuna mixed with onions and capers, my own eggplant and mushrooms pickled in August. It was just my sense of a shift, a slight change that shouldn't have been a big deal to me, but was.

Al came up behind me and kissed my neck as I was rolling prosciutto to put around the edge of the platter.

"You're going to make the antipasto too salty," he murmured as I dabbed my tears with the handkerchief I kept in my apron pocket. "She's married now. She's got her mother-in-law staying with her. Give her a chance to be a good daughter-in-law, like you are."

Al had a way of easing me into a better frame

of mind. He knew he could soothe me with a nuzzle or a kiss. I was fifty years old but I felt like a teenager when he put his arms around me. And he was right. I remembered how I'd felt trying to adapt to Al's family when the difference was only the distance between Naples and Calabria—a few more hot peppers than I was used to. Toni had a lot more to cope with, and I had to stop myself from wishing time could stand still.

"She's coming to dinner, even if she isn't here in the kitchen," Al murmured.

When Manny had a free minute, he danced over to the counter and rolled a few dozen slices of Genoa salami before slicing the fennel and arranging it on platters with green and black olives.

"We'll get it done, Mama Rose."

And we did.

Manny whisked the turkey gravy at the last minute, freeing my hands to fry the batter-dipped broccoli and cauliflower in hot oil.

Al and Mike each carried out one of the thirty-pound turkeys we'd roasted; a third one we kept in the warmer for second helpings.

The place was pandemonium that year—so many kids. We had a children's table for the ones old enough to sit by themselves, although more than one of my nieces had to cut the turkey on their kids' plates. We had at least three in high chairs at the big table.

Hazel seemed overwhelmed at first by the noise and confusion, but I saw how attentive Toni was to her mother-in-law, introducing her to aunts and uncles, serving her graciously. And I have to admit, I watched to see if Hazel appreciated it—my daughter's care and our food. She ate like a bird, only putting little spoonfuls on her plate of the unfamiliar parts of the meal, but at least she tried things and didn't turn her nose up at the antipasto or manicotti before tasting them. And each bite seemed to soften her expression, widening the smile on her lips the more she ate.

After Thanksgiving, Mike sat on Manny to get his college applications done. He even drove him down to Rhode Island to see a school where he could get both the chef's training and the management courses he'd need. But while they were there, they heard from one of the other families visiting the school about the new Culinary Institute of America in Hyde Park, New York. Manny's attitude up to this point had been resignation. He knew we weren't willing to back down from insisting on college but his heart wasn't in it and he was just going through the motions.

He was ready to get in the car and go back to Boston, but Mike decided they should keep driving and take a look at the Culinary Institute.

"What have we got to lose, except a few hours?" he said to Manny. "Who knows, maybe this is the one."

And it was.

When Manny and Mike got back from New York, Manny couldn't shut up about what he'd seen and the people he'd talked to. He also realized how hard it was to get into and was suddenly on fire to put together the best application he could.

Al wasn't crazy about the fact that he was only going to get an associate's degree and I wasn't happy that the school was hours away in New York instead of just down the expressway in Providence. But Mike spoke up for Manny.

"I talked to some of my restaurant clients at the bank, and they all say this place is the best. If he's accepted, it's like going to the Harvard of the cooking world. If you make him go to a lesser school, even if it's close to home and he comes out with a bachelor's degree, he'll just be wasting his time. Look, we've finally got him excited about school. Let him try for this. To him, it's like being drafted for a Red Sox 'A' team."

When the acceptance letter arrived in the mail, I could hardly wait for him to come home from school. I propped the envelope up against a glass at the table. When he came into the kitchen for something to eat, he headed first for the refrigerator and grabbed some leftover *pasta e piselli*. He was going to eat it cold, but I took it from him.

"Sit and let me warm it up for you." I steered him to his chair and waited for him to see the envelope staring him in the face. He let out a whoop and then held it for a minute, weighing it in his hand.

"Okay. Time to face the music." His hands were shaking as he picked up a knife and slit open the envelope. Then he read out loud from the letter: " 'Dear Mr. Dante, we regret to inform you . . .' "

My heart sank. It wasn't what I'd expected. Oh, boy, he was going to need a lot more than my pasta. And then I noticed the impish grin and the sparkle in his eyes.

" '. . . that we have turned down countless qualified candidates to make room for someone as brilliant and talented as you.' "

I flipped the dish towel in my hand at him. "That's not what it says!"

"You're right. It says, 'Congratulations! Now you're *really* going to work your ass off.' "

I hugged him and he got up from the table to dance me around the room.

"Go downstairs and tell your father. And call Mike!"

We sent Manny off to CIA in September and suddenly the house and the restaurant were too quiet. Mike and Papa were still with us, but Mike was almost never home, between his job and the social life he had, which seemed, as it always had, to center around the bars that were flourishing down near the waterfront.

The run-down wharves on the edge of the neighborhood were being bought up and turned into offices and apartments right on the harbor. They drew a lot of young people and Mike, never one to miss an opportunity to make friends, had quite a circle that made the Rusty Scupper bar their home away from home. When they got hungry, he led them like the pied piper to Paradiso.

He was usually surrounded by friends but never seemed to have one special girl. I knew young people were taking more time than our generation had to settle down, but he was already twenty-six with no one in sight.

I asked him about it one night when he was actually home before midnight and he sat in the kitchen with me. It was a chance I didn't want to lose, and although I was bone-tired, I heated up some 'scarole soup with the little meatballs he'd loved as a kid.

"Ma, you don't have to feed me. I can do it myself. Why don't you go to bed?"

"It's okay, sweetheart. I don't see you much, even though you live under the same roof. How's work?" I started out with the easy stuff.

"It's fine. But I might make a change. I don't think banking is the right place for me."

"I have to tell you, Mike, knowing who the bankers were when I was at Shawmut, I didn't think you were cut from the same cloth. You like your good times too much."

"Is this going to be a lecture on my extracurricular activities?"

I threw up my hands. "Excuse me, I'm only your mother."

"Don't worry, Ma. I know you think I spend too much time partying. I bet you want to ask me when I'm going to settle down. It's all I heard at Thanksgiving, not just from the aunts but also from my overly fertile cousins, who seem to believe it's their mission in life to triple the Italian-American population of Boston."

"I want you to be as happy as Daddy and me, that's all. I'd hate to see you go through life alone. Sometimes I wonder if you have it too good here at home. Not that I want you to leave. I can't believe I'm saying this, but I don't want you to become a mama's boy, so tied to my apron strings that you can't find a girl who lives up to your expectations. Like your father's brother Rocco, who still eats at your grandma Antonella's every night and never got married. If you ask me, he got trapped taking care of his mother twenty years ago and wound up feeding her cats instead of his own children. I'd kick you out in a minute if I thought you'd still be here when you're forty."

"I haven't found the right person yet, Ma."

"Do you honestly think the right person's going to be sitting next to you some night at the Scupper?"

I sighed; I could see we weren't getting far. "Change of subject," I said. "What did you mean earlier, about changing jobs?"

"One of my customers at the bank is looking for an accountant. We've been talking."

"What kind of business?"

"He runs a magazine in one of the converted buildings down on the waterfront. He's the smartest guy I've ever met, a real Renaissance man. He knows a lot—art, science, business. Like Leonardo da Vinci. I feel I could learn a lot from him."

"How long has he been in business?"

"About ten years. The magazine is solid, doing well. And he's thinking about expanding. That's why he's hiring."

"So what are you waiting for? You have any doubts about this?"

"I guess, despite my party-boy reputation, I'm still a numbers guy, and I want to run a few more before I make a commitment. I think I learned that from you, if I'm not mistaken." He smiled.

"I don't think you're asking for my advice—or are you?"

"You're a good businesswoman, Ma. Not just a great cook and mother. What do *you* think I should do?"

"Bring me a copy of this magazine. And invite him to dinner next week."

And so, instead of figuring out where Mike was headed in his love life, I got to pass inspection on his possible new boss. I wasn't sure what to expect from Mike's description. Was he going to be an egghead, talking over my head? I had subscriptions to *Life, Ladies' Home Journal* and a restaurant trade magazine. If I had time to sit down and read, it usually wasn't a magazine. So I couldn't really be helpful on that front. But I'd always been a pretty good judge of people. I knew I'd be able to tell if he'd do well by Mike.

I liked Graham Bennett the moment he looked me in the eye and shook my hand. He wasn't a big man physically, but he carried himself with confidence. His eyes behind his black-rimmed glasses were warm and direct. In spite of how smart Mike claimed he was, he wasn't showing off his intelligence at my table. He showed respect for Al and me, and seemed to understand what it took to run a successful restaurant. I wouldn't have been able to tell if his magazine ideas were going to work, but his answers to my questions about how he ran his business satisfied me.

I gave Mike my thumbs-up in the kitchen when

he helped me get the coffee. Mike handed in his notice at the bank a week later and right after Christmas started working at the magazine.

If only finding him a steady girlfriend could be this easy, I thought.

## Changes

PAPA PASSED AWAY in the spring of 1974. He was eighty-nine and it seemed as if he'd decided it was time to go. His failing eyesight had excluded him from the card games he loved to play at his club, and most of his *compares,* who for years had whiled away the afternoons with a demitasse of espresso and a cigar with him, had one by one slipped away. He was practically the last one left. Once again the whole family gathered for a funeral, ten years after Mama's death. The last month I'd spent almost constantly at his bedside, watching the life seep out of him. The little he spoke was in Italian, as if the closer he got to the end, the more his mind returned to his beginning, his childhood in Italy. With his passing, I was now the oldest generation. Both my mother and father were gone, and without them as anchors, we started to drift apart as a family.

Thanksgiving 1974 was the first time that all my sisters and brothers and their families didn't gather together at Paradiso.

"The family's getting too big and the kids are too widespread for us all to come to Boston," my sister Bella said, calling from Albany to excuse herself and her family.

My brother Sal and his wife decided to take a cruise since their kids were going to their in-laws.

It bothered me. It is not that I took it personally, that they suddenly weren't coming to *my* place. It was just how quickly, without Papa, they no longer considered it important for the family to be together. Maybe I should've seen it as less work for me and less *agita* all around. In a family as large as ours, somebody always had a beef; there was always a burning topic that people were never in agreement on—the Church, the president, the football game.

I should've appreciated the fact that it was going to be a quieter holiday than we'd had in many years. Even Toni, Bobby and the baby were going to Indiana. I knew I'd cook too much food. Nobody ate the way we used to. For days before, I was slamming cupboard doors and making and remaking lists as one family member or another called with his or her excuses.

"Rose, what's eating you?" Al asked me. "Is it too much to do Thanksgiving this year after

Papa's death? You want somebody else to take it on?"

"No! That's the last thing I want. I'm disappointed, that's all. I feel like the family's splintering and I should be able to hold it together, like Mama did."

Al gave me a neck rub as I sat at the kitchen table refiguring quantities.

"Your sister Bella hit the nail on the head. The family is now so many families, with all the kids getting married and having babies. Maybe it's time for them to each have their own traditions."

"I know you're probably right, but I'm not ready. Thanksgiving to me is a room full of people, all talking at once and enjoying my food."

"So, let me get this straight. It's a room full of *people,* not necessarily *family?*"

"Well, if I can't have the family, I guess, yes, I'd still want a full house."

"Then let's fill the house. I bet Mike's got friends with no family in town. And I bet those classmates of Manny's from other parts of the country aren't going home."

And that's how we made up for my own family's absence that Thanksgiving and began to throw open the doors to friends who had nowhere else to go.

Mike's boss, Graham Bennett, came that year. It surprised me that he wasn't married, a successful man like him and nearly thirty-five. But I figured when you start a company, there's not much time for starting a family, too. Al and I were lucky that we were together and had already begun having kids when we opened Paradiso. I couldn't imagine not having a family.

The next few years were peaceful ones for us. To begin with, nobody died. Manny graduated from the Culinary Institute in 1976 and came home with his hair four inches longer and his head full of ideas. He and Al jostled each other so much for control of the stove that, for the sake of my sanity, I told them they had to work different shifts. It was time Al got a break, anyway.

In the winter of 1977 we took a whole month off for our trip to Florida. As Joey had gotten older and Toni got pregnant again, she was more willing to leave him with us so she could get some rest. And when her second son, Benjamin, was born, it seemed like the right moment to take Joey to Florida with us for his first excursion to Disney World. That gave Toni a chance to devote all her attention to Ben and us a chance to spoil our grandson.

Around this time, the neighborhood was changing, ever since the city had spruced up Quincy Market, a derelict collection of old warehouses, and turned it into shops and food stalls and restaurants. One of the restaurants was a high-end Italian place and the owners had a cooking show on public television. She was British and he was Italian, and frankly, she made him out to be a buffoon. She was supposedly explaining Italian food as if she were the expert and he'd get all emotional over the seasoning in the meatballs. It was embarrassing. I also went to eat at their restaurant and it wasn't so good. They were trying too hard to make the food elegant instead of satisfying.

But Quincy Market turned out to be good for our business. It attracted a lot of tourists following the Freedom Trail, which guided people around all the historical sights in Boston. Even though Quincy Market was on the other side of the expressway, people would come over to the North End to find Paul Revere's house and the Old North Church and then stay for dinner.

Manny should've had a cooking show. He had a flair in the kitchen and was a lot better looking than Luigi and his snotty wife.

Manny had learned growing up in the restaurant that we treated our customers like family. Al always came out from the kitchen during the evening to see how people were enjoying their meals, especially if they were regulars. Manny started doing that on the nights he was cooking. Some of the old-timers remembered when he'd been a busboy. He had an excellent memory and would greet people by name the second time they came to eat.

He also began to attract a new clientele for us—young, very pretty women. Once word got out about the good-looking chef at Paradiso, the girls from the offices and banks along the waterfront started to flock to the restaurant on their lunch hour or on Friday nights.

The place was packed. When we heard the building next door was going up for sale, Al and I both had the same idea. We could break down the wall on the first floor and expand. We'd hesitated to do it before; the original restaurant had been all we thought we could handle. But with Manny, who was eager to do more—enlarge the menu, open up the kitchen so diners could see the meal prepared as it if were a show—we decided it was the right time.

Manny joked about naming the new section the Inferno and having an open-hearth brick oven in the front of the house to bake pizzas. But Al nixed that idea.

"Not everybody will get the joke, and I don't want people saying, 'I'm going to Hell,' when somebody asks where they're eating dinner."

It took more than a year to get everything done once we'd made the decision. Permits, loans, an architect who cost an arm and a leg but who came recommended by one of Manny's teachers at CIA. The whole thing was a headache for me, especially acting as a buffer and a go-between for Al and Manny. Al liked the tried-and-true, the traditional, comfortable place we'd built from nothing over thirty years. Manny, a little too full of himself and his education, kept pushing for this or that.

"Everything has a cost. Show me how we make them up at the cash register, your fancy ideas. We're not Stella Mare down on the waterfront. We're on Salem Street."

In the end, we compromised. We deferred the brick oven but put a half wall in the back of the new section so people could watch the grill; we also added more Northern Italian to the menu.

When we finally had the grand reopening Al and Manny were speaking to each other again, Toni was pregnant for the third time and Mike, at twenty-nine still wasn't married.

He did, however, decide to move out. He just went upstairs. The Boscos, who'd rented the apartment on the top floor for forty years, decided after the blizzard of 1978 that they'd had enough of Boston winters and bought a mobile home in Palm Beach Gardens.

Mike jumped at the place when I started worrying about finding someone to rent it.

"Let me take it, Ma, and pay the rent. You said yourself you don't want me still living with you when I'm forty."

"I *meant* that you should be living in your own home with a *wife*."

But I gave in. He needed his own place,

married or not, and if he didn't go upstairs, sooner or later he'd move, maybe out of the neighborhood. I half expected Manny to want to go with him, but Mike was pretty quick to quash that idea, and we wouldn't have let him, anyway. He was too young, too headstrong and there were already too many beautiful girls chasing after him at the restaurant. I didn't need them trooping up the stairs, too.

For our fortieth wedding anniversary, Al took me to Italy. I didn't think he'd be willing to leave the restaurant for that long, but Manny was proving himself, even at twenty-four. What a trip! We treated ourselves to *la dolce vita,* staying at first-class hotels and eating at the best restaurants in Rome and Florence and Venice. Al and I made mental notes on the dishes, comparing them to what we offered at Paradiso.

"They're using rosemary in this bean dish."

"I like what they did with the prosciutto and figs. We could do it in the summer."

After a whirlwind tour through the famous sites, we relaxed on Capri for a weekend. I'd bought a new maillot swimsuit for the beach but I felt like an old woman when I saw everyone else, even women my age, in bikinis. Al noticed, too.

"You could be wearing one of those, Rose. You've still got the body for it."

At lunchtime, when we walked back up from

the beach, he stopped at a shop that had bathing suits displayed in the window and pulled me in.

He flipped through the rack and pulled out a couple of colorful bikinis, all in shades of aqua and green. I tried each of them on and watched Al's face light up in admiration. We bought one of the suits and then strolled back to the hotel arm in arm. The Italians have the right idea about siesta. There's nothing more relaxing than going to bed in the middle of the afternoon with the sound of the sea outside your window and a ceiling fan rotating slowly above your head.

I couldn't remember when Al and I had last been able to enjoy lovemaking with such disregard for everything else in our lives. We had no responsibilities. Not an aging and ill father or kids struggling through one crisis or another on the way to adulthood or a business that demanded so much of our energy and attention. That was the true luxury of this vacation, not the fancy hotels or the celebrated restaurants. We'd been so busy swallowing up as much of Italy as we could that we'd forgotten to take the time just to enjoy each other. But Capri changed that.

Al couldn't wait to get me back to the hotel. He took me in his arms as soon as we were inside the door.

"Do you have any idea how good you looked to me back in the store?"

"I think so." I smiled through the kisses.

We pulled back the covers on the bed and stretched out. That delicious first contact of skin on skin sent ripples through me. Even though I knew every muscle, every line and scar on his body, it still felt thrilling to me. I hoped we'd never tire of this, because in many ways it was what had helped us survive. We were crazy about each other. In all the years of our marriage, through all the ups and downs, Al's arms wrapped around me, holding me close, always reminded me what was important.

In the final days of the trip we rented a little Fiat and drove to Calabria to visit cousins of Al's on his father's side. They didn't have much, a small farm in an out-of-the-way village. The women, my age or younger, looked years older, worn out by the hard work and their large families. I saw old women in the marketplace who could have been my mother, their heads wrapped in the kind of kerchief Mama wore when she was cleaning the house. They were bent with age but still moving with purpose, haggling over the price of a sack of onions or half a pound of tripe.

If Mama and Papa hadn't left for America, this was the life she would've led. Who am I kidding? This was the life *I* would've led. I shook my head at the poverty in the village. Most of the houses didn't have toilets. Al's cousin at least had plumbing in his house and even a washing machine, but it was like the tub and wringer Mama had used forty years ago. I felt that Italy was two countries—the postcard country of the Sistine Chapel and gondolas, and this forgotten place in the hills of the south, where time seemed to have stopped a hundred years ago. Some people might think it was romantic, like the hippies in America living in communes. But I thought it was horrifying.

When Al and I were getting ready to leave, I felt we needed to do something for his cousins, who, despite how little they had, willingly shared it all with us.

"Do you think they'd be insulted if we gave them money as a gift? They need so much, I don't know where to begin to help them."

"Tino has his pride. I'm sure he'd refuse it if we tried to give him an envelope."

"What if I gave it to his wife? Or we put it on the dresser with a thank-you note? I remember when my aunt Cecilia came back to visit her sister, she told Mama she felt she couldn't go without leaving some cash, even though she'd brought gifts for everybody."

We wound up tucking several hundred-thousand lire notes in a card I'd picked up at St. Peter's in Rome. Maybe all I was doing was easing my conscience, since we were the lucky ones, the ones who'd made it in America. But I can remember my parents sending money to

Italy when we were young. When Papa came home every week with his pay, Mama would parcel it out into envelopes—so much for rent, so much for food, so much for those left behind in Italy. It was what you did for family.

# ROSE
## 1980–81

# Disintegration

THE SPRING AFTER we returned from Italy, our granddaughter, Vanessa, was born. I went up to Bedford and stayed with the boys while Toni was in the hospital. Joey was already in first grade and Ben was in nursery school, and Toni didn't want them to miss any days.

We had fun, the boys and I. We baked cookies and built Lego space stations and I even got them to sit still for a couple of Tomie dePaola stories that I found on the bookshelf in their room. I liked that Toni had Italian stories for the boys. *Strega Nona* made me laugh, reminding me of the old women in the neighborhood with moles on their chins and bowls of water and olive oil for warding off the evil eye. They used to scare me to death when I was a kid. But *The Clown of God* was my favorite. One of the nuns at St. John's had told us the story one day in church, in front of the statue of the Madonna with the Christ Child on her lap holding the golden ball. After I heard that story as a seven-year-old, I used to sneak into church to see if He ever played with the ball the juggler in the story had tossed Him.

"Did you ever see Him throw the ball, Nana?" Joey asked me, wide-eyed when I told him about the statue in St. Leonard's. I wasn't sure these kids had even been in a church after their baptisms.

What *wasn't* fun was spending time with my son-in-law. I thought he'd get home to have supper with his boys, or at least kiss them goodnight. But it was almost ten before he walked in the door the night after Vanessa was born. Okay, I thought, he's been spending the evening with Toni and Vanessa at the hospital. I didn't find out till later that he'd barely made an appearance at Mt. Auburn's maternity ward after Toni gave birth.

I was crocheting in the family room, wearing my nightgown and robe, when he got home.

"You want something to eat, Bobby? I made veal cutlets and string beans tonight."

"No, thanks, Rose. I'm not hungry. I'm just going to have a drink."

He poured himself some bourbon from one of those big jugs people get at the New Hampshire state liquor store across the border in Hampton. It was already half-empty, and from the size of the glass he poured for himself, it probably hadn't taken him long to get it there.

He couldn't sit still, jumping from one thing to the next. He flipped through the mail, tossing aside what looked like bills without even opening them, grabbing *Newsweek* and turning a few pages before leaving it open on the counter.

Despite telling me he wasn't hungry, he rummaged through the fridge and cabinets for junk food—Cheetos, ice cream with fudge sauce, a bag of peanuts whose empty shells he left scattered across the coffee table while he watched the Celtics game.

He didn't say anything about how Toni and the baby were doing until I asked, and he didn't seem to care how the boys had spent the afternoon.

He finally grabbed his drink and went down to the garage where he tinkered with his motorcycle until two in the morning. I went to bed around eleven but when I got up to go to the bathroom, I heard him still down there.

In the morning he was gone before the boys and I were up. I didn't know how he was managing to work with so little sleep and so much whiskey. Maybe he was just coming to terms with the fact that he'd fathered three kids in eight years. Maybe he saw these few days while I was taking care of the boys and Toni was in the hospital as his last opportunity to have a break before the reality of what he was shouldering set in. I tried to tell myself he was acting normally. But I was truly frightened for my daughter and my grandchildren if this was what life with him was going to be.

"I'd like to stay for a few more days after Toni gets home," I told Al. "You and Manny will have to manage without me. I'm worried, Al. I get this sinking feeling that Bobby doesn't care a damn about those children. I don't even know if he still loves Toni." My voice broke at the prospect of something so terribly wrong in my daughter's marriage. When your children hurt, you hurt, maybe even more than they do.

"You want me to come up there and talk to the son of a bitch?"

"Let's wait it out. I don't want her to feel we're butting in, and it's better if they can work it out themselves. I just figure if I'm here to take care of the kids, she'll have some time to give to her marriage. Who knows, maybe that's all it is— that she's been so tied up with the boys and teaching and this pregnancy that he's feeling like a neglected husband."

I wished that was the answer. When I told Toni I'd stay another week until she got back on her feet she started to protest.

"It's not necessary, Mom. Vanessa's a good baby and I got lots of rest in the hospital. We'll be fine."

"My experience is they're always good for the nurses in the hospital, and as soon as they get home they have you walking the floor all night long. I can keep the boys occupied, get them to school and put up some meals for you in the freezer. It's not a burden. I'm happy to stay."

I thought she might put up more of a fight. She'd always been so private with her emotions that I knew it was hard for her to have me smack in the middle of her life. But I was *not* going home. Neither of us mentioned Bobby. She didn't say to me *Bobby will help* or *I'm not alone.* And I didn't ask, because I already knew.

In the next week I did my best to stay out of the way when Bobby came home to give them time together. But it seemed that he was doing everything possible to avoid Toni. He wasn't even sleeping with her, on the grounds that Vanessa was keeping him awake. Toni was breast-feeding and had Vanessa sleeping in a cradle next to her side of the bed.

Although she can't have sex for six weeks or so after she gives birth, a woman still needs to be held and cherished in bed. That Toni was being denied this comfort really bothered me.

"Do you think he's got another woman?" Al asked me during one of our daily phone calls.

"I don't know. But it seems like more than that. He ignores the boys, too. And I don't think I've even seen him pick Vanessa up. Not that I'd want him to after he's been drinking all night. He's completely disconnected. In another world. Toni's putting on a brave face, but I don't think I can keep my mouth shut any longer."

"I'm coming up there. We'll talk to her when he's not around and the boys are in school."

Al came for lunch that afternoon. I made some pasta fazool, one of those comfort foods I knew Toni loved.

She greeted Al with a hug. "Daddy! What brings you here in the middle of the day?"

"I missed your mother," he said, sweeping me into his arms for a kiss. It was something the kids had grown up witnessing, Al and me always greeting each other with a passionate kiss. But I caught a glimpse of pain on Toni's face as she watched us, a question forming in her head—Why don't Bobby and I have this?

"But I also wanted to see you. Your mother and I are worried about you, honey. We want to help you if you'll let us."

"But you *are* helping me. Mom's been great. My house hasn't been this clean since before I had kids, and I've got enough meals in the freezer to feed my family for a year."

Her mouth was set in a forced smile.

"We think you need more than a cleaning and catering service. How are things between you and Bobby?"

She looked from Al to me. At first she threw me a "What have you been telling him?" glance of irritation, as if I'd betrayed some secret of hers. But she hadn't confided any secrets to me, and it began to dawn on her that what she was going through was only too clear to somebody who loved her.

The phony smile was gone. "Bobby's sick."

"You don't have to make excuses for him, Toni."

"I'm not. He's mentally ill. He's seeing a psychiatrist. He's supposed to be taking medication, but I think he stopped."

"He's medicating himself with a bottle of bourbon."

"He's always had more to drink than you've been comfortable with, Mom. It's part of his culture."

"He has no culture," Al muttered.

"That's not fair, Daddy."

"What do you want to do, Toni?" I asked softly.

"His moods go in cycles. He's just in a down phase right now. I've weathered this before."

"How long has it been going on?" Al was having difficulty believing that she'd been able to keep something like this from us.

"A couple of years. It started around the time Ben was born."

"Why didn't you tell us?"

"Because I knew it would upset you, like it's doing now. And because it was under control. There wasn't anything you could do, anyway. You can't cure what he has by having a man-to-man talk about his responsibilities to his family."

"Why the hell did you have another baby?"

"Al!" I was shocked he'd said that to her.

"Its fine, Mom. Legitimate question. We were actually doing reasonably well last year. And my idea of a family has always been three kids. We weren't really trying, but we thought if it happens, great. If it doesn't, that's okay, too."

"But it wasn't okay."

"He started to slide about two months ago and I braced myself. Look, I've made my bed, as you've so often told me. You two didn't give up on each other when things got tough. Especially you, Mom."

"How can we help you?"

"By understanding that this is something I've learned to cope with, as painful as it is. Don't push me to leave him."

"But what about the kids? It can't be good for them to see their father like this."

"They know that when Daddy gets very sad, it's not their fault. And I give them extra attention."

"I think you're asking too much of them and yourself."

"I'm doing the best I can, Daddy."

Vanessa woke up at that moment and Toni went to get her.

"How are we going to talk some sense into her, Rose?"

"Would you have listened to your parents at her age? Everybody thinks nobody else could possibly understand what they're going through, especially when it comes to marriage. We're on the outside, Al. If she doesn't want to hear what we have to say, there's nothing we can do, except be ready when everything comes crashing down."

"And it will."

"I know. I know."

Al, as usual, was angry that he couldn't protect Toni. And I was hurt that she wouldn't let us do more. I even wondered if I was making the situation harder by staying, but I couldn't bring myself to leave when I saw how much she had on her shoulders. I tried to keep in the background whenever Bobby was home, which, frankly, wasn't often. During the day, I found myself as busy as Mama had been—grocery shopping, cleaning, laundry, cooking. Anything that would take pressure off Toni. At night, I stayed in the guest room and watched TV on the little portable set, trying to block out my worries.

I finally went home when Vanessa was two weeks old. I could see I was adding more stress than I was alleviating. I felt she was putting on an act to convince me that everything was fine. I didn't want to make things worse by having her worry about what I thought of her marriage and her choices.

I left her with a full freezer, a spotless house and a sweater set for the baby. If only that had been enough.

Just before Thanksgiving, as I was peeling sweet potatoes, Toni called. Her voice was flat.

"Mom? I just wanted you and Daddy to know that Bobby's left."

"Left? As in moved out? Do you want us to come? What do you need?"

"I'm okay. If you want to know the truth, I'm relieved. It's over. I can stop trying to save him."

Toni had stood by Bobby during his depressed state, but when he came out of it he decided he needed to move on. He'd quit his job without telling Toni, sold his car and taken off on his motorcycle. Al was ready to go after him and strangle him.

"Let him go, Al. If you ask me, it's a blessing that he's gone. Maybe now she can get on with her life."

All Toni would tell us was that she'd come home from school after picking up the kids to find Bobby in the bedroom packing a suitcase. She thought he had a business trip. He'd been jumpy the past couple of weeks. The slow-moving guy who'd ignored everyone when Vanessa was born had been replaced by someone so full of nervous energy that he couldn't sleep.

She sat on the edge of the bed nursing Vanessa while Bobby moved from closet to dresser to suitcase, talking a mile a minute while he threw things into his bag. He claimed he had a job offer in Boulder, Colorado, the opportunity of a lifetime. He was leaving immediately on his motorcycle.

She made him say goodbye to the boys. She told us she wondered whether she'd even have gotten the meager explanation he'd given her if she'd stopped at the Star Market to pick up groceries on her way home. If she and the kids had been later, would he have waited? Or would he have left without saying goodbye, his empty side of the closet the only indication that he was gone?

She didn't know.

She made supper for the kids and put them to bed like any other night. She called us the next day.

Al wanted her to come home.

"How are you going to manage on your own with three kids way out there?"

"Daddy, I've been living here for over seven years. And most of the time I *have* been on my own, even when Bobby was here. We're fine. We'll see you at Thanksgiving. I'll stay over so you can spend more time with the kids."

We didn't tell anybody else at Thanksgiving dinner about what had happened, except Mike and Manny, of course. Like their father, they couldn't believe what Bobby had done to their sister. It was beyond understanding.

When aunts or cousins asked about Bobby, we

just said he was away. Toni didn't want the whole family discussing her life or making comments, especially in front of the kids.

I thought she'd be on the edge of a nervous breakdown, but I have to hand it to her—she held herself together. She came in with the kids on Wednesday afternoon and plunged right in to help. She even put the boys to work, setting the kids' table. She had Vanessa in one of those baby carriers that hold a baby on a mother's chest, close to her heartbeat. It left her hands free and I was impressed by how much she could get done in the kitchen. And Vanessa didn't fuss.

"I wish they'd invented that thing when you kids were small! Keeping you happy while I was in the kitchen used to run me ragged."

I noticed things over those five days they stayed with us. Toni was calmer than I'd seen her in ages, and the dark circles under eyes were disappearing. Maybe it was that Vanessa was starting to sleep through the night or that Toni no longer stayed up worrying about Bobby. She laughed with her brothers. She moved around the table at Thanksgiving, spending time with her aunts and uncles and cousins, introducing herself to Mike and Manny's friends—time she hadn't spent in years because she always seemed distracted by making sure Bobby was comfortable. They'd always just come for dinner in the past and had often been the first to leave, as if Toni had extracted from him the compromise of attending the meal and nothing else.

In spite of the uncertainty of her future, she seemed to be enjoying herself. She seemed to *be* herself.

I was glad she had those days surrounded by family and activity. Mike took the boys to the Museum of Science. I took them to the new Disney movie. We sat around the dining room table at night and played cards.

I felt like I had my daughter back. I hated that the price to be paid for that was the breakup of her marriage. But if those early days were any indication, it might have been the best thing that had happened to her.

I don't mean to downplay how difficult the next year was for Toni, dealing with the messy details of Bobby's abandonment of his family. More than once, she thought about taking him back, even moving out to Colorado. Apparently she'd been talking to him.

"Are you nuts?" I said to her when she told me she was considering it.

"He's the father of my children."

"And he *abandoned* them. Look at how well they're doing! How good a mother you are. If you go out there, knowing no one, who'll be there for you when it all falls apart again? Because it will."

Thank God she had friends who told her the

same thing. Everybody could see the change in her for the better. And no one wanted her to go back. She finally accepted that it was a fool's mission. She'd bought a plane ticket to go to Boulder for the weekend, "just to talk," she said. She was taking Vanessa because she was still nursing her but realized it would be too hard on the boys. She also didn't know what condition she'd find Bobby in, or even how he was living. But when she got to Logan a massive storm system was moving across the country and flights were being delayed left and right. She waited with Vanessa for five hours. Mike went into the airport to have supper with her and it's a good thing he did. The flight was cancelled at 11:00 p.m. She called Bobby to let him know, and from what Mike could tell, Bobby didn't seem to care one way or the other if she came— that weekend or ever. She wavered about rebooking for the next day, but Mike said, "I think this cancellation is a message. You're not supposed to go, Toni. If Bobby wants his family back, let him come to you."

She burst into tears, but she knew her brother was right. She got into a cab with him and they returned to our place. She never talked about following Bobby to Colorado again.

She got a lawyer after that, somebody Graham Bennett recommended, and started divorce proceedings.

When we heard she was selling the house, Al urged her to move back to the neighborhood.

"Let us help you, Toni."

"Daddy, it's wonderful of you to offer. I can't tell you how important it's been these past few months to have you all around me. But I need to be on my own for a while. Besides, with my job at the high school, living here in the city would be too far to commute. I'll find a place to rent that I can manage financially, and I promise to be here every week for dinner with the kids."

She stood her ground. As much as she'd become one of us again since Bobby had left, she held on to that private part of herself that I knew had always been there.

"She doesn't want to be smothered, Pop," Mike explained to Al after he'd tried again to convince her to take an apartment in one of our buildings.

"She's a thirty-year-old woman. What does she think, that we're going to treat her like a teenager?"

"Wait till she starts dating again. I guarantee you, you'd be watching who goes up the stairs, and whether or not he comes back down."

"Don't be smart!"

"Pop, you don't want to know everything that's going on in our lives. Trust me!"

I reminded Al what a difference it had made when we'd gotten our own place after living with my parents.

"Don't you remember what it was like? Mama, no matter how much I tried to keep our problems from her, saw and heard everything! And had an opinion about it."

"Yeah, but you've said yourself you wish the family wasn't so spread out. The farther people move from the neighborhood, the looser the bonds that keep us together. Look at what happened after your father passed away. I just want her close enough to protect her. If we'd known sooner what was going on when she was married to that jerk, maybe things would've turned out differently."

"I want her close, too, Al. I hurt for her in ways I didn't know were possible. Let's give it time. Look how much more often she's with us. She's not keeping us at arm's length like before. If it makes sense for her to stay in the suburbs, let her be."

Toni was the first one on either side of our family to get a divorce. She wouldn't be the only one, but in 1980 it was still cause for shame and disapproval. People who didn't know what they were talking about and who had no business saying anything saw fit to criticize my daughter. Someone even had the nerve to suggest that Toni was at fault.

"Who'd walk away from his children unless he thought they weren't his?" That was one of the outrageous comments that got back to me. Of course, nobody dared say anything like that to my face. But the phone lines were humming the minute after Toni told my niece Annette, the cousin she was closest to. Naturally Annette told her mother, my sister Ida. By the time word got to Bella in Albany, I was bracing myself for the questions and advice.

"Is she going to get an annulment? Tell her to talk to the priest. If she doesn't, she'll be cut off from the Church. How's she going to raise those children if she can't receive communion?"

I didn't bother to tell my sister that Toni probably hadn't taken communion in years, and that I didn't think a little wafer would make any difference in how well she brought up her kids. She was already doing a fantastic job.

I have to admit the idea of divorce was unthinkable to me, too—until it happened to my own. You see the world changing all around you but you don't believe it'll reach in and grab *your* family. I used to think that people who couldn't keep their marriages together were weak, quitters, selfish. But after what I saw in my daughter's house and how she struggled to make peace with her situation, I began to understand why, for some families, it's the only choice.

Accepting Toni's divorce, as painful as it was, made me realize that sometimes the ideas we've believed for a lifetime get shaken up and tossed in the air—like clowns on one of those round nets at Ringling Brothers. When those ideas come back down, they're slightly lopsided.

I thought I'd made enough adjustments in what I expected to see in my children's lives. The little things, like Manny's taste in music or the length of his hair—a ponytail! Let me tell you, Al was not happy. The bigger things, like Mike's lack of a girlfriend. But nothing prepared me for the blow that seemed to come out of nowhere one day in June 1981.

I never go to Beacon Hill. My friends don't live there. The stores on Charles Street charge prices that might impress the people who shop there, the kind of people who like to carry around the fancy shopping bags proclaiming that they're rich enough to afford the baubles inside the bags. But on this particular day I was down there to pick up a small painting Toni had taken to be framed at Boston Art & Framing. I didn't know it was a parade route. Lots of people were milling around on the sidewalk and, in spite of gray clouds that were spitting rain now and then, people in apartments and offices on the upper floors had their windows open and were looking up the street. I got caught in the press of people and couldn't make it across, so I waited along with everyone else.

"What's going on?" I asked the woman next to me.

"Gay Pride Parade," she said, as if I were an

idiot. That's what I mean about Beacon Hill. Am I somehow stupid because I live on the other side of the expressway? Do I have *Italian from the North End* tattooed on my forehead?

I inched my way to the curb, curious to see why the parade was attracting so much attention. I could hear the strains of music approaching and then a wave of applause from the onlookers lined up along Charles Street. Men and women passed by in lavender T-shirts and carrying banners— *Harvard*, *BU*, *UMass* were the ones I could read. They didn't all look like college kids, though. Some were older. Behind them came more groups, some without signs. They didn't seem to mind the rain; they were waving and dancing to the beat of the music coming over a loudspeaker on a van. And then my heart stopped.

Approaching the corner, in the middle of a small group, was Michael. Next to him was Graham Bennett, and they had their arms around each other. He was smiling.

I slipped back into the crowd and almost dropped the package with Toni's painting. You think you know your children, understand their heart's desires.

I walked slowly back home, the sounds of the music and the cheering from the parade growing fainter as I put more distance between myself and Charles Street. I tried to figure out how I'd missed that Mike was gay. Maybe he wasn't, I told myself. Maybe he was just marching to support gay people, the way he'd protested for civil rights when he was at Holy Cross. But I reminded myself that he'd never been serious about a girl. Other than that, he didn't fit the idea I'd always had of gay men.

I didn't consider myself a naive woman. I read the *Globe;* I went to the movies. I knew there was something called a "gay subculture," especially in cities. I just never imagined that my son was part of it.

I didn't really know what to do with what I'd learned about Mike. He'd been keeping it a secret from us. Did he think we wouldn't understand? Did he think we'd be angry with him for not meeting our expectations?

My heart ached with the knowledge. I knew it couldn't be easy for him to be a gay man in our neighborhood. There's always been too much emphasis on being a "tough guy" in the North End. No wonder he'd spent so much time at the bars on the waterfront that attracted an outside crowd of more sophisticated young people. I'd assumed it was because he was more educated than a lot of the boys he grew up with. The ones who did well had become cops and firemen. The ones who didn't went in the other direction. He didn't have much in common with either group.

I couldn't sleep that night. I couldn't bring myself to tell Al or Mike what I'd seen on

Charles Street. How many secrets do mothers hold in their hearts? I remember Mama telling me she never stopped worrying about us, even after we were adults.

"*Especially* after you were adults," she said. "The hurts when you were small were easy to fix. When you grew up, I couldn't fix anymore."

I thought I was spiraling into despair. A daughter abandoned with three children; a son leading a double life. I felt betrayed by motherhood. I wanted to crawl into bed and pull the covers over my head. I wanted to blame somebody and call curses down on them. But then I remembered the last time I'd felt like this. I *had* hidden in the stupor of pain and forgetfulness after Al Jr. was killed in Vietnam.

The next day, I drove out to the cemetery. I spent about an hour weeding and cleaning up in front of Al Jr.'s headstone and I planted an azalea bush, a purple one. By the time I was done, sweat was running down my forehead and my fingernails were caked with dirt. I sat back on my heels and cried.

And I said to myself, Toni and Mike are *alive.* Toni's children may not have a father, but they have a loving mother and grandparents and uncles who adore them.

I picked myself up and went home.

I didn't ask Mike about the parade. I decided when he was ready, he would tell us. In the meantime, I welcomed Graham like another son and stopped pressing Mike to find a girlfriend and get married. As well as I could, I started preparing Al so that he'd be ready to hear what Mike had to say. I began by telling him about my trip to the cemetery and the peace I found there, grateful for what we had in Mike and Toni and Manny and the grandchildren.

And I let Toni take her time figuring out what was best for her family.

# TONI
## 1980–98

# Safety

I GAVE UP TRYING to live on my own with my kids after my apartment was broken into. I walked into the front hall with six-month-old Vanessa asleep in her car seat. The boys, thank God, were at school.

I heard clattering at the back of the house and thought one of the neighborhood cats or, worse, one of the brats from upstairs had somehow gotten into the pantry.

"Hey!" I yelled and marched over there in a fury to chase away the nuisance.

But as I moved through the dining room into the kitchen, my eye caught the disarray. The drawers of the built-in china cabinet were pulled open and the Venetian lace tablecloths I'd received as wedding presents and never used were strewn about the floor. The glass door above the drawers hung ajar, swinging gently on its hinges as if someone had just pulled it open.

I was still furious, thinking the kids had done more mischief than I'd imagined they would dare. When I got to the kitchen and saw that my bedroom door was open I thought they'd hidden in there. In an instant of recognition, though, coupled with a sickening sensation in my stomach, I realized it couldn't have been cats or kids. The contents of all my drawers had been dumped on the bed. My jewelry box was wide-open and empty. The pillowcase had been stripped from one of the pillows and was missing. Like the teenagers in the neighborhood who marched around on Halloween with pillowcases as their trick-or-treat bags, the intruder had taken one of mine and filled it with everything valuable in my crummy apartment.

It made me want to throw up. Some stranger's hands going through my underwear, fingering the pieces of jewelry my ex-husband, Bobby, had given me, back when he was still in love with me. Even my diaphragm case had been opened.

I turned from the chaos and saw where the door to the porch had been jimmied open. Still seething, I ran out onto the porch, but all I saw was the rustle of leaves on the lilac bush where the thief had probably jumped the fence.

Vanessa started to whimper.

I picked her up and dialed 9-1-1. Then I called my brother Mike.

"Don't tell Mom and Daddy yet. But I need somebody here tonight. I don't want to be alone and I don't want to scare the kids. Can you come?"

I knew I could turn to Mike. We'd always had each other's back—he, the big brother who'd defended my independence when my parents thought I was defying them; I, the sympathetic and accepting listener when he revealed to me that he was gay. I knew it hadn't been easy for him, growing up in a neighborhood like ours with its macho culture. I'd hurt for him, knowing how unhappy he was at not being able to be himself. But then he met Graham Bennett, and their relationship evolved from colleagues turning out a hip magazine to life partners who loved and cared deeply about each other. Although they hadn't come out to my parents, Rose and Al treated Graham like another son. Both men were wonderful uncles to my kids.

Having him with me that afternoon was a solace.

When he arrived he found a board in the basement and nailed it across the back door. The police weren't hopeful of tracking down the thief.

"Probably some addict just grabbing enough easily fenced stuff to buy his next fix. You got insurance?"

I pulled myself together and cleaned up the dining room, where the thief had emptied my silver chest. Everything was gone, including the baby spoons my three kids had received at their baptisms. I couldn't deal with my room or even think of sleeping in my bed that night. The only thing I did was bundle up the sheets with my clothes piled in the middle and carry it to the washing machine in the basement.

Mike met my boys, Joe and Ben, at school and told them we were going to Friendly's for dinner. They ate their burgers and fries, then listened solemnly and wide-eyed as I told them what had happened.

"Did the robber take my Transformers?" asked eight-year-old Joe.

"No, honey. He didn't touch any of the stuff in your room. He only wanted jewelry."

"Why would a robber want jewelry? He couldn't wear it, could he?"

"That would be pretty silly, wouldn't it? No, he took it to sell so he could get money."

"Mommy, is he going to come back and take more stuff?" It was six-year-old Ben, who worried enough for us all.

"No, Ben. He's not coming back."

I answered him with conviction, keeping my voice calm and my eyes focused on his, willing myself to see his innocence and absolute trust in me instead of my pink bra dangling over the edge of my bed, my stockings spilled in a crumpled pile on the floor.

I had to protect them from my fears as well as their own. It had been easy to sweep away the monsters under their beds, even after Bobby left me and the kids. He'd stopped taking his meds and decided he needed his freedom.

When he left for Colorado, I felt only relief. I believed I could hold my family together. While Bobby was disintegrating in front of my eyes, it took all my strength, all my energy. After he was gone, I no longer had to take care of him *and* the kids. I wasn't waiting up at night till three in the morning, listening for his car in the driveway or the phone call from the police telling me he'd driven into a tree. I didn't have to bite my tongue to hold back the accusations and doubts that had already spilled into every crevice of our lives together. After he was gone, I took a deep breath, gathered my kids around me and promised to be their strength and protection.

Now, faced with my shattered back door and equally shattered confidence, I faltered.

"You know what?" I said to them to gain some time. "Let's have a slumber party tonight! We'll all sleep in the same room with our sleeping bags."

"Even Uncle Mike?" Joe looked at Mike hopefully.

"Yeah, squirt. Even me." Mike smiled at him.

We made a big deal out of pulling mattresses onto the floor in the boys' room and shaking out sleeping bags that had been rolled up in the closet since before Bobby left. He'd gotten excited about introducing the boys to the "wild" outdoors during one of his manic phases and ordered a pile of gear from L.L. Bean that, like many originally enticing objects, he quickly lost interest in. I had neither the time nor the desire to take the kids camping. I was a city girl, whose entire experience of nature growing up had been class trips to the Boston Public Garden.

Joe and Ben whooped, jumping from one mattress to the next, as Vanessa watched, propped up in her infant seat, sucking on her binky.

I finally got them settled enough to listen to a story and they crowded around me, sprawling across my lap, giddy with the novelty of sleeping on the floor. I read several chapters of *The Chronicles of Narnia,* not wanting to dispel the lulled mood that came over them as they listened. I was grateful they'd become lost in the story instead of caught up in remembering that an intruder had violated our home.

Ben nodded off first, his head heavy and damp on my thigh. Joe asked for one more chapter and I acquiesced. He was asleep before I finished.

I eased myself out from the tangle of their limbs and checked on Vanessa, asleep, as well—at least for a few more hours.

Mike was in the living room, sipping a beer he'd found in the back of my fridge and watching TV.

"Do you think you're going to want to stay here—long-term, I mean?"

I hadn't really thought about it yet. I'd moved

to the duplex in Arlington two months before, after I'd sold the Bedford house Bobby and I lived in for the seven years of our marriage. I'd never been comfortable there, a brand-new house in a suburban development with no sidewalks. But Bobby, a WASP from Indiana, had this vision of what home was supposed to be. I remember the first time he brought me to meet his widowed mother. It was for Thanksgiving in my last year of college. I was an art student at the School of the Museum of Fine Arts in Boston, studying printmaking. I'd met Bobby at a bar in Kenmore Square one night after a Red Sox game. He'd been at the game with a bunch of his buddies. I'd stopped for a beer after working late at the studio to finish a project. My cousin Annette worked as a bartender there and we often took the Green Line home together late at night.

I had paint in my hair and was wearing one of Mike's discarded work shirts, spattered with the inks and chemicals I used. Apparently Bobby found me intriguing and struck up a conversation with me at the bar, where I was listening to Annette complain about her mother, my mother's sister Ida. He bought me another beer; we talked. There was no way I was going to leave with him that night, not with Annette watching and ready to take whatever she saw straight back to the neighborhood. But I agreed to meet him for supper and a movie later in the week.

We saw *The African Queen* at the Brattle Theater in Harvard Square and afterward ate roast-beef sandwiches with Russian dressing at the Wursthaus. It always astounded me, this kitschy German restaurant, complete with leaded glass windows and flower boxes filled with geraniums to look like some Bavarian village inn, serving bratwurst and schnitzel, and it was owned by Italians.

Bobby astounded me, too, back then. He was so American, so unhampered by the snarled web of family that seemed to enmesh me anywhere I went in Boston. He was exuberant, curious, full of boundless energy—and interested in me. I assumed his fascination with me had to do with what must have appeared to him as my exoticism. I was an artist, ethnic and urban. He was a six-foot-six blond engineer from a Midwestern suburb whose mother belonged to a garden club. But he continued to pursue me, and I was both flattered and curious myself. What I didn't realize until later—much later—was that his exuberance and intense interest in me had more to do with the manic phase of his illness than it had to do with loving me. But as I said, that was later.

When he invited me to Belle Arbor, Indiana, for Thanksgiving, I said yes. My mother, however, voiced her objections.

"What do you mean you're going to Indiana

for Thanksgiving! Thanksgiving is here, with the family, like always."

"He wants me to meet *his* family, Ma. Please let me go."

"When a man takes a woman to meet his family, it means something. He's looking for their approval of someone he sees as more than a movie date. You ready for that?"

"You read too much into things, Ma. He's just doing what Americans do—invite guests for Thanksgiving."

"Hah! Don't be blind *and* stubborn, Toni. Are you ready for him to ask you to marry him? Because that's what this trip to Indiana is all about."

"So are you going to let me go?"

"Tell him to have his mother call me. Then I'll decide."

After my mother talked to Bobby's mother, she discussed the invitation with my aunt Cookie, my godmother Patsy and finally my father. The women had concurred. I was old enough and Bobby serious enough about his intentions; I would be allowed to go. My father, faced with these three women and their conviction, threw up his hands and gave his approval. I hugged him.

My mother, in the midst of preparing Thanksgiving dinner for the family, made extra for me to take to Belle Arbor. We were driving with Bobby's sister, Sandra, and her husband, who lived in Portsmouth. My mother made a lasagne with the handmade fennel sausage that she got from my uncle Sal, the butcher who supplied the restaurant.

"I froze it so it'll keep in the cooler while you're driving. Tell Bobby's mother, one hour at three hundred and fifty degrees and keep it covered with tin foil till the last ten minutes."

She also put together a basket of her own preserves—a quart of plum tomatoes with whole basil leaves floating among them; eggplant strips pickled in olive oil, wine vinegar and hot pepper flakes; marinated wild mushrooms she'd picked herself in some secret pocket of the urban landscape she'd discovered years ago.

Belle Arbor, Indiana, is a long way from the North End. I should have recognized what that trip foreshadowed about my marriage to Bobby.

Hazel, Bobby's mother, while politely grateful for the provisions I had brought, clearly had never encountered anything like them and didn't know what to do with them. Out of deference to me she did actually bake the lasagne and we ate it for supper on Saturday night—not as a pre-turkey course on Thanksgiving Day as my own family did.

The meal we sat down to in Hazel's elegantly decorated dining room, with monogrammed silver on the table and striped silk upholstery on the Chippendale chairs, resembled nothing I had ever eaten, except for the turkey itself. She served scalloped oysters, which, I discovered, consisted mostly of crushed soda crackers and lots of cream and butter; succotash with corn, lima beans and an ample amount of paprika; corn bread stuffing—which Hazel called "dressing"—and an aspic made with V8 juice that had stuffed olives, celery and green peppers suspended in its shimmering middle.

The rest of my stay in Belle Arbor featured equally unfamiliar meals as Bobby, Hazel, Sandra, her husband and I were invited to the homes of one after another of Hazel's social circle. I was fed breakfasts of cheese grits and scrapple, lunches of Smithfield ham salad coated in homemade mayonnaise and dinners of pork tenderloins smothered in cream gravy. I consumed more dairy products in four days than I'd tasted in four months back in Boston.

The culinary journey wasn't the only revelation. I noticed that everyone in Belle Arbor—at least, everyone Hazel knew—had a green living room. Various shades and textures of green, to be sure, but all green. Refined, subdued, punctuated by bowls of freshly cut flowers and untouched coffee-table books about the Silk Road or the Great Barrier Reef. The bookcases were filled with books and not overflowing with family photographs. I encountered no flocked velvet wallpaper or white-and-gold furniture upholstered in wine-red brocade—the staples of my mother's and aunts' living rooms.

Throughout the visit I felt as if I were on display, like Pocahontas in London. The strange native of the Eastern city who had captivated Bobby and turned his head from the daughters of Belle Arbor, who were waiting with their Tupperware containers full of tuna casserole and braised short ribs—if only he'd sit at their tastefully decorated tables.

We returned to Boston with a slab of Smithfield ham and a container of Quaker grits to which Hazel had thoughtfully taped the recipe for cheese grits. For Christmas, she sent me a copy of the *Joy of Cooking* with all of Bobby's favorite dishes carefully bookmarked. It was the first cookbook I'd ever used. I grew up watching my mother cook with no recipes at all except what was in her head. She would taste and adjust, with a handful of chopped parsley or a fragment of cheese hand-grated and tossed into the pot. I used to think she'd been born with the knowledge of how to cook, something she'd absorbed in the womb.

Following a cookbook was a new experience for me, but I threw myself into learning how to produce the dishes Bobby had grown up with. Once a week I took the T to his apartment in Kendall Square near MIT, carrying a shopping bag filled with ingredients I'd never seen in my mother's pantry. I made pot roast with carrots and potatoes,

Cornish hens stuffed with rice and onions, and pork chops with sauerkraut.

After I started to cook for him, Bobby and I became lovers. We'd leave the dishes on the drop-leaf table, a hand-me-down from Hazel, and slide into his narrow bed. I never spent the night. I lived at home and there was no way my mother and father would have condoned or understood such behavior. They didn't even know I was cooking for him, because they would've disapproved of my being alone in his apartment.

On the nights I did cook, I told them we were going out to dinner.

"Why do you always go to strangers to eat?" asked my mother one night. "What's wrong with bringing him to Paradiso once in a while?"

I rolled my eyes, memories of the dining rooms in Belle Arbor rising up alongside the dusky interior of Paradiso, its mural of the Bay of Naples stretching like a fresco across the rear wall, the bud vases of silk flowers on each table, its antipasto table covered with platters of provolone and soprasatto, olives, anchovies and cherry peppers. I had a hard time envisioning Bobby finding something he'd want to eat on the menu.

I slipped further from my family and my neighborhood with each recipe I mastered in the *Joy of Cooking*. I made buttermilk pancakes from scratch, separating the eggs and beating the whites into lofty peaks. I made hors d'oeuvres. Hors d'oeuvres! A nonexistent concept in my family, along with the daily Belle Arbor ritual of cocktail hour. My mother and father didn't drink before dinner. They were too busy cooking it. But I learned how to pile crabmeat and cocktail sauce on cream cheese and surround the platter with Triscuits. I hard-boiled eggs and deviled them with Hellmann's and paprika and mustard. I wrapped bacon around water chestnuts and chicken livers to make rumaki.

Bobby ate it all, reveling in each dish. When the weather got warmer, I prepared foods we could take on picnics. He bought a Kawasaki motorcycle in April and on Sunday afternoons, when Paradiso was closed and I didn't have to waitress, we headed out Route 2 to Walden Pond or Mount Wachusett and ate homemade biscuits stuffed with ham salad and sweet pickles and drank iced tea laced with mint.

Bobby was brilliant and funny and wild about me. I sketched him as he leaned against a tree, his leather-clad legs stretched out, his calf nestled against my hip as I quickly moved my charcoal across the page. He smiled as he watched me, his blue eyes intently following the movement of my hand.

"Have you thought about what you'll do when you graduate?"

"I've applied for teaching jobs. If that falls

through, I can always increase my hours at Paradiso. My parents would be happy to see more of me." I spoke those words dryly. As much as they were true—that my mother and father wanted me close to home and in the business— Paradiso was the last place I intended to spend my future.

"I just got a job offer out here in Concord. I was thinking about moving out of Cambridge, finding an apartment closer to work."

"That would certainly alter our pattern. I can't exactly hop on the T and get out here."

"Actually, I was thinking you could move in with me."

"Right. Over Rose's dead body, as my mother so colorfully likes to emphasize when one of her kids wants to do something she regards as outrageous."

"Would she say that if I were to marry you first?"

I stopped sketching and looked up, into his face, at the smile twitching at the corners of his mouth.

He leaned forward and pulled me into him, crushing the sketch pad between us, blurring the lines of the face on the page.

"Will you marry me, Toni?"

And I said yes, for all the reasons, right and wrong, that we say yes when we're twenty-two and the future looks vast and lonely. Did I love him? Yes, in that sense of wonder and awe I had for this gorgeous man who knew how to make me feel alive and beautiful. Did I acknowledge to myself that he was my escape route from the confines of Salem Street and all it represented? I knew deep in my heart that the only way my parents would let me go would be in marriage. My memory of the twinkle in my mother's eye and her conviction—that the only reason a boy invites a girl home for Thanksgiving is because he wants to marry her—was floating in my brain. I had resisted the idea back in November, hadn't really considered marriage for myself—with Bobby or anyone else—despite the fact that girlfriends and cousins were busy getting fitted for bridal gowns and asking casts of thousands to be in their wedding parties.

I had vague plans to develop my craft as a printmaker. My master teacher at the Museum School, Peter Ricci, sat with me one night while I waited for an acid bath to complete the etching on a plate I'd finally finished—a portrait of a wild-haired man I'd sketched one afternoon at the Boston Public Library.

"You have to make a commitment." Peter was frustrated by what he saw as my divided loyalties. He knew I was taking courses to get my teacher certification and he thought it was pulling me away from my true work, diluting my art.

"You have talent, Toni. But you're not putting time and energy into developing it. I thought you were serious about your art, but this last year you've become—I don't know—conventional, predictable."

He threw up his hands, weathered, nicotine-stained, bearing fine white scars where gouging tools had slipped.

"Go be a teacher, if that's what you want. Find some nice middle school in Lexington where you can demonstrate the color wheel and show them how to do collages of their favorite sports or animals. Don't take risks or experiment. Because that's where you're heading, and you'll never be an artist if you think you can straddle both worlds."

I recoiled emotionally as if he'd struck me. I loved the work I did in the print studio. It was in the basement of the school, a warren of rooms lit by hanging lamps that cast pools of warm light on the scarred wooden workbenches and left pockets of dim shadow in the corners that reminded me of the chiaroscuro of Caravaggio's *Christ at Emmaus*. The play of light and dark, illuminating and obscuring. Even the smells were familiar and comforting—the bite of the hydrochloric acid in the shallow tubs that lined the wall; the metallic taint of the inks; the distinctive odor of the hard rubber rollers I used to ink my plates. We were a secret society, we printmakers. Unlike the painters who craved the light, we were a clan of cave dwellers working in the dark because of the light-sensitive films we used on our silk screens. We were pale, our eyes attuned to seeing what others often missed.

The hours I spent in that basement were precious to me. A hiding place. But I knew I couldn't stay there permanently. For one thing, my parents had imbued me with a work ethic. You had a duty, a responsibility—to your family, to yourself—to put food on the table, keep a roof over your head. We all worked in the restaurant—me, my brothers Mike and Manny, even my grandparents.

My parents were proud that I had gone to college, but as far as they were concerned, there was a straight line—unbroken—from graduation to a job. Printmaking was not a job. My father called art "a casino," a gamble as tenuous as sitting at a blackjack table in Vegas.

"I don't care how beautiful your work is. If it's not bringing in a steady paycheck, it's not work."

"You could teach, Toni. A girl as smart as you. Look at Marie Filizolla. She gets the summers off. You could help out in the restaurant during the tourist season."

Little by little, I felt my mother shaping my unfinished parts, rounding me out to fit the mold of Italian womanhood. Slightly updated, of course, for the education she had never attained.

Marriage, a teaching job and beautiful hand-printed Christmas cards that she could hang in Paradiso and boast about to customers. "My daughter's artwork. She's the one who painted the mural on the wall."

Let's face it. I was too scared of the unknown, too unsure of my own talent to embrace Peter's view of my possible future as an artist. I got the teaching job. I married Bobby. I knew what I was doing. I was staying safe.

## Return to the Neighborhood

I SHOULD HAVE UNDERSTOOD that safety is an illusion, especially after reading C. S. Lewis and Madeleine L'Engle stories to my children. Heroes and heroines don't hide from danger and the unknown. They plunge into it, even though they're terrified, and come out the other side scarred but wiser and in possession of whatever is necessary to save the world.

All I wanted to save was my children, and at first, after Bobby left me, I thought I had to do it on my own. I felt like the cliché of my generation—educated professional woman, single mother, in possession of half the wedding gifts. I got the Cuisinart and the vacuum cleaner. He got the stereo system and the color TV. Bobby traveled light when he left on his Kawasaki, but his lawyer made sure his share of the household goods were shipped to Colorado, along with half the proceeds from the sale of our raised ranch when the time came.

The loneliness and exhaustion were nothing new to me. Bobby had been emotionally missing from our lives long before he walked out the door. I joined a single-parent group that had just formed in Cambridge, people who were exploring the idea of living communally, or at least matching up fragmented families. It was like "let's see if my jagged edges fit into your empty spaces." I met with three different people and their kids—a tortured dad who seemed to have self-pity oozing out of his pores, a British woman, several years older than I, whose main interest in the arrangement was to find a live-in babysitter, and a woman about my age whom I liked well enough but whose child drove me bananas. With three children of my own, including an infant, I wasn't considered a prime catch. I made a list for myself, one of those two-column charts, placing in the plus or minus column the issues I'd identified in each household. Some were as simple as "not enough bedrooms," while others were more complicated, like "doesn't believe in setting limits." I had almost nothing in the plus columns for any of them.

The kids and I went to Sunday dinner at my parents' shortly after the robbery. My mother got down on the floor with Vanessa and played finger games with her. Manny and Mike taught the boys how to play Pong. The sweet aroma of Mom's chicken salmi wafted into the living room from the kitchen. Outside the windows the sun was shining and the street was bustling. The plus column was getting crowded. After we ate, I spoke to my parents.

"Mom, Dad, when did you say that apartment would be vacant?"

We waited until the school year was finished, and then the kids and I moved in over the summer. I enrolled Ben and Joe at St. John's and kept my job at Bedford High. I spent July and August showing the boys the neighborhood—how to cross the street safely, where the playgrounds were, who had the best lemon ice.

When Mom sent Joe on his first errand, to walk down to Giuffre's fish market on the corner and pick up an order of octopus and squid, he started out looking over this shoulder as he passed each doorway while Mom stood on the stoop at Paradiso, smiling and waving at him. He finally ducked into the store and out of sight.

Mom remained in the doorway, her eyes glistening with tears.

"How many times have you stood here, watching one of us walk down the street?"

She picked up the corner of her apron and wiped her eyes. "I'll never tire of it. It's the first taste of independence any of you got. And you always knew I'd be waiting for you right on this spot when you came home."

A few minutes later Joe strode down the sidewalk carrying a bag that was almost as big as he was. He was bursting with what he'd seen.

"Big bloody buckets of fish heads the guy was chopping off, and spiky things with slippery insides and black ropy things he said were eels. It was really gross!"

For a kid who'd grown up in a subdivision with three different models of houses repeated endlessly along winding streets with names like Meadowlark and Robin and Cardinal, Joe adapted to city life with unbridled gusto. Sharing a playground with a bunch of other kids—especially one on the edge of the harbor—was far superior to playing with his kid brother on his own swing set.

Ben, on the other hand, was slower to warm to all the changes in his life. No longer the baby, not quite understanding where his daddy had gone and having to sleep in a strange room for the second time in a few months, all took their toll. He didn't want to go to the playground. He would only eat pasta with butter and cheese. He would've been quite happy to spend the whole day in front of the TV playing Pong if I'd let him.

"Give him time," Mom said. "Once he goes to school in September and makes some friends in the neighborhood, he'll be a changed boy."

I wanted to believe in my mother's simple conviction that the rhythm and patterns of life in her familiar and close-knit world would heal us. But I knew enough about Bobby's mental illness to be aware that his children were more likely to develop it than children who didn't have a parent who was manic depressive. In her own way, though, my mother was right. Biology wasn't the only determinant. I was most concerned about Ben, but I was determined to give all three of my children the love and stability that coming back to the neighborhood represented.

I kept them occupied with treks to the aquarium and the Children's Museum, the children's room at the library, the wading pool in the Boston Common. We put Vanessa in her stroller and set out on foot with juice boxes and animal crackers. If nothing else, the excursions exhausted them and they fell asleep without complaint at the end of the day. If I'd learned anything growing up in my mother's house, it was that keeping busy dispelled, or at least disguised, sadness. I raised the activity level for Ben's sake, but I was doing it for myself, as well. I didn't want to sit still for too long, because that gave me time to think about my life.

When the kids were in bed I painted the

apartment, made curtains, refinished old dressers and, as summer neared its end, organized my lesson plans and arranged field trips for the fall.

Now that I was living in Boston, I decided to meet with the educational program directors of the museums in person and coax them into special tours and behind-the-scenes visits for my students.

I asked Mom to watch the kids the day I scheduled appointments along the Fenway at the Museum of Fine Arts and the Isabella Stewart Gardner Museum. The last time I'd been at either one I'd been shepherding a raucous group of students who saw the trip as a day off from the classroom. Very few had appreciated what they'd seen. The rest had only paid enough attention to fill out the worksheet I'd distributed on the bus.

I'd given myself time when scheduling the appointments to wander through my favorite galleries. When I was done, my mission at both museums accomplished, I came out the side door of the MFA. Across the street was the Museum School. I hadn't been back since I'd graduated. It wasn't the sort of place that invited alumni back for reunions.

I was curious enough to make my way into the building. I told myself I was gathering information from the admissions office for my few serious students who were thinking about applying to art school.

But if I'd been honest, I'd have realized that I was looking for a lost part of myself. I felt like an interloper, an impostor, when I walked into the building. The school had a summer session and was swarming with students—intense, paint spattered, arrayed in a wild panoply of colorful, mismatched, funky clothing.

I was so out of place. I'd dressed as the suburban mother of three and schoolteacher that I was for the meetings at the museums. The Toni who'd once roamed these halls cringed at the Toni now stepping carefully into the lobby. And not just because of how I looked.

I almost turned around and left. But I followed my nose and my memories down the stairs to the print studio, not quite sure what I was seeking. I hesitated before opening the door.

*You don't belong here anymore,* a voice inside my head scolded. *You gave this up a long time ago. You can't go back. You can't undo that decision. Stop before you make a fool of yourself.*

I took my hand off the doorknob, ready to listen to the cautionary voice. But someone on the other side of the door pushed it open and rushed through, knapsack flying. She didn't close the door behind her and I found myself standing in the hallway looking into my past.

The late-afternoon light slanted across the floor through windows as dirty as they had been years before. The few people in the room were bent over workbenches and didn't bother to glance up at the stranger in their midst. I took a deep breath and crossed over the threshold into the studio.

"Excuse me." I addressed no one in particular. "Do you mind if I look around? I'm an alum, an art teacher."

The student nearest me shrugged. "Go ahead."

I started moving around the room. Prints were hanging from wires strung across the middle of the space above the worktables. Many of the pieces were striking. Dramatic abstract images. Nothing at all like the work I had done, which had been very personal—figures revealing stories. All that work had been packed away in portfolios for years.

I could hear voices coming from the pressroom beyond the studio and the sound of one of the larger presses being cranked. Not wanting to disturb what was under way, I began to walk back to the entrance of the studio. Then I heard my name.

"Toni?" The questioner's tone was a combination of surprise and disbelief.

I turned in response to see Peter Ricci standing by the pressroom and felt his eyes sweep over me in appraisal and instant judgment. I expected that he was congratulating himself on his accurate prediction. The talent he'd once recognized and tried to nurture had been diluted by years in a suburban high school. I stood there in my gray linen suit and my Capezio pumps, my hair pulled neatly in a ponytail, and regretted that I'd even gone into the building.

Peter moved toward me, his hand outstretched in greeting, formal and without warmth.

"What a surprise! What brings you back? In town for a day of the arts?"

I couldn't blame him for thinking I was a "lady who lunched." Someone who came into Boston for a few hours to do some shopping in Copley Square, have lunch at the Ritz and take in the latest exhibit at the MFA. "I live in Boston now. I had appointments to set up field trips for my students and I thought I'd stop at the school to pick up admissions information. I couldn't resist the opportunity to poke my head in and see the state of the art. Despite the age-old methods, your students are doing some very modern stuff."

"It never gets old to me. These kids continually find new ways to express themselves. So you're still teaching? Did you continue your printmaking?"

I shook my head. "Life took over after I graduated."

"That's a shame. A waste, actually. You were one of the most remarkable artists to come through here."

"Thanks, I'm honored that you thought so, but what I see here today is far beyond what I was doing back then."

"If you'd continued, who knows where you'd be today."

The longer we talked, the more uncomfortable I became. I wasn't willing to have my choices questioned or to be reminded of lost opportunities. I had a family to support. My father had been right; art was a gamble, one I couldn't afford.

I looked at my watch and made my apologies.

"I'm so sorry. I've got to get back to my family. It's been good to see you."

"Come again, Toni. Bring your class next time."

"Thanks. I'm sure they'd love it."

And I escaped. I felt claustrophobic. Riding back to Government Center on the Green Line I wished I hadn't gone down to the print studio. It had unsettled me and raised painful questions about how much I'd changed. The talented artist Peter had recognized no longer existed. We both knew that, and I didn't know which one of us regretted it more.

School started, and in October I brought my seniors into town for their field trip to the MFA. I decided not to take Peter up on his invitation to his class. The last place I wanted to be was the studio.

Hazel wrote, asking me to bring the kids to Belle Arbor for Thanksgiving. I suspected she might be trying to bring Bobby and me together. I'd heard from Sandra that her mother had been distraught about the divorce. What she didn't tell me seeped back to me from friends of mine who also knew Sandra. Hazel found it incomprehensible that Bobby would leave his family. She was convinced I'd done something so unforgivable he had no choice but to leave. More than likely, she thought, Vanessa wasn't his daughter.

I was hurt and outraged that she'd even entertain such a thought. Throughout my marriage I'd tried to be a good daughter-in-law.

"She's an old woman whose faith in her son has been shattered. She's grasping at any explanation to feel better about him. Let it go. But don't go to Indiana." This was the advice from my brother Mike, who, in the months since we'd moved back to the neighborhood, had become my confidant.

I sent a letter and pictures of the kids, the subtle message of their blond hair and blue eyes underscoring that they were decidedly Templetons. Even though it had been more than a year since Bobby left, I still felt raw and vulnerable.

A few days after Thanksgiving, just before Paradiso was booked solid for office Christmas parties, Mom tripped on the cellar stairs and broke her ankle. She was effectively off her feet until Christmas.

"Toni, I've got a deal for you," she told me that afternoon when I got home from school. Her foot was propped up on a kitchen chair. "I'll watch the kids in the evenings if you'll take over hostessing downstairs."

I wanted to ask who would do my lesson plans and grading, but I knew I'd fit them in somehow.

Considering everything my mother had done for me, I could spell her for a few weeks in the restaurant.

"Put some makeup on and find something a little softer to wear than those suits of yours."

I'd grown up watching my mother open boxes from my father every year on her birthday and Christmas, boxes filled with gorgeous dresses, cashmere sweaters, diamond bracelets. I thought that's what all men did, but I'd learned otherwise. I didn't have a thing in my closet that would meet my mother's requirement for how the Paradiso hostess should dress.

I enlisted my cousin Annette to go shopping with me.

"How tarty do you want to look?"

"My mother doesn't dress like a tart!"

"She dresses like a movie star from the 1960s. Think Sophia Loren. Gina Lollobrigida. Elizabeth Taylor in *Butterfield 8*."

"Do you think I can pull it off?"

"Toni! You've got my uncle Al's smoldering

bedroom eyes and jet-black hair, and my aunt Rose's figure. We are not talking Audrey Hepburn here, although the black dress from *Breakfast at Tiffany's* wouldn't be a bad start."

Annette poked through racks and threw things over the dressing room door. In the end, I settled on a short black skirt and a couple of sweaters, "sexy but elegant" in Annette's assessment, and a red dress for the catered parties.

"You're a 'winter,'" she told me, based on some *Cosmo* article that categorized flattering colors by the season. She also made me buy a pair of stiletto heels.

"I wore nurses' shoes when I waitressed during college," I protested.

"You're not a waitress anymore. You're the woman with the power to banish someone to the hell of a table near the restrooms or bestow upon them the gift of a seat by the window, where anyone walking by can see how favored they are. You may not be the queen Aunt Rose is, but you are the princess and you should look the part. Besides, you never know who might walk into Paradiso tomorrow night and be struck dumb by your beauty."

"I'm not ready for that."

"You never will be if you continue to dress like you're going to a PTA meeting. Our next stop is the lingerie department. You need sheer black stockings and a push-up bra. You know, Toni, I don't remember you dressing so conservatively when we were kids. You were a lot more of a free spirit. It's good to have you back in the neighborhood, cuz."

She put her arm around me, guided me through intimate apparel and then marched me to the cosmetics department.

"My friend Elaine works for Lancôme. She'll set us up with what you need."

The next afternoon, after getting home from school, giving the boys a snack and making sure they'd done their homework, I got dressed in the new clothes. I herded the kids downstairs to my mother's apartment at four-thirty.

"Turn around—I want the whole effect," she said when I walked into the kitchen. Vanessa, who'd been with my mother all day, was clamoring for a hug and a kiss. I scooped her up, nuzzled her and then let her squirm out of my arms to toddle over to her brothers, who were on their way to the TV.

"Don't let them watch too much," I said.

"Don't worry. Manny is sending up some ziti in about an hour and then we'll play cards. Let me see you! Nice. Very nice. Eventually a haircut would be a good idea. Enough with the hippie folksinger look. But on the whole, you look enticing."

"Gee, thanks, Ma. Glad you approve."

"Now go downstairs before your father starts

getting *agita* that there's nobody in the front of the house."

And so began my new role as the hostess of Paradiso. I'd like to say my performance that first night was as successful as my appearance, but it took me a while to learn how to balance the flow and recognize who should get the best tables. It had always looked so effortless when Mom had done it. I was exhausted by the time I got upstairs.

The kids were sound asleep. Mom and I had already talked about having them spend the nights with her and Daddy, so I slipped off my heels and padded up the stairs to my own place alone. I washed off the unfamiliar makeup and went to bed.

I was into my second week when Peter Ricci came in for dinner. I don't think he recognized me at first, especially since I'd taken the plunge and had my hair styled, again with Annette by my side. We went to a salon on Newberry Street, where I paid a fortune, but came out with a look that was all tumbling waves.

Both Manny and Mike gave me the thumbs-up sign, which was a relief. Mom thought it was a little too tousled. "Bed hair," she called it. But she agreed it was better than the Joan Baez look. I'd never had so much attention paid to my appearance.

It finally dawned on Peter who I was as I handed him his menu.

"Toni? What are you doing here? I thought you were teaching."

"I am. This is my family's place. I'm helping out for a few weeks. Enjoy your meal."

I sent over a small antipasto on the house for him and his date.

I wasn't crazy about seeing Peter Ricci again. It was too much of a reminder of how sharp a turn my life had taken. Unfortunately Peter didn't realize how unwelcome his presence was, and he actually got up from his table and asked me to come over and meet the woman he was dining with.

"I've been telling her about you."

Great, I thought. A cautionary tale of unfulfilled potential. Watch out, or you, too, could become a lapsed artist, fallen away from your calling to show slides of the *Mona Lisa* and Michelangelo's *David* to bored teenagers.

"Maybe you know her work," he said as we walked back to their table. "She's Diane Rocheleau."

Of course I knew her work. She'd emerged in the late sixties and had several shows in New York that had garnered critical acclaim. The last I'd heard, the Whitney had held an exhibition of her work. She was a printmaker.

"What's she doing in Boston?" I'd begun to wish I'd seated them at a better table.

"She's a guest lecturer at the school for a

couple of weeks. Why don't you come down to one of the evening classes next week? That is, if you can get away."

Good. He'd given me an out. "It's hard to do. This is a busy season for us. I'll try to make it, but no promises. Thanks for the invite."

Diane was gracious, and even though I tried to detect a note of condescension, she was genuine and down-to-earth. I was grateful that neither one of them asked me what I was currently working on. How would I have answered? Finding the right shade of yellow for my daughter's bedroom?

"The meal was wonderful," Diane said. "Our compliments to the chef."

"Thanks, I'll let him know. My brother's cooking tonight. It's always a little spicier when he's in the kitchen."

After they left I tried to brush away the glimmer of reawakening longing that had surfaced. Now, more than ever, I told myself, I don't have what it takes to be an artist. I picked up a stack of menus and turned up the wattage on my smile as I saw the mayor's chief of staff walk in the door.

Peter Ricci's invitation wasn't an idle one. He stopped by the restaurant two days later, not to eat but to give me the schedule of Diane's demonstration classes.

"You look great, by the way. Different than you

did this summer. City life seems to be agreeing with you."

"My mother's influence. She thinks the sizzle shouldn't just be in the frying pan if you're going to run a successful restaurant."

He laughed. "You know, I've eaten here many times and never realized this was your family's place. I bought a loft down on Union Wharf a few years ago and have adopted this neighborhood. It reminds me so much of where my grandparents lived in New York." He paused. "I just had a thought. I started a neighborhood art program last year at the community center. I scrounge whatever supplies I can for the kids, and I've twisted a few arms among the faculty at the Museum School to get them to come down here and teach a class or two. You've probably got your hands full with your own teaching load and the restaurant, but if you were interested, I could use someone with your talent and experience."

It was my turn to laugh.

"Besides my teaching and the restaurant, I also have three children I occasionally try to see, Peter. I wish I could help you, and I'm flattered that you asked. I think it's wonderful of you to be doing this. But at this point in my life, it would be impossible. For the same reasons, I know I can't make it to one of Diane's classes. But thank you."

I hoped that the wall I was erecting around me was high enough not to be breached. I wanted to say to him, *Stop trying to reclaim the Toni who was your star pupil. She doesn't exist anymore.*

"Okay. I understand. I didn't realize you had kids. But if you change your mind, give me a call. Here's my card."

I stuck the card in my pocket, but I didn't intend to use it.

I had spent too many years allowing someone else to define who I was. My parents. The nuns at Sacred Heart. Bobby. Even Peter, who thought he knew who I was when I'd been his student. I'd returned to the neighborhood for the sake of my children, so they could grow up surrounded by love. But I was determined not to go back to the old definitions of myself. I was trying to shed masks I'd accumulated over the years, masks that had come at great cost to the original Toni, whoever she was.

In the final year of my marriage to Bobby I'd been in hell, caretaker to his disintegrating personality as my own identity disappeared. After he left I found myself in a kind of limbo. Neither pain nor joy made its way onto that neutral shore. The weekend my plane to Colorado was canceled, I'd abandoned the ridiculous notion that Bobby and I might reconcile, eliminating the opportunity to even open the discussion. Mike had been at the airport with me and Vanessa, and rather than read me the riot act, he was very quiet and thoughtful. His comforting presence forced me to think through what I really wanted, and I knew it wasn't resuming my life with Bobby, in Colorado or anywhere.

But I hadn't a clue yet what I *did* want. At night, after my kids were settled in bed and my work organized for school the next day, I sometimes sat in my darkened bedroom looking out at the city. My room was in the front of the building now. Like the old ladies on the street who know everyone's business because they sit at their windows all day watching the neighborhood as if it were a soap opera, I sat and watched late at night. The street had an emptiness then that echoed my own loneliness. The few people out and about were moving quickly in the cold, their footsteps and muffled voices bouncing off the brick facades of the buildings. I wondered if they were hurrying home or racing to the arms of a lover.

I was not moving at all. Frozen. Rooted. Behind a wall not of brick, but of ice.

Annette, emboldened by the success of the makeover she'd engineered, decided to push on to higher stakes. I thought she'd be content when she managed to entice me into getting a manicure regularly.

"The first thing people see will be your hands as

you distribute their menus. Well-manicured nails reflect on the quality of the house. If you don't believe me, ask your mother, who never misses an appointment with Bernadette up the street."

I got my nails done—just a shaping and a coat of clear polish. But for Christmas, I picked out a deep burgundy to go with the velvet dress I was wearing to Christmas Eve dinner, and I stayed with that shade.

But Annette wasn't satisfied.

"Now that you have a new look, it's time for a new man."

"No, it isn't. I told you, I'm *not* ready."

"Not ready to get married again, with that I concur. But you are certainly ready to enjoy life a little."

"I enjoy my children. I enjoy my family. I enjoy my work."

"That's wonderful. Commendable for the Italian mother and daughter you are. But why, if I happen to be looking out my window late at night and glance across the street, do I see my cousin pensive and sad at her own window?"

"Are you spying on me?"

"Don't deflect from the point I'm trying to make. Enjoying family life in its many Dante forms is all well and good. But there's a piece missing from your life. Whether you believe this or not, Toni, you deserve the attention of a man. And it's my next mission in life to find you one."

"Don't, Annette."

"Nonsense. We're not talking about *the* man. You're right about that. It's too soon. You're too miserable to attract him."

"Thanks a lot!"

"I am talking about injecting some light-hearted fun into your overly responsible existence. A movie date. Dinner at some place other than Paradiso with somebody whose meat you don't have to cut."

Annette reached out to her network and started setting me up on blind dates. The son of one of her father's customers, who took me to Pier 4 for lobster and popovers and then expected a nightcap of sex while my children slept down the hall. I left him firmly at the door. A minor-league hockey player who appeared to have been rammed against the sideboards a few too many times and had difficulty carrying on a conversation that consisted of more than two or three words.

"Annette, I'm an art teacher. I read books. My idea of a good time is an exhibit at the MFA or a play at the Colony Theater."

"Okay. I'm working on it."

She found me an accountant and a stockbroker, both educated and well-groomed and totally boring. One talked only about himself, without a single question to me. *Am I invisible?* I asked myself. *Or just a mirror reflecting back his glowing opinion of himself?* The other was too inquisitive. I felt as if he had a mental checklist for the ideal woman as he questioned me about my life. When we got to how I felt about kids and I started describing the wonder and delight and physical exhaustion of being a mother to three unique beings, the questions stopped. It was clear he had no idea I'd been married before and had children; his eyes glazed over.

"I thought this was supposed to be a fun-filled romp for me, Annette. Frankly I'd rather have all my wisdom teeth pulled than go out on another date. I'm done. This is worse than being lonely."

My mother had gotten back on her feet after Christmas and no longer needed me to do nightly hostessing at Paradiso, but I found I missed it. Manny had talked my parents into keeping the restaurant open when they went to Florida in January and he asked me if I'd fill in again. A few more weeks of turning outward instead of inward, on my feet and chatting with customers instead of sitting morosely by my window at night, sounded more than appealing. My cousin Vito's teenage daughter Mira came over to watch the kids and I went back downstairs.

I discovered during my stint as hostess that I enjoyed the theatrical aspects of the restaurant business. Manny had understood that we were putting on a show every night and had been making changes at Paradiso ever since he got back from school. My parents had established the reputation of Paradiso with the quality of the food, but Manny was generating attention that was starting to draw a hipper crowd. It used to be rare for a neighborhood place like Paradiso to be significant enough for a restaurant critic to notice. I think most of the Boston food writers dismissed North End restaurants as nothing but tourist traps offering a list of standards—meatballs, sausage, eggplant parmigiano and lasagne —smothered in red sauce. We'd always presented a more varied menu, and our regulars knew that. Manny was finding ways to attract new customers who were looking for something adventurous. So word spread, the critics started coming around, and Manny and I wanted to put on a good show. I flirted with the men; I complimented the women.

"I love your earrings! They really set off your face."

"Welcome to Paradiso! As Beatrice said to Dante, come sit awhile at my table. Enjoy your meal!"

I started bringing each table a small plate of tidbits to nibble on while they read the menu— olives, celery stuffed with Gorgonzola that had been mashed with olive oil and lemon juice, a couple of anchovies rolled around capers. On weekends, when the place was busiest and guests often had to wait, I brought them spiced nuts and chatted with them to make the time pass more quickly. I roamed the floor, making sure everyone was content. I'd grown up watching my mother welcome guests to the restaurant as if it were her dining room upstairs. She'd put her hand on someone's shoulder as she stopped at a table. If she knew the people, she'd ask about the family. If she didn't, she'd tell them they'd made a good choice in whatever they were eating.

"My favorite," she'd say. "My mother's recipe."

One night, Peter Ricci showed up. I hadn't seen him since I'd turned down his request to help at the community center.

I felt myself stiffening, the defenses going up, but I put on my hostess face and welcomed him.

"Happy New Year, Peter! How many in your party tonight?"

I continued my usual performance as the evening wore on, trying not to notice that Peter was watching me as I moved around the room. Probably sharing with his fellow guests, none of whom I recognized, the sad tale of my wasted potential. I forced myself to return to his table as their meal was winding down. I was gracious. I recommended the panna cotta for dessert. I kept talking so he couldn't bring up art.

When they were leaving, he told his companions to go ahead, he'd catch up with them, and then he turned back to me.

Here it comes, I thought. He hasn't given up yet, has he?

"It was great to see you tonight, Toni. I missed you the last time I was in. Uh, this may sound a little off the wall, but do you enjoy dance?"

Dance? Not, Have you created any lithographic images lately or etched a sheet of copper?

"What kind of dance?"

"Modern. I've got two tickets for the Nederlands Dans Theater at the Metropolitan Center next Thursday. Would you like to join me? I saw them in Europe last summer and found them compelling. I thought you might . . ."

I wasn't quite sure where he was headed with his invitation. Warning bells deep in my brain were signaling that any contact with Peter Ricci, no matter how unrelated to my lost talent, would not be a good thing for me. But instead of the self-assured master teacher, the in-your-face, knowledgeable professor, what I was seeing was a vulnerable adolescent asking me out on a date. To do something that actually appealed to me.

I said yes. My brother Mike agreed to host for me; my cousin Annette watched the kids.

The dance company was as compelling as Peter had promised—dramatic and thought-provoking. We walked back to the neighborhood after the performance, so caught up in conversation about what we'd seen that we ignored the cold.

When we got to Salem Street I noticed how red his nose was.

"Can I offer you a warm drink? I'm sure Manny still has some espresso or cappuccino in the kitchen."

He accepted, and we went into the restaurant. The last table was being cleared and Mike had already gone upstairs to relieve Annette. I led Peter to a booth, then walked into the kitchen to get us some coffee.

Manny was sipping a glass of wine and about to dig into a plate of linguine carbonara. He was always famished at the end of the evening.

"How was your date with the art teacher?"

"Intriguing. Fine. Why do you ask?"

He smiled. "The guy's been waiting for you for months. Every time he came in for dinner he asked about you. Showing up last week wasn't a coincidence. I'd mentioned that you'd be working when Mom and Pop went to Florida."

I threw a sugar packet at him. "You don't need to be my matchmaker."

"You had a good time, right?"

I left the kitchen with the coffee and a plate of biscotti.

Peter smiled as I slipped into the other side of the booth. I didn't know what to do with the knowledge that his invitation hadn't been spontaneous.

It had been years since I'd felt someone genuinely interested in me. For once, I took Annette's advice and decided to enjoy it. Peter and I talked until the coffee grew cold, not about art but about life. His growing up in Rochester, New York, with a father who worked at the Kodak plant and a mother who was a hairdresser. The inspiration provided by a high school teacher that had propelled him to the Rhode Island School of Design.

I shared with him a condensed version of my life since graduating, sparing him the melodrama of the collapse of my marriage. I was still wary of tainting new friendships with my own misery.

"I was an asshole ten years ago to have criticized you for becoming a teacher," he said.

That was unexpected. He went on.

"I'm a product myself of a wonderful teacher. I think I equated what I saw happening to you, your art, with your decision to teach. But, in fact, it was something else, not the teaching. You were shutting down emotionally. I don't know what it was—and you don't have to tell me—but it was still there when you came into the studio this summer.

"But you've changed since then. Not just physically—although, believe me, that's been striking. I've watched you here at the restaurant. You're vibrant. You cast a spell on people."

That was when he leaned across the table to kiss me. It was soft and inviting and filled with longing. When he stopped, he looked at me, cupping my face in his hands.

"You're an amazing woman, Toni."

The lights went off in the kitchen. It was late. I reluctantly said good-night to Peter.

"I had a wonderful time. Especially our conversation."

"Shall we continue it tomorrow?"

"I'm hostessing again. Why don't you come by near closing time. I'll ask Manny to whip us up a late supper."

He kissed me in the vestibule before I went upstairs.

Mike was watching the *Tonight Show* on the couch with Vanessa sprawled across his chest. I gathered her gently into my arms and settled her in her crib, but she woke up. I wound up walking the floor with her to get her back to sleep, wondering what I'd been thinking when I opened myself up to Peter. I couldn't afford to let a man into my life the way Peter Ricci seemed to want. The intimacy of our conversation that evening, despite my reticence, had been both satisfying and draining. I couldn't imagine being able to sustain that. Not with everything that was pulling at me for attention—my children, my teaching, my responsibilities to my family.

When I finally got Vanessa to sleep, I crawled into bed and wrapped the comforter around me for warmth. I longed to have Peter beside me, holding me, making love to me. But at one in the morning, exhausted and already anticipating the start of another day—with kids to rouse and feed and get off to school, traffic to face, classes to teach—I realized that wasn't going to be possible. Better to accept that now rather than make a mess later. I was afraid I'd be doing all the taking from Peter and have nothing to give in return.

The phone rang. I answered quickly so Vanessa wouldn't wake up again.

"It's Peter. I'm sorry if I woke you."

"You didn't. I just got to bed."

"I couldn't sleep. I feel as if I left things unfinished."

"Peter . . ." I wanted to stop him.

"I'm in a phone booth down the street. Can I come up?"

I sat up in bed. I told myself I should say no. I should say I can't go any further.

"Yes."

In the few minutes it took him to reach the building I opened the drawer in my night table and took out the new diaphragm Annette had encouraged me to get as part of my transformation. As with her other suggestions, I had protested at first. But my hand trembled when I took it out of the case. I felt both relieved to have it and in a state of joyful disbelief that I might actually need it. When the intercom rang, I tiptoed down the hall and buzzed him in, listening to his footsteps as he climbed the stairs.

He stepped inside the apartment, picked me up and carried me down the hall to my bedroom.

Bobby had stopped making love to me months before Vanessa was born. And before that, our lovemaking had been sporadic and more a physical release than an expression of love or even desire. I didn't realize how much of my pleasure in sex had been deadened, wrapped in layers of neglect and abandonment. I'd forgotten what it felt like to be caressed and cherished. I thought I could live without passion. That night with Peter threw me off balance, opening a rift in the shell of protection I'd constructed. It exposed a need so raw and hungry that it frightened me.

He was an extraordinarily tender lover. When we got to the bedroom he sat on the side of the bed and I sat with my legs wrapped around him. At first, we simply rocked to a lullaby that emerged from our kisses and sighs. His kisses moved from my lips down my neck to the opening at the top of my nightgown. His hands moved down my back and slid the fabric up over my head. Once free, I lifted my arms to unzip his jacket and unbutton his shirt. I forgot about the chill in the room as he pulled me down and we lay facing each other, his bare chest against mine. I somehow managed to get the rest of his clothes off in a blur of movement, my mouth continuing to kiss him as my fingers released the five buttons on his jeans. Peter was nearly forty, but his body was lean and strong, cradling me with a fierce warmth. I responded to his exploration of my body with a ferocity of my own. It wasn't a sweet reawakening of my long-dormant sexuality. Instead, it was explosive, driven, frenzied. We both seemed to be in a state of want that only the other could fill.

I didn't know myself.

We finally collapsed, hearts beating wildly against each other, our breathing gradually subsiding into a steady, synchronized rhythm. We hadn't spoken a single word since the phone call hours before. Talking had been superfluous. Our means of communication was tactile, the responses unfiltered by judgment or caution. Our lovemaking had been intemperate. Insatiable. And we clung to each other afterward, unable or unwilling to break the connection. I was trembling, and he held me tighter, gathering the covers around us as I had earlier, when I thought I'd come to terms with my loneliness.

We slept. Around five, the tenuous thread connecting us broke when Vanessa began to cry. I groped for the nightgown shed with everything else I thought I knew about myself and went to my daughter. It was still dark. By the time I settled Vanessa, Peter was up and pulling on his jeans. We looked at each other across the room, an acknowledgment passing between us that what had happened during the night had been inexplicable, arising out of some unfulfilled hidden need neither of us had understood. Then we moved toward each other in an embrace.

"Thank you." We both murmured it at the same time.

As much as we'd taken from the other, we'd also given.

And then he was gone.

I stood at the window and saw him cross the street and round the corner, heading toward the harbor.

I got through the first part of the day on autopilot, filling bowls with Cheerios, making peanut butter and banana sandwiches, packing Vanessa's diaper bag and leaving her with Manny to drop off at my aunt Ida's later in the morning. My makeup disguised the dark circles under my eyes, but not the haunted expression in my eyes.

"You look like hell."

"Thanks, dear brother. Vanessa was up a couple of times during the night. She'll probably sleep for a couple of hours now. I've got to get to work. See you tonight."

I drifted more than once at school, feeling like an adolescent caught in the hazy euphoria of remembered passion. No wonder I'd sealed myself off from sex. It rendered me dysfunctional.

When I got back to the neighborhood I met the boys at their school and walked them to Aunt Ida's. She was watching them for this last night before my parents got back from Florida.

"You don't mind keeping them overnight? Fridays are always late for us."

"It's not a bother, honey. They're good kids. We have fun, don't we, guys?"

I kissed them all and walked down the street to my place to shower and change. I pulled out the red dress I'd bought in the fall with Annette. I put my hair up to accentuate the neckline of the dress, which bared my shoulders.

I was downstairs by four-thirty, reviewing the reservations and taking calls. It was going to be a busy night.

"You're looking better," Manny said when I poked my head in the kitchen. "You want a bite to eat before we open the doors?"

"No, thanks. Not hungry." I didn't tell him I hadn't been able to eat all day.

I kept things moving, not rushing people, but mindful of those waiting for tables. I started watching the door around ten o'clock. I didn't know when to expect Peter and tried not to panic with each passing quarter hour. The euphoria I'd experienced during the day was draining out of my veins, reminding me of the cost of a night like the one I'd had.

By eleven I was convinced he'd fled, overcome with regret or self-loathing. He had a wife and had decided to go back to her. He was lying in an emergency room somewhere paralyzed, as Deborah Kerr had been in *An Affair to Remember,* unable to keep her assignation. I thought I was going to be sick to my stomach. I was blowing out candles when I felt two familiar hands around my waist and heard my name whispered in my ear. I turned to face him. He kissed me, urgently. The taste of last night lingered in the familiar softness of his mouth on mine.

"How was your day?" he murmured, planting a second kiss on my bare shoulder.

"Distracting. I felt like I was underwater most of the day."

"Me, too. When will you be done here?"

I nodded toward the two tables still occupied. "Not until they leave. Are you hungry? Manny made roast pork in almond sauce tonight."

"I've had no appetite at all today. It's as if I have no room for anything else except you."

"I've been the same way. Is this what addiction feels like?"

The last of the guests finally left. I spent another thirty minutes supervising the breakdown of the dining room, then said good-night to Manny. He didn't miss the fact that Peter was with me.

"Have fun." He grinned.

I took Peter by the hand and walked upstairs with him.

"I've been thinking about slipping the rest of this dress off you ever since I walked into the restaurant tonight and saw your shoulders. They set off such a wave of memory of your body." He was already unzipping the dress. It fell to the floor and I stepped out of it.

We made love for hours, as hungry as we'd been the night before but with a deepening awareness of each other's needs. And we broke the silence. In moments of repose, as our bodies came back down from their heightened states where nothing existed except pleasure, we spoke to each other.

"The minute you walked into the studio in August I felt a jolt of recognition. I thought the pain I was feeling was that of a failed teacher who'd lost his star pupil. I saw what I *thought* you'd become—a comfortable suburban matron who 'appreciated' art but no longer created it herself."

"And you've been trying to save me ever since?" I was propped up on my elbow facing him, stroking him gently with my free hand as if I were sculpting clay.

"I tried. But you were remarkably resistant to saving. I began to see a strength in you that I hadn't perceived before."

I frowned. "Is this seduction just one more way

of convincing me to return to art?" My hand stopped sculpting.

He grabbed the stilled hand and kissed it.

"God, no! I asked you out because I realized my interest was no longer that of a teacher for a student, but a man for a woman. I was probably drawn to you ten years ago and unable to admit that my anger with you for giving up on your talent was muddied by my jealousy."

"I knew back then that your disapproval was intense. I even felt it in August. It never occurred to me that it was so personal."

"I was a selfish jerk. Forgive me."

"Forgiving you is easy. Despite your blurred intentions, you were encouraging me do to what I loved. Forgiving myself is a lot harder. I've made a real mess of my life because I didn't trust my own talent. And I'm afraid that by coming back here, I'll slip into another kind of complacency."

"At least in coming back, you've reentered *my* life." He smiled, then continued. "Don't beat yourself up about returning home. First of all, you need to heal and be taken care of, and it seems that your family—especially your brothers—are more than willing to do that. Second, and more important, this place, this life, is the root of your talent. It's what nurtured you. Tap into it again."

"I don't know if it's there anymore."

"Is that doubt enough to stop you? That doesn't sound like the Toni I've seen emerging over the past several months. Or the Toni who's made love to me the past two nights."

I felt my face redden. "I don't know that Toni. She's a revelation to me."

"Then get to know her. Even if it's just to let her move your hand sketching—the way she's been moving your hand over my body."

"You're talking like a teacher again."

"No. I'm talking like a man who's in love with you."

When we woke in each other's arms the next morning, the lovemaking was languorous and unhurried, gentler than the night's quenching of an endless thirst.

"Let me cook for you," I said when we finally stirred, the winter sunlight cutting across the bed and the sounds of the street rising up—metal shutters clattering open at the greengrocer's and my uncle Sal's butcher shop, delivery trucks backing into narrow alleyways.

I surveyed my refrigerator, filled with provisions for feeding three children—yogurt cups and peanut butter and applesauce, leftover meatballs and fusilli. Not much for entertaining a lover. But I found some eggs and day-old bread and cinnamon. I didn't have any vanilla left, the bottle emptied the last time I'd made chocolate-chip cookies. I dug around under the cabinet in my pantry and unearthed an old bottle of Drambuie. I splashed a dollop into the beaten eggs and presented Peter with a platter of French toast garnished with my mother's peach preserves.

I set the table in the dining room and used my good dishes, not the sturdy but scarred pottery that had withstood years of children. I felt as if I were creating a bubble, insulated from the rest of my life, where for one more hour it was only Peter and I, sipping coffee and holding hands in the midst of warmth and sweetness and nourishment.

"What are you doing today?"

"Picking up the kids at my aunt's. Grocery shopping for me and my parents, who get back from Florida this afternoon. Spending time with the kids. Saturdays they know they have me to themselves."

"Do you want to bring them over to the community center later? We're holding an open house. The kids can get their hands dirty—finger painting for Vanessa, clay and woodworking for the boys."

"Is this a ploy to get me to volunteer?"

"No expectations. I know how much you have on your plate. I just thought it might be fun for the kids."

"Okay. We'll try to stop in."

"I should leave and let you get on with your day. I know this is a tough question, with your parents returning, but when can I see you again?"

I looked at him. There was nothing I wanted more at that moment than to have him back in my bed, in my body. And there was also nothing I feared more, to be as consumed as we had been by each other.

I kissed him. "We'll find the time, when it's right."

When he left, I stripped the bed and put the sheets in the washing machine, grabbed my coat and went across the street to bring my children home.

We *did* go to the community center after lunch. Joe was the least enthusiastic. He would much rather have gone to the rink and played hockey, and dismissed the art studio as stuff for babies. But when we got there, he gravitated to a table where some older boys were making monster masks and he stopped moping that we only did things that were fun for Ben. I knew Ben liked to draw. Much as I did as a child, he'd use any blank space as a drawing tablet—the margins of his notebook, the backs of envelopes. He could go through a pad of newsprint in an afternoon, sketching rocket ships and imaginary space creatures. The teachers at the community center had wrapped an entire wall in paper and handed kids multicolored markers when they walked in. Ben chose a corner, sat cross-legged on the floor in front of it and began a meticulously detailed air battle.

Vanessa, as Peter had predicted, found her calling at the finger-painting table.

The room was humming with color and activity. A Raffi album played in the background. I looked around for Peter but didn't see him, which was both disappointing and something of a relief. My reaction to being near him was still too visceral and I didn't trust myself to disguise my pleasure. There were too many people from the neighborhood here, parents from St. John's, customers who ate at Paradiso. I wasn't quite ready for it to be so clear that Toni Dante Templeton had a boyfriend.

Vanessa was growing bored with the finger painting and starting to make a mess. I cleaned her up and collected the boys to go home. One of the volunteers, a student from the Museum School, snipped Ben's drawing off the wall and rolled it up for him. Joe put his mask on. Vanessa's painting was still wet, so the student hung it on a clothesline strung across the room and I promised I'd stop by on Monday to pick it up. She handed me a sheet of paper with the studio hours and class schedule.

"Please come again!" She was cheerful and efficient and the kind of person I'd be happy to have working with my children. We trooped home and I asked the boys if they'd like to go to the studio again. When they both answered in the affirmative I began to see a way to spend time with them *and* offer help to the program.

We welcomed my parents home from Florida late in the afternoon and the kids spent the evening with my mother as she unpacked and I worked the Saturday dinner shift. As the late diners started dessert, I hurried upstairs to retrieve the kids. My mother went down to set up for the next day.

I carried Vanessa to her crib, ushered the boys to their bunk beds and retreated to my room. The bed was still bare, not yet made up. The light on my answering machine was blinking.

I listened to Peter's voice, apologizing for not being at the studio. He'd been called to the Museum School because of a burst pipe that had left several inches of water in the press room. No damage to anyone's work, but a mess to clean up.

"I know you need to spend time with your parents. I won't disturb you this evening. But give me a call when you get in if you want to talk."

I hauled the sheets out of the dryer and made the bed before climbing into it and calling Peter.

"Where are you?"

"In bed. I thought it wouldn't seem so empty if I settled in with at least your voice close to me."

We talked for two hours.

The next week I started volunteering one afternoon a week at the community center. After facing the indifference of high school students, the exuberance of the children was infectious. They played with their art unselfconsciously, and their playfulness became one more source of encouragement, one more incursion into the wall of restraint I'd built around myself.

## *The Sketchbook*

PETER GAVE ME A gift for my birthday. A small bound sketchbook and a set of charcoal pencils.

"Carry it with you. Use it like a journal and record what you see, only for yourself."

"Thanks, Teach." I was ready, I realized, to resume what had been a daily practice for me before I'd married Bobby. The book was beautiful, with heavy pages of pale cream that beckoned to be filled. I put it in my knapsack. The first time I used it I was pushing Vanessa in her stroller through the square to Old North Church. It was an unseasonably warm day and the old men were out on the benches arguing with one another and punctuating the air with their gestures.

Vanessa had dozed off, so I parked the stroller and pulled the notebook out of my backpack. I quickly sketched two of the men, one using his cane as an extension of his arm, the other shading his eyes from the sun with a rolled up copy of the *Herald*. It took me just ten minutes, and then we were on our way again.

Within a month I had filled the notebook. It surprised me. But I had trained my eye to see small squares of life. Some were as minute as a gnarled hand grasping a plum tomato from the basket on the sidewalk in front of the greengrocer's. Others were more expansive, like the shanks of prosciutto hanging from hooks in the window of my uncle Sal's shop or the cityscape framed by my bedroom window.

One night after the kids were in bed, I sat with the book and examined the pages. Some were better than others, but on the whole I'd captured a substantial number of images I was pleased with. The next day I went downtown and bought myself some sheets of watercolor paper, inks, brushes.

I chose one of the images in the notebook and recreated it in pen and ink with a soft wash of color.

It was on my dresser drying when Peter saw it there. We'd found a rhythm to being together that seemed to balance feeding the hunger we had for each other with the demands of everything else in our lives—especially my children's hunger for me.

I had introduced Peter to my parents a week after they returned from Florida by inviting him to the Sunday dinner my mother continued to prepare; it was how she got us all to sit down at the same table at least once a week. Bringing him to that meal was my way of hiding him in plain sight. He had a number of labels attached to him—former teacher, current colleague, neighbor, Paradiso regular. Enough to distract and deflect from the primary roles he played in my life, those of lover and friend. Even though most thirty-two-year-old divorced mothers of three probably had sex lives, to my parents sex remained something reserved for the marriage bed. I assumed Manny, who was still living under their roof, fulfilled that side of his life away from home in the beds of any of the lovelies who were ratcheting up the popularity of Paradiso. For me to spend even a couple of hours away from home in Peter's bed was nearly impossible. Too many questions. Too much judgment. But bringing Peter in the front door, making him a very visible presence, actually reduced speculation.

He got to know my boys at the community center and turned out to be an adept craftsman who was helping them collaborate on a scale model of a spaceship Ben had designed and Joe was constructing in their bedroom. When the children were around, Peter and I exchanged penetrating looks full of the promise of things to come. Once they were asleep, we shared a few hours made more pleasurable by the anticipation.

It was late spring when Peter saw the pen-and-ink wash on the dresser. He hadn't noticed it when he'd first come into the room because we'd been too intent on getting each other out of our clothes. But afterward, as he was dressing in the soft light, he saw it and picked it up. I hadn't shown him the notebook. As he'd promised when he gave it to me, it was mine alone. Not an assignment. Not an expectation. He turned to me with the sheet outstretched.

"It's wonderful."

That was all. No questions about how I felt to be creating again. No suggestions about what to do now that I'd plunged back in. He let me be, which was an even greater gift than the notebook itself.

I knew the piece was wonderful. I'd once found a quotation from the author James Dickey when I was a student that I kept tacked to my bulletin board—about the moment of revelation when, as a writer, you realize what you've created is "damn good." I'd had that moment. And I wanted more of them.

I bought another sketchbook. And filled it with more images from my life, my neighborhood. Manny hovering over a saucepan, the veins in his arms tracing a path of intensity as he stirs and then lifts the spoon to his mouth to taste; my parents sitting side by side at Joe's fourth-grade concert, my mother's diamond-bedecked fingers entwined with my father's withered hand.

I kept going.

In August 1983, my parents rented a place down on the Cape for a couple of weeks and offered to take the children.

"You need a break. Have some fun. Make plans with your girlfriends," my mother said.

Peter took me out to dinner the first night they were gone.

"I have something important I want to talk to you about." He didn't elaborate until we were seated on an outdoor terrace. We'd driven all the way to Gloucester.

"Hear me out," he said when I asked him to stop keeping me in suspense. "Don't respond until I tell you everything.

"Walt Bergeron has decided to retire."

Walt was Peter's colleague on the faculty, a printmaker like himself.

"He's ill and wants to spend whatever time he's got left making art instead of teaching."

"I'm so sorry for him."

"I am, too. He's a good friend as well as a colleague. And I understand why he'd up and leave. But it also creates a huge gap in the department just before term begins. Which is why I wanted to talk to you."

I started to speak, but he reached up with two fingers and touched my lips gently.

"Please wait. I want to offer you the chance to join the faculty, teach printmaking. You're more than qualified, especially with the ten years you've taught in Bedford."

The prospect of having students who *wanted* to be learning, the opportunity to be back in a studio . . . It was tantalizing. But I saw one major obstacle.

"How can I take the job when I'm your lover? You'd be my boss, right? That sounds like a situation the school would frown on."

"But if you weren't my lover anymore, they'd have no reason to complain."

I felt tears rising. "Are you asking me to choose?" I was incredulous.

"No, Toni. I'm asking you to marry me."

He took my trembling hands in his. Now he was the one with tears in his eyes.

"Please say yes."

Peter and I were married on Thanksgiving Day in the courtyard of the Isabella Stewart Gardner Museum. It wasn't a church and we didn't have a priest, but my parents put aside their expectations, recognizing that even with those blessings there were no guarantees that a marriage would flourish.

My mother was anxious that I was marrying again "too soon."

"Mom, it's more than three years since Bobby left. Peter and I have spent two years learning about and loving each other, and we had four years before that, as well. I'm sure of him, Mom. He makes me happy. And I know I do the same for him."

We held the reception at Paradiso. Faculty members from the Museum School with their funky hairstyles and shabby-chic clothes mingled with our Italian relatives—mine from the neighborhood and Peter's from Rochester—in their beaded dresses and flashy sports jackets. My boys got their first suits for the wedding, and Vanessa was old enough to be a flower girl. My mother went overboard and got her a dress from Priscilla of Boston, the shop that created Grace Kelly's wedding dress.

On my mother's dresser was a photograph of her in Trinidad that had been there for as long as I could remember. In it, her back is to the camera, her arms outstretched touching the frame of the open doorway in which she's standing, and her head is turned over her shoulder. She is wearing a Japanese kimono, embroidered in flowers.

"Where is the kimono now?" I asked her one afternoon before the wedding. "Do you still have it?"

She did, packed away with other mementos of Trinidad. It was exquisite—navy blue silk with a riot of color spilling down the back. I asked her if I could wear it for the wedding.

"Are you sure?" she asked, recalling that I'd worn her gown for my first wedding.

"This is something else, Mom. Daddy gave it to you, right?"

We agreed that a gift of love, like the kimono, could only be a good omen, and that is what I wore.

Manny created the menu. Because of the larger crowd than we normally fed at Thanksgiving, he decided to make rolled turkey breasts instead of roasting whole turkeys. He flattened the breasts and layered a mixture of sausage, cheese and eggs with fresh sage leaves and slices of mortadella, then rolled the breasts up and roasted them, basting them with white wine. We had the usual accompaniments of sweet potatoes, stuffed mushrooms and broccoli and cauliflower florets sautéed in olive oil with garlic and lemon peel.

Between courses Peter and I circled the room to greet our guests. He kept his hand on the small of my back, a point of connection that he didn't break. It was a source of energy for me, propelling me, warming me, protecting me, as I stepped into the next stage of my life. One of the first things I did was let go of the Templeton name and take back Dante.

We decided to keep both our homes. Peter moved into my apartment when we married. It was large enough for all of us and didn't disrupt the kids' lives. We kept Peter's loft on Union Wharf as a studio for both of us—a place to retreat and to work.

I kept filling sketchbooks and began turning my pen-and-ink interpretations into prints. I experimented with etchings and lithographs until I found a process that conveyed what I was trying to achieve. I held my first show as part of the faculty exhibition at the school.

I loved teaching at the Museum School. The atmosphere was so charged and the ideas so explosive that I was continually challenged by my students about the definition of art. Peter and I started a tradition of dinners at our home for our students; they often evolved into spirited debates that went on into the early hours of the morning.

Peter embraced my children and gave them time to accept him as their stepfather. We tried to have another child, but it wasn't meant to be. Instead, we became surrogate parents to our students and the friends of our children who gravitated to our home.

After the exhibition of my work at the faculty show, I was invited to participate in shows at Smith College and Brandeis. A publisher of art books saw my work at the Smith gallery and approached me to do a collection of prints entitled "Faces of the North End."

In fifteen years of marriage, the passion that had brought us together that first cold winter night continued to burn. We never grew tired of each other or bored in bed. We were bound together, our connection forged in the soul-baring heat of our lovemaking.

We weathered the challenges any marriage faces—the adolescent traumas of the children, the aging of our parents, upheaval at work. My worries that any of the children might inherit Bobby's bipolar disorder faded as they reached adulthood.

We were content. When Vanessa graduated from high school and started her freshman year at Harvard, we had dinner alone and toasted each other. We thought we'd not only survived, but flourished. That we'd made it up the steep side of the mountain and had earned a glimpse from the summit. But we were wrong.

# VANESSA
## 1998

# Freshman

I GREW UP ABOVE my grandparents' restaurant—Paradiso on Salem Street in the North End of Boston, the city's Little Italy. My grandparents, Rose and Al Dante, live on the second floor of the four-story brick building; my mother and father, my two brothers and I on the third; and my uncle Mike on the fourth.

My earliest memories are redolent with the aroma of Grandma Rose's gravy. Huge vats of her Neapolitan marinara bubbled softly on the back of the range in the restaurant kitchen. If I was hungry before dinner she tore off a chunk of crusty Campobasso bread full of air pockets and skimmed it across the top of the pot, where the pockets filled up with tomatoes and basil and garlic. She put the bread on a saucer and handed it to me.

"*Mangia,* sweetheart. But not too much or you won't have room for macaroni later."

When I was ten, I helped Grandma Rose fill the lidded bowls of grated Parmigiano on every table. When I was fourteen, I folded the napkins that came in every morning from the laundry. Grandma Rose didn't believe in paper napkins.

When I was sixteen, I waited on tables on the weekends.

My mother, Toni, is Paradiso's weekend hostess. During the day she usually wears jeans and a Cape Cod sweatshirt picked up in Orleans during the two weeks in summer when the restaurant closes and we all go down the Cape to the same cottage we've rented since I was a baby. But in the evenings, when Paradiso opens for dinner, my mother puts on a black V-necked sequined sweater, a tight-fitting black skirt, high heels and makeup.

Watching my mother get dressed late every Friday afternoon was my first lesson in transformation. She might've been scrubbing the toilet or making my brother Joe sit at the kitchen table and do his algebra homework, but once she puts on those clothes, her mascara and her Estée Lauder #148 Hot Kiss lipstick and goes downstairs, she's like an actress stepping out of a limousine onto the red carpet.

She's the first impression people have when they walk into Paradiso. She greets everyone with a voice that flows over them and makes them feel like she's been waiting all night for them to arrive and she saved the best table just for them.

I haven't figured out how to do that yet.

My mother was okay with my waitressing at Paradiso—after all, the whole family is involved in the business. But she wanted more for me and my brothers.

"You're too smart to go to the nuns for high school," she declared the summer before I went to eighth grade. High school was a whole year away, but everybody in the neighborhood went to Catholic high school when it was time.

"I want you to study for the entrance exam to Boston Latin," she said. And that was that. I studied. I got in. While my girlfriends at St. John's were buying their uniforms for Cathedral, I was at the library checking out books on the summer reading list. Chaucer. Milton. Emerson. Aristotle. Even Dante.

My grandfather Al liked to tell us how the family got its name when his father landed on Ellis Island from Calabria. His name was Bernardo Alighieri. The immigration clerk couldn't pronounce or spell it.

"Like Dante!" my great-grandfather exclaimed in exasperation. And that's what the clerk wrote down on his papers.

I did my summer reading sitting at a corner table in the restaurant before the dinner crowd showed up. Some people think my mother pushed me during high school, like I was her last hope. My two brothers, Ben and Joe, are five and seven years older than I am. Ben was a sophomore at Northeastern studying computer science when I started Boston Latin. Joe had gone to

Bunker Hill Community College, but stopped there. My mother's uncle Carmine got him an apprenticeship in the electricians' union and he's happy enough.

But people who think it was my mother's thwarted ambitions rather than my own that propelled me out of the North End would be wrong. It wasn't just the gap in our ages that made me different from my brothers; we have different memories because of that gap.

Joe and Ben remember our biological father, for example, and I don't. A month after I was born, Bobby Templeton quit his job, emptied his closet in our suburban raised ranch in Bedford and took off for Boulder, Colorado. Joe and Ben remember a daddy who occasionally played catch with them in a backyard that had a sandbox and a wading pool. But they also remember a household that was cast in the shadows of our father's mental illness—or lack of moral compass, depending on which member of the family is describing it.

I have none of that. I don't even remember the apartment in Arlington that my mother rented after she couldn't afford to keep the house in Bedford. Where she tried to be independent and strong and hold our fragile family together.

My memories and my boundaries are tightly defined by the bricks and mortar of Salem Street, by the demands of a family restaurant, by the enveloping and, yeah, sometimes smothering love of my Italian family.

Going to Boston Latin, even though it was only across the city, blew open my world. Some people might think it didn't lead me far. After all, I'm only across the river now in Cambridge. But let me tell you, Harvard Yard's a world away from the North End.

It's a little weird, being a freshman at Harvard when you've grown up in an enclave like the North End. It's especially a disconnect because people don't get that I'm Italian. Not only do I have Bobby's quintessentially Middle-American last name, but I also have his blond hair and blue eyes. So all the private-school, country-club kids believe I'm one of them and don't understand why I'm not flying to Jackson Hole or Saint Kitts for Thanksgiving break. And all the gritty, urban, ethnic kids who wear their heritage on their hard-working, rolled-up sleeves believe I'm some privileged legacy, with a long line of alumni in my family preceding me.

But frankly, I'm working too hard to worry about it. Boston Latin was a piece of cake compared to this. My mother was right: I'm a smart kid, but so is everybody else here. I hole up in Widener Library until it closes, my yellow highlighter furiously moving back and forth across the pages of my plant physiology textbook. I AP'ed out of bio, chem and American history, so

I'm taking 200-level courses. Grandma Rose fusses that I don't come home often enough.

"What could it hurt to get on the T and come for a good meal now and then, Vaness'?" she asked me when she'd called me one Sunday afternoon.

"Tell me when you're coming and I'll make your favorites—the ravioli with the porcini mushrooms and a torta Milanese with spinach and red peppers." Rose accepted my being a vegetarian, unlike my brothers, whose idea of a balanced meal is a steak and a beer.

"I can't, Grandma. I've got two papers due this week and a midterm. I'll be home for Thanksgiving."

"Okay, sweetheart. I'll see if I can find that fake turkey you told me about. What's it called again?"

"Tofurkey, Grandma. Hey, thanks. Gotta go— my study group's meeting before supper. I'll see you soon."

"Vaness', before you go. You know if you've got any friends that have nowhere to go for Thanksgiving, you invite them here, you understand?"

"Yeah, Grandma. Thanks. I'll do that."

I didn't think about Thanksgiving again for another week. Too much to do, to worry about, like keeping my scholarship. When the Monday before Thanksgiving rolled around, I was in the dining hall with my dorm mates. I live in Canaday, an anomaly—architecturally speaking—in Harvard Yard. If you're thinking ivy-covered, eighteenth-century, high ceilings and fireplaces in the common rooms, you'd be totally wrong. Canaday was built in the 1970s and, although it's brick, that's the only resemblance it has to anything else on this hallowed ground. It's all sharp angles and flat roofs, with six separate pods, each possessing its own utilitarian entrance cluttered with bikes and an overflowing bulletin board. The floors alternate male-female, something my mother and I mutually agreed not to share with my grandparents. Mom was cool about it, though. I feel she's come to terms with the ramifications of pushing me out of the nest at such a high altitude.

So I was at dinner in Annenberg Hall with the other girls on my floor—my roommate, Megana, who comes from Roslyn on Long Island, but whose parents are from Mumbai; Sonja, from Minnesota, who grew up in a town exactly like Garrison Keillor's Lake Woebegon; Elise, from Savannah via Miss Porter's School; Kelly, a hockey player from Buffalo; Naomi, from the Bronx High School of Science, another urban exam school, like Latin; Jessica, from Salt Lake City and the first Mormon I'd ever met; and Raquelle, from San Antonio, who had once regaled us with the extravagance of her

*Quinceañera.* Harvard Dining Services, like every other institutional dining room in the Boston area, seemed to think that students needed more than one Thanksgiving dinner that week. Turkey with all the trimmings—sweet potatoes, gravy, corn, cranberry sauce—was arrayed on the steam tables of the cafeteria line. They had thoughtfully provided tofu burgers for us vegetarians.

The menu, of course, got us talking about the holiday—plans for trips home, families we missed or could live without. Everybody was babbling away except for Sonja, who seemed focused on her plate.

After the meal, walking back to the dorm, I caught up with her.

"Hey, are you heading back to PBSville on Wednesday?"

She shook her head. "I'm hanging out here. Don't really have time to go back." She didn't seem to want to expand on the reasons.

I remembered Grandma Rose's directive and considered asking Sonja to come home with me. I hesitated, surprised by my own ambivalence about opening a window into the life I'd left in the North End when I was trying to figure out my new life here at Harvard. I didn't want to acknowledge that I was feeling slightly embarrassed by my family. There were just too many of them to control. But I also thought about how, despite their rough edges, it was hard to feel lonely or unloved in their midst. And Sonja looked truly adrift at the prospect of spending five long, empty days in the dorm. I pushed aside my reservations and plunged in.

"My grandmother has issued an open invitation to her Thanksgiving feast. She doesn't believe in eating alone, no matter what the occasion. Why don't you come across the river to Grandmother's house with me? It's not exactly through the woods, but I can promise you a meal better than you got tonight."

She wavered for a minute, the Norwegian martyr—"Oh, no, I couldn't trouble you. Just let me eat my bread and water here by myself"—trying to emerge. But then I told her it would be a favor to me if she came. It would put my family on their best behavior with a stranger at the table.

She said yes. I gave her the address, but told her I'd meet her at the Park Street T station if she wanted me to. She seemed grateful for that, not having ventured very far beyond the environs of Harvard Square in her three months.

I warned her. "My grandparents shut down Paradiso for the day and cook for the family. Um, that means there'll be about forty people—aunts, uncles, cousins, in-laws. Just so you don't think it's going to be a nuclear family event. It's an ever-changing guest list that shows up at Paradiso on Thanksgiving."

I didn't want to frighten her away or overwhelm her. It probably would've been better for both of us if I'd said, Hey, I'll stay here, too, and we can go eat Indian or Chinese and watch movies. But that would've been an impossible choice for me, incomprehensible to Grandma Rose and unacceptable to my mother. So Wednesday afternoon I packed up my knapsack, pulled on my Harvard sweatshirt and went back to the neighborhood.

## Dangerous Games

PETER RICCI HAS BEEN the only father I've known. He taught me how to roller-skate, suffered through my piano recitals and made me apologize to my mother when I was thirteen and the daughter from hell, slamming doors and yelling, "You're ruining my life!" because she wouldn't let me hang out at Waterfront Park after dark. He adores my mother and resides only a notch below my grandpa Al in the eyes of Grandma Rose.

"Peter is cut from the same cloth as my Al. He gives with his whole heart. Take my word for it, Vaness'. When it's time for you to choose a man, compare him to your father to see if he measures up."

In spite of everything Peter had done and been for me, in spite of how much I loved him, I found myself one dreary winter afternoon in Widener Library looking for Robert Templeton on the Internet. I was mildly curious. What becomes of a man who decides to reinvent himself, freed of familial responsibilities? What did he look like?

Any photos my mother had of the early years of her marriage to Bobby had been put away by the time I had memory. When I was sixteen I found their wedding album among some old boxes in the basement and had turned the stiff and yellowing pages in secret, trying to see in Bobby Templeton's eyes some reflection of the demons that had driven him away from us. But he looked content, optimistic and a lot like me. Maybe that's why I let the seed grow inside my brain, why I allowed myself to wonder where he was, what had become of him.

Although Grandma Rose has preferred to wipe his existence from our family history, my mother has been relatively comfortable with it, considering. Her attitude is, "Hey, this happened and it sucked. We can let it eat away at us, or we can thumb our nose at it and move on." Until my other grandmother, Hazel, passed away, my mother kept in touch with her. She always ordered extra copies of our school pictures and had us make cards for her on Mother's Day and her birthday.

My brothers wrote Bobby Templeton off a long time ago, especially Joe, who seems to have absorbed my grandmother's philosophy of "He's dead to me." Ben is more closed about his internal life. If he cares at all about who Bobby Templeton is, he doesn't share it with any of us.

I think I was just bored that first time I typed Bobby's name into a search engine. I was in the procrastination phase of writing a paper on Nabakov for my Comp. Lit. class and *any* diversion was welcome. Robert Templeton is a fairly common name, I discovered. The search bounced back fifty-nine references. I clicked on a few, entertaining myself with the possibility of our Bobby Templeton being a physics professor at Gonzaga University or a state senator in Louisiana or a late-night radio jock in Lincoln, Nebraska. Then I got sensible, preferring not to be up until 4:00 a.m. writing my paper, and stopped playing on the computer.

It really was just a game to me at first, my own version of *Where's Waldo?* I didn't mean for it to become anything more than clever stories to entertain my dorm mates. It was nothing. Until it became something. It kind of took over, feeding some need in me that was more than curiosity.

This must be what adoptees feel like, trying to find their birth parents, I told myself. I tried to justify it on medical grounds. What if he's a diabetic? What if he's passed on some genetic disease that's a ticking time bomb? But it was more than that. I wanted to look Bobby Templeton in the eye, not in an aging photograph but in person, and understand who he was. And who I was.

I found him when I stumbled across a photograph online, one of those stiff, formal company portraits, the corporate equivalent of yearbook pictures. Well, at least he wasn't a homeless derelict living in a cardboard box, which is the fate I think my grandmother had envisioned. He lived in Nashville, Tennessee.

I e-mailed him. I didn't have the money or the nerve just to show up on his doorstep, like one of those movies where the adorable little girl drops into the life of the confirmed bachelor, throwing his carefully established routines into chaos and ultimately winning his heart. I'm not adorable. I'm what my friends charitably call "edgy" and what my brothers define as a pain in the butt. I'm either direct or brutally honest, depending on your perspective. I tend not to sugarcoat things.

I somehow thought he'd jump at the chance to know his daughter once she presented herself. It didn't occur to me that he'd known where I was for eighteen years and could have made my acquaintance at anytime. But didn't.

It will come as no surprise that he did not respond. However, I chose to ignore his silence and began sending him regular updates—dispatches from a college freshman.

And then, on my birthday, he sent me a card. Not one of those sappy "To a Dear Daughter" confections you find in the racks at CVS, but a hilarious Far Side cartoon. The guy had a sense of humor.

I sent him a thank-you note and we then began a regular exchange, via e-mail.

Does your mother know you've contacted me? he asked, like a responsible adult.

I thought about blurring my answer. But I reluctantly admitted to myself that keeping my relationship with Bobby a secret from my mother and, yes, father was probably a stupid idea. Hey, I go to Harvard. And even though my grandfather suspects that my classmates were born with high intelligence and low common sense, I'd spent enough time in the world before Harvard to know that reaching across the rift to Bobby was bringing him not only into my life, but into everybody else's, as well.

So I told my mother.

We were in the pantry between the kitchen and the dining room. She leaned back against the counter with her arms folded across her chest.

"Why didn't you tell me you were interested in finding Bobby? I could have saved you the search."

"You knew where he was?"

"He wasn't hiding."

"You're not mad at me?"

"No, sweetie. Dad and I expected that sooner or later you'd want to know something about him. Just . . . well, don't expect too much. I don't want you to be hurt."

Okay. That went better than I'd expected. She didn't jump on me, yelling, What were you *thinking?* If she had, I couldn't have answered her. I don't know why I wanted to find Bobby. I don't know what I wanted *from* Bobby. An apology? An explanation?

I was going to find out. He'd told me he had a business trip to New York. Close enough to rent a car and drive up to Boston. He offered to buy me dinner in Harvard Square.

He took me to Upstairs at the Pudding, the sort of place where families treat their offspring to graduation dinner. The place takes reservations months in advance.

"A fancy dinner is not going to compensate me for nineteen years of desertion," I said during the appetizer.

I asked what he'd been doing while he was gone. He told me. He'd remarried, had two kids, gotten divorced.

"Do they know about us?"

"My ex-wife, yes. The kids, no."

"Why did you send me the birthday card?"

"It was your birthday."

345

I made a face. "That doesn't answer the question."

"I wanted to know who you were. And let you know I hadn't forgotten that I left a family behind."

"You left a wreckage."

"I'm sorry."

"That's supposed to make up for what you did?"

"I was young. I was sick."

"I'm young, but I know you don't do that to your wife and kids. No matter how bad a shape you're in or how hard life is."

"If you're so angry with me, why did you try to find me?"

"I wanted to know what kind of man you are. I didn't contact you to forgive you. I contacted you so I could figure out who *I* am, where I came from."

"You look like me."

"Duh."

"Other than the superficial traits I seem to have passed on to you, I don't think I had much to do with the young woman you've become."

"Are you happy?"

"I have two failed marriages, four of my five children are not speaking to me and I'm a prime candidate for a heart attack. You tell me."

"What do you want, Bobby?"

"Redemption."

"I can't help you with that. I was a baby when you walked. I can't restore you to the self you were before you deserted us because I don't remember you. Did you even hold me before you left?"

"In the delivery room."

"After that?"

"No. I couldn't. It hurt too much. I knew I was going to leave. I was in hell, Vanessa."

"It sounds to me like you still are. Look, I'm a kid. I may have scored 1580 on my SATs, but I'm not smart enough to figure out what you need."

"Do you think your mother would see me?"

"I can't answer that. She knows you're in town. I told her."

That was when I really began to understand what I'd done by bringing Bobby back. Dumb. Dumb. Dumb. I started to cry.

"Don't you dare wreck our lives again!" I got up from the table without finishing my crème brûlée and ran back to my dorm. He didn't try to stop me.

When I got to my room the phone was ringing. I didn't answer it and let it go to voice mail. It was my mother.

"Hi, sweetie. I just called to see how you were doing after your dinner with Bobby."

I picked up the phone.

"Oh, Mom, I'm so sorry! I wish I'd never found him."

"What happened, Vanessa? Are you okay?" I could hear the rising note of anger tinged with hysteria that was the signature of the women on my grandmother's side of the family. My mother, normally a reasonable and even-tempered woman well in control of her emotions, could be pushed over the edge if she thought one of her kids had been hurt.

"I'm okay. I'm just so stupid. He doesn't care about me. He's using me to get to you."

The other end of the phone was silent.

"Mom?"

"I'm sorry, Vanessa. I'm sorry he's hurt you. Do you want me to come over?"

I'm not much of a mama's girl. Ordinarily I would've turned to one of the girls in the dorm to calm down. But I didn't think any of them would understand. And I was worried about my mother. I felt I needed to inoculate her against Bobby. I didn't think I could stop him from getting in touch with her. But she needed to know what a loser he was.

"Yes, please, Mom. Thanks."

"I'll be there in twenty minutes."

When she got to Canaday I made some tea and we sat curled up on my couch. I'd stopped crying, but I was still upset I'd been such a fool.

"Don't beat yourself up, sweetie. There was nothing wrong in your wanting to know what had become of Bobby. But seeking knowledge like that has its costs. The important thing to remember is that, despite Bobby's absence from your life, you've turned out great! You're an impressive, resilient young woman, and I'm so proud of you!"

"Your life's turned out great, too, Mom. Don't let him drag *you* down. He's miserable. I felt contaminated by his unhappiness."

"Don't worry about me. I've got a hazmat suit on when it comes to Bobby Templeton."

By the time she left I felt reasonably certain she could kick Bobby's ass if he came groveling at her door. I imagined her in her hostess regalia, sequins flashing, long red fingernails tapping the table list as she sized him up as an out-of-town nobody she could stick at the worst table in the dining room.

Bobby disappeared from Boston without contacting my mother, and my systems backed down from high alert. Unfortunately he was only regrouping.

My mother had an exhibition of her prints at a gallery in New York a couple of months later. I took a day off from school and joined her for the opening reception. My father was in Italy with a group of students on an exchange program.

Everything was going well. Some hotshot critic from the *New York Times* had shown up and my mother, in addition to having mounted a brilliant show, looked her ravishing, Italian-actress best. My aunt Annette had done it again. I keep telling her she ought to launch a new career as a stylist.

My mother was entertaining the critic, champagne flute in one hand, the other flowing through the air as if she were conducting an orchestra.

The critic was nodding; Miles, the gallery director, was beaming and I wandered off to watch the crowd milling around the prints. I liked to eavesdrop on what they were saying about her.

I had my back to one cluster of people, trying not to be obvious that I was listening.

I heard one of the men say he thought this was her best work yet.

"I've been following her career since she began," he said. "In fact, I own several of her prints."

"You sound like a devoted fan," a woman responded.

"I am. As far as I'm concerned, no one else comes close."

My pulse was screaming in my ears when I recognized that the voice speaking so passionately about my mother's art belonged to Bobby Templeton.

I slid away from the group, hoping he hadn't seen me. I wanted to warn my mother, but she was still talking with the critic. I retreated to the bar, where I grabbed another glass of Apollinaris and had a pretty good view of the room.

As soon as the critic moved on I headed toward my mother. But I was too late. To my horror, Bobby slipped up next to her. I saw a flicker of surprise on my mother's face. Her hand holding the champagne flute was trembling.

"Don't kiss him!" I almost shouted out loud. The evening had been filled with far too much of that phony art-world kiss-kiss. But she didn't. I watched her stand, listening to whatever he was telling her, trying to decipher from her face what she was thinking. I should have gone up and interrupted them, broken whatever connection he was trying to reestablish. But I didn't want to talk to him. And apparently he had no desire to talk to me, either. His attention was totally focused on my mother.

The conversation only lasted a few minutes. Other guests wanted a piece of my mother. She'd shaken her head a few times, then finally nodded. I could read her lips well enough to see that she'd mouthed the word *okay.* As he moved away from her, he brushed her hand. My mother turned to the others with her warm hostess smile. "I'm so happy you could make it!" But I could see, even from a distance, that there were tears in her eyes.

Bobby left the gallery after that. I was relieved

until things were winding down and my mother approached me.

"Vanessa, I'm sorry to do this to you, but Miles wants me to go to dinner with a client. His assistant has offered to take you out for something to eat. I'll meet you back at the hotel."

I wanted to protest. To tell her that I knew the "client" was Bobby. I was so pissed with her for doing this, and didn't want to admit I was the one who'd set this whole mess in motion.

"I thought this was supposed to be time for us to spend together."

"I know, sweetie. I really *am* sorry. Look, we'll go to the Tavern on the Green tomorrow for brunch and then go shopping. Okay?"

"Fine." I found the anorexic assistant, assuming she'd watch me while I ate, and left my mother to lose her soul.

# TONI

# The Commission

I WAS UNPREPARED for the sight of Bobby approaching me in the gallery. Miles had told me that some avid collector had arrived, eager to meet me and interested in discussing a commission with me. When I saw it was Bobby, I thought, *What a line!* But then he launched into how moved he was by my work and how happy he was that my talent had been realized. He told me which of my prints he owned and why he'd selected them. What meaning they'd had in his life.

Every fiber of my will was stretched taut with the effort of resisting the emotional depths he was pulling me toward. I wished I hadn't had the two glasses of champagne I'd been blithely sipping as I greeted guests. I should've known better. I was working this exhibit, not just the celebrated guest. Bobby's tale was as compelling as it had ever been. It stunned me that after almost twenty years he could suck me back into his troubled world. He made my heart ache for him, as futile as I knew that was.

It seemed he truly did want to commission me. "I'm asking you to capture the image of my children in print. I don't know of any other way to hold on to them."

"Which children?" I asked. I knew I was being brutal.

"All of them."

"No. I won't give you mine. They are no longer your children. You abandoned them. You didn't even pay child support."

He stepped back as if I'd slapped him.

"Okay." He acquiesced. It wasn't like him to accept less than he had asked for. I was wary. This was probably not the end of it.

"There are other people here waiting to talk to me. You can talk to Miles about the details."

"When the reception is over can we talk some more? Let me take you to dinner."

"I can't. I have plans."

"Please, Toni. Just hear me out this one time. That's all I'm asking."

I saw the pain in his eyes and reluctantly said yes. I knew Vanessa had been watching our exchange, and my heart sank. She wasn't going to understand. No one was going to understand.

When I got back to the hotel Vanessa was still up studying. She didn't speak to me.

I went into the bathroom to get ready for bed. I looked terrible, pale with dark circles under my eyes. The conversation with Bobby had drained me. I took a shower, trying to relax my tensed muscles and wash away the residue of his guilt and remorse and sense of being misunderstood that had settled on me like ash from a newly awakened Vesuvius.

When I came out of the bathroom Vanessa was waiting by the door.

"I know you were with Bobby."

"Yes, I was."

"What are you going to do?"

I wanted to reassure her, to tell her it was going to be all right, that his presence tonight was not going to disrupt our lives. But I couldn't. It was too late. The disruption had already occurred, and at that moment I was furious with her for triggering such an upheaval by bringing him back into my life in the first place.

Her face twisted in anger and fear, and with clenched fists she pounded on my chest. "You can't! You can't let him in! Don't do this to us!"

She went into the bathroom and locked the door.

"Vanessa!" I didn't have the energy or the will to deal with her at that moment.

"Go to hell."

She finally crept out and climbed into her bed about an hour later, her eyes red and swollen from crying.

I turned out the light.

In the morning she got dressed in silence and only spoke to me as she picked up her knapsack.

"I'm taking the train back to Boston."

I checked out of the hotel and went downtown to the gallery to wrap up some paperwork with Miles. He told me Bobby had bought two of my most expensive prints.

"That guy from Nashville seems obsessed with your work. He told me he owns eleven of your prints. Are you going to do the commissioned piece for him?"

"I don't know yet. It's complicated." I didn't want to explain to Miles what I could hardly explain to myself—that I was both repelled by Bobby's intrusion into my life and compelled by his need to provide what little solace I could with my art. He'd made me feel powerful, as if I could give him something he so desperately wanted, and that power was seductive.

I was exhausted. From being on my guard with Bobby, from the fight with Vanessa, from the energy I'd poured into mounting the show and schmoozing the guests at the reception. I climbed into my car around noontime and drove back to Boston.

When I got home all I wanted to do was crawl into bed. But I checked the mail and phone messages first. Peter had sent a postcard from Pisa, an image of one of my favorite frescoes from the Camposanto Monumentale of a woman holding a falcon. The message was detailed, written in Peter's rapid, angular hand, full of the minutiae of shepherding a group of wide-eyed students on their maiden voyage to Italy. I missed him. I wished he'd been with me at the gallery, an anchor holding me fast against the turbulent storm that had blown in from Tennessee. I propped the card on my night table and picked up the phone to retrieve my voice mail.

The second message was from Peter. His voice was tight, cold.

"Toni, what the hell is going on? Vanessa called me, hysterical, that you'd abandoned her in New York to be with Bobby Templeton. Call me."

I started to shake. I'd done nothing the night before except listen to Bobby, but I'd underestimated how out of control Vanessa was in her reaction. That she'd called Peter and instilled in him a sense of betrayal chilled me. I didn't know how I could have a conversation with him without revealing my own confusion about my reaction to Bobby—and to Bobby's interjection of himself into my life. Why would I create a work of such personal meaning for him?

I looked at the clock, hoping it would be too late to call. Almost four o'clock in the afternoon, ten in the evening in Italy. Peter had left the number of his hotel in the message and I dialed it.

"Peter, it's Toni. I just got home and picked up your message. I'm sorry Vanessa was so upset."

"What happened?"

"I asked Miles's assistant to take her to dinner so I could discuss a commissioned piece with Bobby."

"He shows up after nearly twenty years and wants you to paint a picture?" Peter's voice was incredulous. "Is that all? If that's what he's telling you, I don't believe him."

"I'm not naive. I know this isn't an ordinary commission."

"Then why are you even considering it? I don't understand why you'd give him anything as precious as your talent. Do you really want that? Because if you do, you're not the woman I thought you were."

I didn't have an answer.

"I can't talk about this over the phone, Peter. I haven't agreed to anything. When you get home on Friday we can discuss it. I need your help to sort it out, but you're no help if you're going to prejudge me."

"Do you have any idea how angry this makes me? Not for *me,* but for what it could do to you. Don't let him pull you back to where you were emotionally after he left you."

I didn't tell Peter that I was dangerously close to being there already. I was a wreck. And for the first time in our marriage, I felt he didn't understand me.

"I'll see you in a few days. I hope the rest of the trip goes well." And I hung up.

I was too agitated to sleep.

I grabbed the keys to the studio and walked to the harbor. Once inside the studio I sat by the windows for a while just looking out to sea. I love the light that comes in through the floor-to-ceiling expanse of glass on the eastern wall. I watched as night descended on the ocean, the sky deepening from lavender to violet to indigo. When it was too dark to see the water I got up and turned on the lights.

I made myself a pot of tea—Sleepytime. It was the only tea I drank when I was nursing and, after nineteen years, its aroma brought me right back to that time when I was the sole source of nourishment for my children. It had been so simple to meet their needs then. Hold them close, suckle them, rock them, sing to them. Vanessa's favorite song had been "Somewhere over the Rainbow," and I'd sung it to her constantly—in the car stuck in traffic, walking the floor with her at night.

What could I sing to her now to reassure her?

I paced the floor with my mug for a few minutes and then went to the bookshelf where I kept my sketchbooks. They were arranged chronologically, so it was easy to pick out the early years. I pulled two books off the shelves and sat at my workbench on a high stool, slowly turning the pages I'd created before my marriage to Bobby. I was looking for a reminder, a sign, of who I'd been back then.

Like most of my work, the sketches were intimate portraits, attempting to capture the essence of the individuals in the lines and contours of their faces. I was startled to see how many of the sketches were of Bobby. I'd forgotten that I'd often used him as my subject. In some, his face was ravaged; the eyes staring out at me were blank. In others, he was looking away, unaware that I was sketching him, and he had a softness about his lips and his eyes, almost as if he was asleep. Perhaps he had been. When I first met him, I'd been swallowed up by his physical presence. I used to watch him, the way he moved with the confidence of a man used to being admired, his long, lean body proportioned like one of Michelangelo's sculptures.

It disturbed me that I still found him so physically powerful. When our marriage had begun to dissolve, his withdrawal from my bed—long before he swung his leg over his motorcycle and rode away—had been wrenching. To have that primal need reawakened was frightening.

A chill had drifted into the studio after the sun had set; despite their modernization these old buildings were drafty, their cavernous spaces quickly dissipating the heat. Rather than turn up the thermostat, I opened the potbellied stove, built a nest of crumpled newsprint and twigs and lit a fire. We still had a small supply of logs left after the winter. With the fire going and a second cup of tea in my hand, I continued to turn the pages of my notebooks. But it wasn't just Bobby's face, in all its variations of mood, that I was seeking. It was the artist herself. I'd become someone else in the years since Bobby had left. The woman who'd been muffled and silenced during my marriage, constrained first by Bobby's expectations and then by Bobby's needs, had finally emerged after his abandonment. Why would I risk losing her?

I finally fell asleep on the daybed, too tired to walk back home, too unsettled to resume my domestic life. I was startled by a ringing sound early in the morning and it took my groggy brain a few seconds to grasp that it was a telephone, not the alarm clock I was unsuccessfully groping for. I shivered as I put my bare feet on the floor and wrapped the quilt around me. I picked up the phone on the counter.

"Hello?"

"Toni? Oh, thank God that's where you are! I worried all night when Joe told me you weren't back."

"Sorry, Ma. I came over to the studio to do some work and was too exhausted to go home late at night. Didn't mean to have you worry."

"Are you alone?" Her voice was sharp, expecting the worst.

"Of course. Who else would be here?"

"I talked to Vanessa last night when you didn't come home. I thought maybe you'd stayed in New York with her. She told me Bobby Templeton showed up at the gallery."

"And you thought I was spending the night with him while my husband was away?" I was incredulous that my mother would imply such a betrayal.

"You're angry with me, but from what Vanessa told me you're treading on very thin ice, Toni. Are you crazy to be jeopardizing everything you hold precious in your life?"

"Ma, I'm not sleeping with him. I'm not even remotely considering the *possibility* of sleeping with him. It's a business transaction, nothing more."

"Don't be a fool, Toni. And don't ruin your life. Come home, take a shower and remember who you are now." And she hung up the phone.

I wondered who else would berate me as word spread across the family that the devil himself had returned.

I cleaned up the studio and left for home. It was only seven in the morning. Maybe my mother was right. If I got back into the rhythm of my life I'd be able to calm the storm Bobby had created in my mind. I hoped so.

I threw myself into the frenzy of activity that I'd watched my mother and grandmother engage in when I was a girl. When trouble hits, clean and cook. I put on my jeans, pinned up my hair and prepared the house for Peter's return, vacuuming and dusting and polishing to keep from brooding on the mess my willingness to listen to Bobby Templeton had generated.

After I finished cleaning, I went down the street and picked up ingredients for Peter's favorite meal—fennel and onions from the greengrocer's, salmon filets from Giuffre's fish market and white wine from Martignetti's. One bottle to cook with and one bottle to drink.

I was carrying my shopping bags up the stairs when my mother opened her door. Her arms were folded across her chest.

"I'm happy to see you back."

"Just to let you know, I had every intention of coming home."

"Have you talked to Vanessa since you got back from New York?"

"Vanessa isn't speaking to me right now, although apparently she's had no problem airing my life to anyone who'll listen. Who else knows? Aunt Bella in Albany? Father Dom?"

"Toni! She's your daughter, and this escapade of yours affects her, too!"

"It's not an escapade! Look, I've got to get the fish in the refrigerator. If you still need to tell me how terrible I am, then come upstairs instead of yelling at me on the landing."

"I'm not yelling at you. And I don't think

you're a terrible person." She was following me up the stairs, taking one of my bags.

In my kitchen she helped put things away.

"You've been cleaning."

"Thanks for noticing. I learned it from my mother." I tried to smile.

"How about a cup of tea?" She already had the kettle in her hand.

I was going to refuse, tell her I had work to do. But I knew that sooner or later she'd manage to have this conversation with me. My mother was indefatigable. She gave up on nothing and no one.

"Sure," I said, and let her bustle around getting cups and tea bags.

"Listen, sweetheart, I'm only trying to tell you what I see happening to you and what I've learned from what's happened to me. I'm so proud of you! Look at what you've accomplished in your life. You've raised three wonderful children, married a man who adores you and made a name for yourself with your beautiful artwork. I see all this, the Toni sitting here at the table with me, and I compare you to the Toni of nineteen years ago, weighed down by the burdens of marriage to a selfish, immature man who didn't love you."

I opened my mouth to protest, but she held up her hand.

"Don't tell me he loved you. A man who loves

doesn't do what he did. That's why I cannot understand why you would even listen to him, let alone do 'business' with him, as you put it. He has no right to even ask you!"

I didn't know how to answer my mother. I saw so many shades of gray where she only saw black and white. I couldn't explain to her what I was feeling because I didn't understand it myself. The memories of the Bobby who'd once drawn me into his orbit were jumbled together with those of the Bobby who, as my mother so accurately and painfully described, had not loved me, and the Bobby who was so deeply troubled by his mental illness and addiction to alcohol.

"I feel pity for him."

"You can't save him, Toni. You tried before. All it did was drag you down. Why do you think you can help him now? Believe me, this will bring you heartache. And it will drive a wedge between you and Peter. Even if it's only a stupid picture. Because that won't be enough. He'll keep taking more. Please, sweetheart."

She stretched across the table to squeeze my hand.

"I hear you, Ma. I know you're speaking your heart, and I understand in my head what you're saying. I'll think about it. I promise."

"I've got to get downstairs. Why don't you eat with us tonight? I'm making tuna and olives with polenta."

"Thanks, Ma. But my stomach's upset. I'm just going to have some chicken soup and try to get a good night's sleep. The daybed in the studio isn't the most comfortable place to spend the night."

"Okay. I'm not surprised you don't feel good. But listen, before you go to bed, call Vanessa. You may think she doesn't want to talk to you, but she needs to hear from you."

She kissed me and left me alone in my darkening kitchen.

When the phone rang, I thought it would be Peter or Vanessa and steeled myself for more lectures and outrage. But when I heard the voice on the other end, I broke into a sweat.

It was Bobby. And he'd been drinking.

"Toni. I needed to hear your voice. Ever since I saw you in New York you've been on my mind."

"Bobby, don't start." I didn't want to hear this.

"You're the best thing that ever happened to me. It took me a long time to understand that, but now I know. I'm not asking you to take me back into your life, but I really need you to listen to me just this once. Just for tonight."

"Bobby, that's what you said the other night. I can't give you what you're looking for. If you were Catholic I'd tell you to go to a priest for absolution. But I can't, I *won't,* absolve you."

He started to sob.

"Where are you? Can I call someone to help

you?" I was concerned that he was alone, in despair.

"I'm in Boston."

I went rigid. *Don't go to him,* all the voices in my brain were screaming. If you step out your door, you're stepping into hell. *Do I abandon him, the way he abandoned me and the kids?* I answered back. *He needs help.*

And then I knew what I had to do.

"Where in Boston?"

"I'm at the Langham Hotel."

"Meet me at the bar in half an hour."

I hung up the phone. But instead of leaving for the hotel I dialed Mike's number, praying he was home. He and Graham had bought and renovated a town house in the South End before gentrification—one of the many collaborations they'd successfully pulled off over their years together.

I was relieved when he answered.

"I need an enormous favor from you," I said.

"You sound like you've seen Nana's ghost on the stairs. What's the matter?"

"Come with me on an errand. An errand of mercy. I need your moral support and I need you to help me keep my resolve."

"I've already got my jacket on. Where should I meet you?"

I walked quietly down the stairs. I didn't want to explain myself to my mother. Once on the street I headed toward the financial district and the hotel. When Mike arrived, I told him what I intended to do.

"And my role in this drama?"

"Keep me in sight and make sure I walk away when I'm finished."

"Do you think he might hurt you? Because if you do, I'm not letting you near him."

"No, he's not dangerous in that sense. But he can suck me into his suffering—he has already—and I have to put an end to his ability to do that."

"Good for you. I know you've been getting it from all sides of the family about this. But you had to come to this decision on your own. I've got your back, Toni. If you start to waver, just look across the room."

"Thanks, Mike. I knew I could count on you. And thanks for not adding to the chorus telling me what to do. Thanks for trusting me."

When we got to the Langham, I went to the bar first. Mike followed a few minutes later and took a seat where he could see me and Bobby couldn't see him.

Bobby was grasping an old-fashioned glass filled with bourbon when I slipped into the seat across from him. He looked as if he hadn't slept since I'd left him in New York.

He grabbed my hand as soon as I sat down.

"You don't know how much this means to me, that you've come. You haven't given up on me, like everyone else in my life."

"Bobby, I'm not *in* your life. I haven't been part of your life for nineteen years. More, if you consider how isolated we were from each other at the end."

"But you're here now."

"I'm here now to tell you what you need to hear. Not to forgive you or save you from whatever demons are clawing at your soul. Including that one." And I pointed to his glass. "The only person who can do that is you."

"But I can't do it on my own."

"You're right, Bobby."

"I knew you'd understand."

"Bobby, I understand that you need help. I understand that you're in pain. And I came here tonight to tell you that. You need help. But not from me. My artwork isn't going to change your life. My listening to you and comforting you isn't what you need."

"But you've already helped me, just by coming."

"Bobby, you need something I can't give you. You're an alcoholic. You suffer from depression. The forgiveness you're seeking has to come from yourself. Get into a program. Find a doctor. You are sick. And I can't heal you. I couldn't when we were married and I certainly can't now."

"I need you, Toni."

"No, Bobby. I'm not what you need. I might be a Band-Aid for some minor cut, but you're bleeding out. Look at yourself in the mirror tonight. And then get on a plane and go home."

I pushed my chair back and stood.

"Don't go! Please."

"No. I've said what I came to say. Anything more is pointless. Listen to me. Go back to Tennessee and do whatever you must to get well."

"Will you do the portraits?"

"No. Untangle your relationships with your kids in Tennessee instead of trying to preserve their images."

"What can I say to change your mind?"

"Nothing."

"Will you write? Can I call you?"

"No. No. When I walk out of here tonight I'm walking out of your life. I don't belong in it. And you don't belong in mine. Goodbye, Bobby."

I was on my feet and moving toward Mike.

"Toni, stop! I love you."

I kept walking. Mike put himself between Bobby and me, and we headed home.

We got to Salem Street and climbed the stairs arm in arm, as quietly as we had when we left. At the door to my place, Mike kissed me.

"Are you okay, sis, or do you want some company?"

"I'm fine. Set free, actually. Thanks. You're the best."

"I'm just returning the favor you did for me by

accepting me when I came out." He smiled that sweet, embracing smile of his that's always made the world seem right, and went on down the stairs.

I called Vanessa as soon as I was in the door. The adrenaline that had propelled me to the Langham and through the conversation with Bobby was rapidly ebbing. I wasn't sure I had enough left to break through Vanessa's resistance *and* keep my own anger in abeyance at the complications she'd precipitated by bringing everyone in the family into this mess. She answered on the second ring, and the brightness in her voice disappeared the moment I spoke.

"I don't have anything to say to you."

"I'm not asking you to. Just listen for a few minutes."

"I don't want to hear your explanations. I'll never understand how you can do this to us, so don't bother trying."

"No explanations, and no expectations. I just wanted to tell you that I told Bobby no tonight. No to the commission, no to his intrusion into my life. I won't let him back in."

Silence at the other end of the phone. I waited.

"Mom? I'm so sorry I opened the door to let him in!" She was crying.

"Oh, honey. This wasn't your fault!"

"But if I hadn't contacted him, he'd never have—"

"He'd have found another way. You did nothing to cause this, Vanessa. And now it's over."

"Really?"

"I promise."

"I'm so relieved. I was so scared you were going to leave us and go back to him."

"I will never leave you, Vanessa. Ever."

"Okay."

"I love you, sweetie. And now I've got to get some sleep."

The next morning I sat by the window in my bedroom, the eastern light illuminating the open page of the sketchbook in my hand. It'd been several months since I'd drawn anything new. Preparing for the show at Miles's gallery had involved translating the rough work of my notebooks into finished etchings and lithographs, and I'd put aside the daily discipline of the sketchbook. But my night of introspection at the studio had reminded me how important a record my sketches were—like a writer's journal.

My hand moved quickly on the page, the soft charcoal pencil leaving traces that revealed the shape of my brother's arm draped protectively around my shoulders; my mother reaching across the table to stroke my hand. And then, emerging under my strokes, a face. Strong, chiseled, with eyes whose gaze was direct, open, vibrant. Peter's face.

# An Open Book

---

WHENEVER PETER AND I traveled separately we didn't see each other off or welcome the other back at the airport. The North End was just on the other side of the tunnel from Logan and it made more sense for the traveler to hop in a cab and be home in ten or fifteen minutes. But this time I decided I couldn't wait at home for the sound of his key in the door. I wanted to see Peter's face when he walked out of customs and throw my arms around him.

I was nervous. We hadn't spoken since the afternoon I'd gotten back from New York, when he was so angry. I stood with at least fifty other people clustered around the international arrivals gate. I realized that many of them were probably the parents of the students Peter had been shepherding.

Finally, passengers began trickling out of customs trundling their suitcases, weary from the long flight. Peter didn't see me when he first emerged. Unlike the others who were scanning faces for family or friend or lover, Peter was focused on getting out of the building.

I called out to him and he turned. I didn't trust

myself to read the expression on his face. Was it relief that I was there and hadn't run off with Bobby? Or questioning and suspicious that I'd shown up at the airport?

I moved toward him, needing to close the distance between us. An urgency fueled me. I was moving so swiftly that my knapsack was flying behind me. I hadn't closed it securely, and as I reached Peter my sketchbook fell out and landed open at his feet.

We both bent to pick it up. He touched it first and, as he started to close it, glanced at the open page. His own image.

His fingers traced the charcoal on the page. My fingers traced his face itself.

He closed the book, tucked it back in my knapsack and took me in his arms.

# ROSE
## 2009

# Epilogue

I DON'T THINK OF myself as an old woman. In my heart, I'm still the young bride sweeping out her first home on the bluff at Chaguaramas and setting out Thanksgiving dinner on plank tables in the sunlight.

I can't even count anymore how many Thanksgiving dinners I've cooked for my family. Some have been more memorable than others. This year was especially so. We had much to celebrate. Toni and Peter's anniversary. Al's survival from cancer. The christening of my first great-granddaughter. Even a trip to Washington to visit Marianne, Al Jr.'s old girl-friend, who lives there now with her family. I found Al Jr.'s name on the wall at the Vietnam Memorial, close to the beginning, and ran my fingers over the letters.

Manny went crazy with the food for Thanksgiving dinner. There's a reason *Boston Magazine* named him chef of the year and the *Globe* has given Paradiso four stars. It *was* paradise to eat that meal. Al and I sat at the head of the table, taking turns holding Olivia, Vanessa's baby. After she graduated from Harvard she went to

Italy for two years and got a master's degree in Italian. We teased her about meeting an Italian boy and falling in love, and sure enough, that's what she did. It kills me that she's so far away, but she and Marcello come to Boston every year. Now, of course, with the baby we want to see them more often.

Al, thank God, got the best treatment at Dana-Farber, and beat kidney cancer five years ago. That's when we decided to make the most of what time we had left. We turned Paradiso over to the kids and moved to Bal Harbour in Florida. He still plays cards every afternoon and we go dancing on Saturday nights.

Toni and Peter are as much in love as ever. He retired in June and my bet is Toni will follow soon, now that Olivia has arrived. They've been talking about buying a place in Umbria to be near Vanessa, and I don't blame them.

Joey and Ben also got married. Joey to a nurse he met when Al was in the hospital; Ben to Jennifer Conti, who was in his fifth grade class at St. John's and has been his best friend ever since. Each couple has a son—Joey's Al, and Ben's Matthew.

Mike "came out" to the family a few years ago. Like me, most of them had figured it out. Even Al. I have to hand it to Al. Of all of us, it was hardest for him to accept. But the cancer changed him. Made him recognize what was precious in life. When Mike told us he and Graham were committed to each other, we both said they had our blessing.

We were surrounded by all of them at the table and, after grace, raised our glasses.

*"Salute!"* we said. "To life."

## Center Point Publishing

600 Brooks Road ● PO Box 1
Thorndike ME 04986-0001 USA

**(207) 568-3717**

**US & Canada:**
**1 800 929-9108**
www.centerpointlargeprint.com